PRAISE FOR THE EMILY KINCAID MYSTERY SERIES

DEAD DANCING WOMEN

"Every woman who's ever struggled with saying no, fitting in, and balancing independence against loneliness will adore first-timer Emily."

—*Kirkus*

"Emily and Dolly's developing friendship, the particulars of small-town Michigan life, and the eccentric characters enliven the story."

—*Booklist*

"Debut author Buzzelli is notable as one of the growing number of women writers who use female protagonists trying to make a life for themselves, such as Sue Henry."

—*Library Journal*

"The mystery is well-plotted … Emily grows more likeable as the mystery progresses and the town and its residents more endearing throughout the investigation."

—TheMysteryReader.com

"More Carolyn Keene than Agatha Christie, Buzzelli captures the quaint quirkiness of country folk with a not-so far-fetched twist on the things they'll do for money."

—The Detroit *Metro Times*

DEAD FLOATING LOVERS

"[An] enjoyable sequel…"

—*Publishers Weekly*

"A mystery that keeps you guessing, together with the story of a woman slowly finding her voice."

—*Kirkus*

"Quirky characters, the life of a journalist and a developing writer of fiction, and the focus on a woman ready to choose her life's direction all add to the story."

—*Booklist*

"Readers will find the same strong sense of place and great characters that are hallmarks of Sarah Graves and Philip Craig."

—*Library Journal*

"Buzzelli is lyrical in her descriptions of the Michigan countryside in the spring and gives nice twists to her characters…"

—*Mystery Scene*

"If you love mysteries that toss in lots of local flavor, don't miss this book."

—*Traverse City Record-Eagle*

"A satisfying tale with a lot of local color, deftly exploring uneasy relationships and deadly situations."

—*Lansing State Journal*

ALSO BY ELIZABETH KANE BUZZELLI

Dead Dancing Women
Dead Floating Lovers

FORTHCOMING BY ELIZABETH KANE BUZZELLI

Dead Dogs and Englishmen

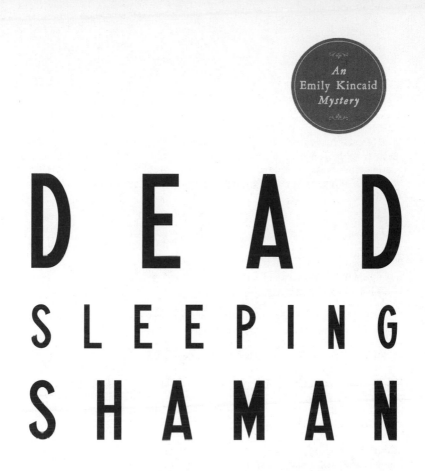

An Emily Kincaid Mystery

DEAD SLEEPING SHAMAN

Elizabeth Kane Buzzelli

MIDNIGHT INK
WOODBURY, MINNESOTA

FIRST EDITION
First Printing, 2010

Book design by Donna Burch
Cover design by Ellen Dahl
Editing by Rosemary Wallner

The unpublished poem "She Meets the Bag Lady (*sans frontieres par excellence*)" is used with permission of the author, Erica Weick.

Midnight Ink, an imprint of Llewellyn Worldwide Ltd.

Library of Congress Cataloging-in-Publication Data
Buzzelli, Elizabeth Kane, 1946–
  Dead sleeping shaman / Elizabeth Kane Buzzelli.—1st ed.
    p. cm.—(An Emily Kincaid mystery ; #4)
  ISBN 978-0-7387-1877-4 (alk. paper)
  1. Women journalists—Fiction. 2. Shamans—Fiction.
3. Michigan—Fiction. I. Title.
  PS3602.U985D445 2010
  813'.6—dc22
                                    2009048235

Midnight Ink
A Division of Llewellyn Worldwide Ltd.
2143 Wooddale Drive
Woodbury, MN 55125-2989
www.midnightinkbooks.com

Printed in the United States of America

For my good friends at Coldwell Banker Schmidt in Kalkaska: Julie Vance for her kindness and endless help, Bob Murray for his wonderful stories, Chad Anderson for his patience, Marti Wilson for sharing the bottom of the totem pole with me, Jeff Fitch for his many "Beautiful Day!" pronouncements and constant good humor, Phyllis Hermes for her laughter, and Jim Williams for his innate goodness.

For my good friends at the Kalkaska Public Library: Kate Mosher, Deb Bull, Shirley Hill, Margaret Beebe, Barbara Joabar, Bonnie Reed, and Janith Ottgen. Also my many thanks to the Kalkaska Library Book Club and the Friends of the Kalkaska County Library for all their support.

And most especially for Greg Hughes. While his technical assistance and his love of mysteries save me from big mistakes in police procedure, any errors found are solely mine.

She Meets the Bag Lady
(*sans frontieres par excellence*)

The bag lady again,
    inhabitant of no city, dweller of dream,
The one dressed in the best of wool,
    the shiniest of thrifty shop of Gucci shoes.
You could not tell but for a slight frayed edge,
    moth bitten hole this side of sleeve.
    In her thrilling dazzling mocha green castor scarf and skirt,
    between you and I and her and Liz,
    she is the best in dress,
    albeit the shine of shoe be made of spit.

This lady of color and of coordination,
    with many wrinkles to her smile and to her face,
    many wrinkles to her thighs and to her belly.
This hallucinatory woman of many wrinkles
    sets her mind to go to Paris,
    sets her will to go on and find Alice,
    that same Alice,
    who with much malice interfered in her love,
        way back when.

So this my lady of fifty, of sixty, of seventy,
    lined incised
    slight trembling fingers
    sets a light to this one last rag,
    soaked in virgin olive, pure oil will not do.
        Sets a light in the tin
garbage can
    in fire and warms her hands
this bag lady of eighty,

And on she goes to catch a bus,
    on her way to find a way to go to Paris,
    to see the tower, to sip the wine, to touch the statue,
    to fall in love and to find the malice.
Last I saw her, the bag lady, she was singing songs inside a barge,
    inside a bus, impeccable as always.

This bag lady
    who likes to be fed on grapes.

—By Brazilian poet Erica Weick

ONE

Monday, October 12

15 days until the end of the world

I FIGURED THE COLORFUL woman under the scraggly jack pine was sleeping off a drunk. She lay propped against the rough tree trunk with her large straw hat drawn over her face. Her hands were crossed in her lap, her legs stuck out straight, the toes of her black shoes pointing skyward. I had no intention of disturbing her. Not that it wasn't odd, that she slept there at the entrance to Deward, an abandoned logging town, but the last thing I wanted, on this, a very happy day for me, was to have to talk to a stranger, share my good news with anyone, or do anything more than sit on my happy letter, which I mean literally, since I'd stuck it in the back pocket of my jeans.

You see, this is the sad and pathetic picture of me when I am "happy." Emily Kincaid, 34, divorced, running out of money, living alone in the backwoods of northwest Lower Michigan, trying to sell a mystery novel nobody wanted, but just that day hearing from a New York literary agent interested enough to ask to see the entire manuscript. Most writers would find such an event thrilling and worthy of a party or at least a few happy phone calls to friends. The friends might want to take me out to a wonderful place for dinner, share a bottle of champagne to celebrate, and share dreams of when I would be famous and mysterious and sought after by conference coordinators and universities which would vie to be the repository of my papers when, and if, I should ever decide to die.

Not me. But then I'm not "most" writers.

It was a long time since I'd had anything to celebrate so I guessed I wasn't doing it very well, walking alone in the sunny autumn woods on my way to do a feature piece about ghost towns for an October special section of the Traverse City newspaper, the *Northern States-man*. I was a stringer there, doing occasional stories for the editor, Bill Corcoran; working for next to nothing.

What I'd really wanted most after Madeleine Clark's letter came that morning was to hide inside my little golden house on my little wild lake with Sorrow, my ugly, black-and-white, young dog. I wanted to lock the door behind us, take the phone off the hook, and laugh my head off. But it seemed I had little talent for happiness left in me. Being at Deward, where a noisy, dirty, ragged lumber camp once stood at a horseshoe bend in the Manistee River, was probably perfect. A normal woman would want to laugh and wave the letter at new friends in Leetsville, the small town closest to where I lived—all those people who'd given up on my ever being a real writer; people who smiled their sad smiles when I mentioned a new book I intended to write and, instead, brought me plots they'd seen on old "Murder, She Wrote" episodes. Their version of pearls before …

Anyway, a cult-like, End of the World group had moved into Leetsville, according to my friend, Deputy Dolly Wakowski, one of Leetsville's finest. They expected the end of the world to begin right there—around the 45th Parallel, and very soon, if I was to believe what Dolly said. She was the one who called to warn me to stay out of town, if I could. "Goin' crazy here. Givin' out tickets left and right." To Dolly that meant true happiness and she was one who actually knew what made her happy.

I kicked along the sandy trail, going over and over the letter; the agent's words circling in my brain, twisting, fluttering, bowing, and giving an uppity sniff... *fetching characters... deep knowledge of your place... very interested in seeing more...* but taking pleasure in being alone, too, hugging my news to myself.

That's when I came on the sleeping gypsy-looking woman.

She seemed comfortable enough under the tall pine with that big straw hat covering her face, thin hands clasped in her lap against the cheap fabric of a wildly colored skirt of bilious greens and shocking oranges. Picture of pastoral innocence, I thought. Well, gaudy innocence, in her bright purple silk blouse and that wild skirt lying in precisely drawn folds around her. Her long-fingered, beringed hands were still and graceful, one on top of the other in her lap. Sketchy dark shadows of bare jack pine under-branches traced the skirt down over her hips and her legs to end at those crossed-at-the-ankles feet in narrowly pointed shoes.

I grumbled to myself. No time for some drunken lady needing rescuing. What I wanted was to get past her without a word since I didn't have a word to share. I had to go to the place where the lumber town once stood, take my photos, make my notes, and be as quiet as the breeze barely ruffling the tree branches.

A turkey buzzard sat, like a Christmas ornament, at the very top of the tree where the woman slept. Below him were three noisy crows, hopping from branch to branch, staring out at me with their beady, bright eyes and giving me a caw or two.

I stopped in the middle of the weedy path, giving the crows a chance to get bored with me and shut their pointed beaks. The woman didn't stir. It must have been peaceful for her, stretched out so comfortably, the way she was.

I put one finger to my lips to hush the crows, pushed my hands down into my corduroy jacket pockets, one hand on my digital camera, one hand on my notebook, and sniffed. I'd get by the woman and keep my back turned if I heard her waken. My hunched shoulders would let her know I was in no mood for conversation. My uncombed, striped blond hair, caught at the back of my head by a red rubber band, would scream I was a woods woman who any sane person should stay far away from.

I followed the path through tall and browning grasses around to where the old sawmill once stood, up on a high switchback of the meandering Manistee, a river so clear and tranquil the few grasses at the bottom lay sidewise, unmoving in the pent current. Color burst from everywhere—blue sky in the lazy river, rainbowed clouds dressing up the water, greens and yellows and reds of trees thick along the shore, and bright gray tangled branches bowing into the river, creating eddies doing slow swirls before moving on. Man-made vees of logs, built to separate the timbers, still cut the river out from shore— the only evidence that men had worked in this place. I made my notes, recorded impressions, and took photographs.

I turned my back to the river, hugging my arms across my chest. There was a small breath of cold coming from the water; the kind of dampness that gets on your skin and lays there like mold, as if it would become a permanent part of you. I shivered, then turned to walk slowly up the path leading to where rows of tar-papered shacks once stood. As I slouched along, I told myself that I should be grateful to have at least one of my books considered worthy. Any sane writer would be standing drinks for everyone at The Skunk Saloon in town about now. Couldn't I just see Dylan Thomas being carried out of a Welsh pub the night he learned he would be a famous poet? *Do not go gentle into that good night*… I'm sure they carted him home and then he drank some more, the drink leading him like a siren's song into what wouldn't be a *good night* after all.

With such a bad example before me, the last thing I wanted was for anyone to know that I was three years' pregnant with possibility, and the elephant I was expecting might very well be still-born despite a New York agent. Happiness was a prelude to misery, as my Irish ancestors would have told you. *Laugh in the morning, cry by night.*

The only reminder of the row upon row of shacks where families had lived were rectangles and squares of reindeer moss outlining what once were brick foundations. I dug into the moss and came up with half a brick stamped W.W.CO. I'd missed the time of reindeer moss in bloom, tiny red flowers almost microscopic they were so small, and perfect. That was in July. This was early October—with the trees fired into a kind of celebration I no longer welcomed, knowing that winter was coming, always sooner rather than later.

I stepped into the woods to walk the outlined shacks. Behind one I bent to pick up something white against the moss. A piece of china, carefully curved; the graceful bend of a soup tureen. I held it in my cupped hand and thought of the poor woman who had cherished this lone piece of elegance; the woman who one day broke this—her pride and joy, the bowl she set carefully before her family, lifting the lid to let the aroma of her soup flow out and around the people she loved. I could almost see her holding the broken bowl in her worn hands, taking it to the dump behind the rows of houses, setting it there—in irretrievable pieces, and turning back to her tar-papered shack, no room left in her for even a single tear.

So, ok. I set the piece of china back under the moss. This was my "happy" day, and I sure as hell wasn't going to end up mourning the soup tureen of a woman crammed, every winter, into a shack with a dozen kids and a husband who could be flattened by a falling tree at any moment. Talk about the failure of hope; that skittish thing with feathers, as Emily Dickinson well knew; a thing you couldn't really trust and can't hold on to. Maybe Emily meant hope was like a bird in the hand, but everybody knows the mess a bird in the hand would leave behind.

I headed back up the path toward the entrance to the town, and home.

First I had to get past the sleeping drunk again. If I wasn't going to see friends, on this happy morning, I certainly didn't want to talk to somebody I didn't know. Especially a stranger who looked as if she could pop up, put her hand out, and demand I give her money in a wheedling voice. There'd been a gypsy on the Greek island of Rhodes, where Jackson, my cheating ex-husband, and I had gone to walk the medieval street of the Knights Hospitaller and the Knights Templar, back in happier times. The young, steamy woman had swayed her way to Jackson's side, stuck her hand into his pocket, and leaned her head against his shoulder, flirting up at him. I think she got a dollar and a lecture since Jackson wasn't one to splurge, especially on gypsy women of no interest. I remembered that Jackson told her to go back to her own homeland and she had asked, "And where is my homeland, Sir?" That answer grew huge to me when I sought out my own homeland; alone, divorced, and seeking an answer to who I really was—when my academic degrees; a good job on an Ann Arbor newspaper; and an abortive, forever, love were all stripped away.

As I got close to the woman I tiptoed, as if the sandy, rutted trail allowed for noise. She hadn't moved. The long, pale hands were arranged exactly as they had been arranged. The folds of the skirt were as perfect as before. I thought of spiders and ants; all things that fly and crawl and leap and could land on your skin if you slept on the ground. The thought of insects creeping into my nose and ears, tickling my arm hairs, and maybe nesting in some shaded part of my body, made my stomach lurch. And wasn't the ground damp? And autumn chilled?

I metaphorically gave a tip of my hat to the sleeping lady— braver woman than I—and put a finger to my lips, shushing those crows again. I was going to pass on by. I was going to take my wild glee at success—of a sort—home. But a thought stopped me. There had been no car out on the two-track leading in. This place was miles from a main road, miles from any houses, back in the forest on land the DNR managed. How had she gotten here? Maybe she'd been dumped, too drunk to know where she was.

Maybe she was sick. Those hands were certainly pale and marble-looking; the nails—now that I really looked—broken. The slightest twinge of conscience hit me. I cleared my throat to see if she would waken. Nothing. I squatted and balanced myself on a splay-fingered hand dug into the sand, then reached out and touched one of the woman's shoes. I gave it a gentle shake.

She slept on.

Quietly, I said, "Ma'am? Ma'am? Are you all right?"

The straw hat slid, more from the foot shaking than from any movement the woman made. I waited, holding my breath, sure she'd snap awake and demand to know what the heck I was doing shaking her foot.

"Ma'am!" I shook her shoe harder. If she was really sick, or unconscious, this was no time to be delicate.

The straw hat slid again. In slow motion, it moved off to the left, down and across her face. The rigid hands in her lap didn't spring up to catch it. The toes of her shoes remained pointing sternly at the fall sky.

The hat moved on, exposing part of the woman's pale cheek. It moved again, until one open blue eye peeked out; one fixed blue eye rimmed heavily with red. The eye didn't blink or focus. I looked at the dead blue eye with horror, falling away from her, scrambling back, breath catching in my throat.

I squatted there and tried to think. Something had to be done. I had to move.

As I watched, still hoping she would wake up and stumble to her feet, a huge black fly crawled from the side of one wide-open, staring eye. It made its way across the pale, almost waxen, cheek to stop, in that dead-still way of autumn flies, to bring its forefeet up, to settle back, and begin to groom its shiny, bottle-green head.

TWO

Still 15 days to go

I WAS A WRECK when I got to Leetsville; in no mood to put up with traffic. Least of all the unusual traffic stretching along both sides of US131, clogging the roadsides. Most of the cars were old, with big REPENT, THE END IS NEAR signs on their doors or roofs. The Chevys and Hondas and anything else that was on its last legs made slow progress along the road—like a bad small-town parade. Some of the vehicles headed north, out toward where I'd heard the cult was staying at an old spiritualist campground. Others were on their way into town. The IGA parking lot was filled, and so was Fuller's EATS restaurant where people stood in a line reaching out the door, all waiting to get inside for Monday's breakfast special.

Sy Huett, a used car dealer from down in Kalkaska, had joined the automobile parade, working his way slowly through town. The big sign on the black hearse he drove read: BEFORE YOU DIE, YOU'LL BUY FROM SY. Nothing like a small-town entrepreneur for creativity. Sy, a skinny guy with a comb-over to rival Donald

Trump's, was obviously betting the world wasn't going to end anytime soon. People buying his used cars had to be betting it would, and he'd never get a dime. I wasn't sure who I was rooting for in this one. Sy had a tendency to be a bit of a pain, especially if you drove a car as old as my yellow Jeep.

A motley group of people walked along the highway—a rare occurrence in Leetsville. Some of them wore pale, rough robes; nubby stuff like coarse linen or wool; something very old. The robes were hooded, closing faces into shadow. Waists were cinched by a length of white cotton rope—à la St. Francis, without the bird on the shoulder. A few of the devotees had thrown back their cowls to show shorn heads. Men and women, both, heads bare of hair. It looked like a Biblical movie being shot, but these were serious folks, come to Leetsville because the end of the world was upon us—only fifteen days away. Which made me wish I'd waited to pay my property taxes—just in case.

Quite a few of my friends among the Leetsvillians had been out to hear the Reverend Fritch, leader of the flock, preach. Some were scared. Some scoffed at the idea that the Four Horsemen of the Apocalypse would be thundering down 131 at exactly noon on October 27. Leetsville, the reverend pronounced, was at the apex of a confluence of something or other—planets, prophecy. Maybe it was that Michigan was almost surrounded by big waters and water attracted cosmic change and Leetsville was at some perceived center of everything.

I waited at the stop sign hoping for a break in the traffic. I had to get to the police station, find Chief Lucky Barnard or Dolly Wakowski, and get back out to that poor woman under the tree.

Damned "happy" day, I thought as I waited for a semi trying to get through town. First I lost my Special K breakfast out there, after watching that awful fly sit on the woman's cheek. Then I had to stop along the dirt road into town to give up the half bagel with cream cheese I'd had before the Special K. My mouth tasted like the inside of a crypt and all I wanted was to be around big, tough cops—like Lieutenant Brent from the Michigan State Police post in Gaylord, with his single dark eyebrow always knitted into a frown, his bald head shiny and tough looking, and his gun strapped reassuringly around a middle thick as a tree trunk.

Behind Sy Huett's hearse, there was an opening in the traffic. I nosed the Jeep forward and across the highway. The station was a couple of blocks over, on Divinity Drive, past the Baptist Church and the wood-sided Church of the Contented Flock sitting under huge old oak trees as yellow as corn silk. The Leetsville Police and Fire Department coexisted in a low, gray, cinder-block building. The hand-painted sign over one of the doors spelled out LEETS-VILLE POLICE.

I parked and suffered a slight twinge of conscience, gripping the steering wheel for balance. Maybe I should have covered her with something? What if a bear found her? What if one of those hungry, green-eyed coyotes came upon her? There were crows there already. And that turkey buzzard—like death itself sitting up in the tree.

I got out, ticking off what I had to do, and slammed the car door behind me. I needed a medical examiner, techs in their crime scene suits and … what else?

Naw, that was Dolly's job. I took a few deep breaths and tried to shut my mind hard against the picture of the dead woman.

Dolly's banged-up patrol car wasn't in the lot, only Chief Lucky Barnard's battered Saturn sedan. I dug into my jacket for a Kleenex, spit on it, and wiped at my jeans where a Special K flake had stuck.

I entered the green-painted, six-paneled door to the sound of the bell Dolly had installed as her early warning system. There was no one in the small lobby, behind the counter, or at the phone. No miserable teenager, who'd been caught batting down mailboxes, sat miserably awaiting pickup by angry parents. No Wilson Parker, our town drinker, snoring in one of the scarred oak chairs, his grizzled chin resting on a big, calloused fist, a bit of drool seeping down to his green flannel shirt.

"Chief?" I called.

It took a minute and then a tired voice yelled, "Emily? Come on back. I'm kind of busy."

Lucky's office was down the hall to the left. Before his office came the two-by-four converted broom closet reserved for Dolly and her files and rolls of toilet paper and a thermos bottle. He sat at his desk, phone to his ear, chin tucked into his chest. He nodded his dark head at me, gave a tired sigh, took a closer look at my face, and got off the phone.

"Better sit before you fall down," Lucky said, his voice a long drawl, his tired eyes wary. I sat and tried to calm myself.

The chief's office was a ten-by-ten room done in cheap seventies pressed-board paneling. Old green filing cabinets stood along the walls, some with the drawers hanging slightly askew. File folders, waiting to go into the cabinets, tilted dangerously on the chief's desk. Chief Barnard was over-extended. Leetsville didn't have a lot of money for their police force. All small towns were cutting back, but the people of Leetsville said they couldn't imagine their town without Lucky and Dolly. "Why, that's the path to anarchy!" Colby Mortenson, the Mayor, recently said at EATS one Sunday morning over blueberry pancakes. Right then and there the townspeople got up a petition which they presented to themselves at the next town meeting, backing the need for their guardians of liberty.

"I found a dead body," I said, happy to have the words out and be absolved of all responsibility.

Lucky's eyes were deeply and darkly puffed. A big man, Lucky could deflate when he got tired enough, lose bulk, and shrink down into himself. He was somewhere in the middle of a meltdown at the moment, blinking a time or two, then sweeping a large hand through his thick brown hair. His lips fell open, his tongue licked out. "Ah shit," he said. "I don't need anything else right now, Emily. Got a missing person; all these nuts in town ..."

"I was out at Deward, doing a story for the paper ..."

"So, where's the body?" He cut through what he must have suspected would be a long buildup.

"At Deward. Under a tree."

He made a face, leaned back in his chair, and shook his head. "You sure? Could be sleeping ..."

"She's dead. I don't know who she is and I don't know how she got out there. I need you ... or Dolly ..."

"Probably be the state police," he said, then thought deeply. "We've got a Mutual Assistance Pact with them and with the sheriff's department. Everybody's so damned over-extended these days. Guess it might be best if Dolly went with you ..." He nodded to himself. "Ok, go get her. She's handing out jaywalking tickets as fast as she can write 'em. Probably by EATS. Or near The Skunk Saloon. I'll call Gaylord. Lieutenant Brent'll come out. You'll need to be there to meet 'im." He snapped into policeman mode, ticking off actions to take as he reached for the phone.

"Geez, Lucky, and all these people in town. I'll probably have to cover this … this invasion for the paper."

"TV already been. Making it worse, if you ask me. And all I can tell you is we've got near a thousand people on our hands and Dolly's giving them tickets while they're laughing at her 'cause they say they'll never have to pay 'em. That makes Dolly mad, so now she's slapping tickets on their trucks and looking into if they've got permits to camp out beyond town, and telling people to get right into the station, here, and pay or they'll sit out the end of the world in our jail."

I took a deep breath and got up. Ah, Dolly on a crusade. Too bad I was going to spoil her fun.

"I'll find her," I said, turning away as Lucky punched numbers on the phone.

"She won't like leaving town right now," he said.

"Too bad. Dolly doesn't always get what she wants."

"Say that again. Better not be a mistake—your dead body. She'll never let you hear the last of it."

He listened as the phone on the other end rang. "Lieutenant Brent and the medical examiner will get out there about the same time as you and Dolly. I'll call an ambulance—in case you're wrong. You don't have a cell phone, do you?"

I shook my head.

"Take Dolly's patrol car. I'll be in touch."

Someone answered and he asked for Lieutenant Brent. As I walked out the door I heard him saying, "Lucky Barnard here. That reporter with the *Northern Statesman*, you know, Emily Kincaid. She thinks she found a body…"

———————

There was no use driving. I was better off on foot, especially when I got out to 131 and threaded my way through robed people and laughing strangers who had the nerve to turn and stare as if I were the weird one here.

In front of EATS, the line stretched out the front door and back around toward the IGA. A lot of the locals waited among the faithful looking like cats caught with their tails in a trap, eyes wide, mouths open. This wasn't a usual day in Leetsville. Our own folks were out in force to get a firsthand look.

Anna Scovil, town librarian, stood straight and unhappy among the robed people pushing hard behind her in the line. She waved and called to me as I wormed my way past.

"Have you ever?" She put a hand out to grab on to my arm. "What's this world coming to? Can't even get into our own businesses. Why these people are taking over…"

"Be happy, Madam," a bearded, robed man behind her chided. "For we bring you the news."

"Well, for goodness sakes! I wasn't even speaking to you." She reared back and fixed the bright-eyed, hirsute man with a glower.

"But I'm speaking to you. We're here with Reverend Fritch to speak to the world. There's not much time. You'd better put your house in order…"

"My house is fine." She turned her back to the man and rolled her eyes at me as I pushed on.

Bob Barley from Bob's Barber Shop stood with George, of the candy store, and Winnie Lorbach, the lady slipper lady, farther up the line.

"What the heck do you think of Leetsville now, Emily?" Bob, gruff voice lost down in the blue flannel shirt he wore, asked. "Ain't this something?"

"Something," I agreed and stood a minute looking over the crowds along the street. It didn't do to be in too big a hurry with Leetsville people. There was always time for chewing over the latest news, or the hottest piece of gossip. This new upheaval seemed to have shocked even the regulars at EATS into near silence.

"Have you seen Dolly?" I asked Bob.

"Saw her down a ways. Trying to give out tickets for jaywalking. Like givin' a ticket to a grackle, you ask me. These folks so sure they're going to die soon they're rippin' up her tickets and handin' them back to her. Makin' Dolly hoppin' mad, I'll tell ya."

I started down where Bob pointed and spotted her in the middle of a sea of white robes, her blue, flat uniform cap bobbing and weaving, the people around her shouting and laughing, making a joyful sound.

I heard her squeaky voice when I got closer. She was yelling for everybody to stand back or they were all going to jail. There was hooting and hollering. The religious folks were having themselves a good time at Dolly's expense. I pushed my way through the throng, caught her eye, and mouthed, "Need you. NOW!"

She frowned, tightening her small features into a bunch at the center of her face. "No time, Emily," she called over. "Got my hands full here with all these lawbreakers."

"I found a dead woman out in Deward," I leaned in and shouted toward her ear.

She snapped back, hands going to her gun belt. Her pale eyes grew huge, the right eye wandering off slightly as she considered what I'd dropped in her lap. "What do you mean, 'a dead woman'?"

"What I said. Lucky wants you to get back there with me and take your patrol car so he can stay in touch."

"You nuts?" Dolly twisted her mouth and nose in opposite directions. "I've got order to keep here in Leetsville. This place is going crazy. They're telling me they don't have to believe in man's law, is what they're saying."

That brought an "Amen" from behind her that was picked up and echoed around the crowd and out toward 131.

"There's jaywalking and littering and parking violations happening all over. Caught one guy with his robe in the air, urinating over behind the gas station. You go. Be Gaylord's jurisdiction anyway."

I shook my head. "You know better than that. Lucky wants you there."

"Hell's bells and panther tracks," she swore, then looked around at the circle of believers, drifting away now that Dolly had stopped threatening them. "You better be sure about this," she hissed at me.

"You think I'd make it up? So I could get a ride in your patrol car with the siren blaring in my ears?"

She made a disgruntled noise, less than pleased that I had inserted myself into her busy day. With one wave at the crowd, she stalked off toward her police car, parked illegally out on the highway. She gave a last "Get back" toward a robed, shiny-headed woman walking in the road.

At the station, Dolly quickly checked in with Lucky Barnard, who said he had called Gaylord. "Medic and an ambulance on the way. Soon as Brent gets his team together, he'll be out. Wants to see you, Emily. He'll need a statement."

Once away from town we didn't pass another car on any of the roads leading to Deward. The siren screamed anyway, wailing through empty space.

"I still think you could've handled this better," Dolly groused, leaning forward over the wheel, staring out the front window, her eyes going from left to right, watching for deer or any animal that would have had to be deaf not to hear us coming.

"And leave you out of it? Since when? You'd have skinned me alive when you found out."

"Not this time. Nothing to do with us. I got plenty going on in town. Bunch of nuts. They're sticking around 'til the twenty-seventh. You believe it? Two weeks more of their crap." She shook her head. "I've got a court date with those Mitchell boys. You watch, Brent'll try to foist this one off on us. Got enough to ..."

"She probably died of natural causes. You'll see what I mean when we get there. Could be a suicide. I didn't look close ..."

"Good thing. We don't need civilians pawing around a crime scene."

"Maybe not a crime scene ..."

She was quiet for a while, the siren the only sound, and that was muffled by the closed windows.

"Can you imagine them believing such crap?" she asked.

"Who? What crap?"

"That the world's going to end."

I shrugged. "Guess so. If you believe in your preacher ..."

18

"Crazy stuff." Dolly shook her head. "You heard about those hoofprints he's predicting?"

"Hoofbeats," I said. "Can't hear hoofprints."

"Whatever."

We drove on a few miles. Dolly picked up speed. "You should've called Gaylord straight away."

I was tired of this reluctant virgin act. "I don't have a cell phone."

"Closer than coming all the way back to Leetsville, where I was busy." She gave me a stern look. "As you could very well see."

"It was all I could think to do."

"You gotta think things out better."

She made a sharp left turn at the dirt road leading to Deward. The ruts in the road made our voices staccato when we tried to talk.

"What you need is to find yourself a real job. Keep yourself busy. Emily Kincaid, Fuller Brush salesperson. Something like that."

"They still sell Fuller Brushes?"

"Think so. You could find out."

"I might have an agent for the book. Think I'll start another one."

"Don't put me in the next one. Bad enough with this dead, dancing thing."

"Wouldn't think of it."

"And don't just copy somebody else's book either."

"I didn't do that on purpose."

"Yeah, well. You don't seem to do a lot of things on purpose. They happen to you." Her voice shivered with the bumps in the road.

"You mean like Jackson hanging around?"

"Whatever …"

She slowed, turned off the siren, and drove carefully onto the two-track sand trail leading into the long-gone town. There were more ruts than I remembered, having come out so fast. She pulled off the trail and parked where the sand wasn't deep, in the same place I'd parked before. An ambulance was there, pulled in toward the entrance to the town. No Michigan State Police cars; no white vans. Dolly reached into the back of her patrol car and pulled out a cloth bag and a clipboard. She checked her equipment, got out, and strode off toward where I pointed.

I didn't want to have to go back to where the woman lay, but I had to. I wished for a whole phalanx of big, strong cops. I wanted deep male voices, and techs working where the body had been. I wanted that woman gone, Deward back to what it was, and those terrible pictures out of my head.

I got out of the car slowly. All I had was Dolly. Like her, I didn't always get what I wanted.

THREE

WE CAUTIOUSLY STEPPED ALONGSIDE the sand trail, trying not to disturb the ground. If there had been footprints, I'd probably already obliterated them. The place was creepy; nothing pretty about the deep blue sky, or all those high puffy clouds. I vowed I'd never come here again. My feet dragged like big cement blocks. I didn't want to get to where she lay. Even more than last time, I didn't want to see her. I was hoping that when we turned the last bend she'd be gone. Let Dolly and Lieutenant Brent think me crazy. I'd take the blame if she'd come out of some catatonic state, gotten up, dusted off her wild skirt, shaken herself, and gone off the way she'd come.

Dolly, ever the sprinter, hurried ahead then turned to give me one of her exasperated, face-wrinkling looks.

"You coming or what?" she demanded, hands at her hips, the drooping gun belt showing under her heavy cop jacket.

"Coming," I mumbled as I took the last turn that would bring me to the woman, all her color, and that moveable hat.

The crows were still on guard, cawing when they saw us. Their numbers had grown. Like astonished spectators at an accident, they bowed and flew in and out of the jack pine, stopping to turn their nervous eyes down toward the woman and then toward us.

The turkey buzzard at the top of the tree was gone. I figured crows can sometimes be too much for anybody.

She was there. The big straw hat had fallen off completely and lay beside her, tipped up against her immovable body. Her blue, red-rimmed, eyes stared out across the path, toward the woods. The look on her face would have been benign if it weren't for the many flies that had gathered, making her features seem to move. Two medics were stepping back from the body.

"That her?" Dolly asked me ingenuously, standing with her feet apart, heavy shoes planted firmly in the sand.

I wanted to say "No, that's another one," but didn't because my stomach was turning again and I knew I had almost nothing left down there to give up.

She looked at me over her shoulder. "Know her?"

I shook my head.

"Me either. Sure dressed funny. Think she's a gypsy?" She bit her lip and looked hard at the woman. "Probably a suicide, you think?"

"How?"

"Poison. Pills."

"You see a pill bottle? Poison?"

She shook her head, set her crime scene bag and clipboard down, then whisked her hands off on her pants. "Could be in her pocket. I'm not touching anything."

Dolly greeted the medics, her hand out. "I'll be the officer in charge on this one," she said. "She dead?"

The two guys wore white suits, booties covering their feet, and clear latex gloves on their hands. Hard to tell what they looked like, other than Pillsbury Dough Boys. One nodded. "Dead all right."

"Anything obvious?"

He shook his head.

Dolly set her bag on the ground, asked the two guys for their names, then wrote them on her clipboard. The men went back toward their ambulance.

"Gotta keep a scene log," she told me as she held her clipboard out importantly. "You're on it, too. Anybody who gets near this woman goes into my log.

"And I gotta tape the area." Dolly busily drew a big roll of yellow police tape from her bag. She handed one end of the tape to me, hollering for me to watch where I walked, then, carefully staying away from the body, she ran the tape around a few of the big trees, making a large square with the dead woman at its center.

"That should do it," she said, eyeing our work. I said I thought it looked fine, the tape taking in the entire area around the body—to the back, both sides, and way down in front. Dolly pulled out her camera and began to take photos of the scene. Behind her, I slipped my camera from my pocket and took photos of my own. Quickly, before she noticed and yelled at me, I snapped the area, not just where the woman lay, but wider shots—all around her. I knelt and took contrast shots. The sun was directly overhead—not much shadow, but still I thought I saw one place that was different from the rest. Standing, looking down, I couldn't see what the photo had shown. I would look at it again, after I got home, I told myself.

Voices came from toward the parking area and suddenly the space around us filled with men and women. Dolly introduced me, calling me "the body finder" which, I supposed, described my role there. Lieutenant Jimmy Brent nodded, his bald head beady with sweat from the walk in, his unibrow forming a single dark cloud over deeply suspicious eyes.

"I'll take a preliminary statement," he said, getting down to business as he pointed me to a quiet place under tall trees, out of the way of the three techs climbing into their white suits. The M.E., old Doc Stevenson, was there, taking photos, then a video of the body, the area, and then of all who were gathered.

I went with Lieutenant Brent to a quieter place, under tall trees, a soft bed of dried pine needles at our feet.

"Mind saying what you were doing out here?" Brent held a pad of official-looking paper and a pen in his flat hands. His voice fell into the deep tones of the accuser as the wind kicked up and swirled dead needles around our legs.

"Assignment."

"That it?"

"Why else?" I knew the police didn't care for nuance—like "I was feeling good and wanted to be left alone" or "I was thinking about writing another book ... "

He raised that eyebrow at me, the look like a shade going up, but under the shade were those eyes. He wrote on his pad of paper.

"Magazine?"

I shook my head. "*Northern Statesman.*"

"On … what … ?"

"You know. Ghost towns. For an October issue."

"And she …," he nodded to where the woman lay, "was here when you got here? You thought she was sleeping, I guess."

I nodded but added nothing, recalling all cop shows where people lawyered up in the face of tough questioning.

"When'd you realize she was dead? I mean, except for the flies …"

I shrugged and dug my toe in, scraping a hole in the needles with my way-off-white sneaker.

"I moved her foot and she didn't respond. Then a fly walked down her cheek."

"You touch the body or anything? I mean other than the shoe?"

I shook my head.

"If we find your fingerprints, that's the reason."

"Why else?" I demanded, getting angry. "Look, I've got to call the story into the paper. My editor will want something ASAP."

"Check with Dolly. I'll keep her informed. Or call me at the police post." The response was grudging. I figured I'd get as much help from him as I had on past stories. The guy was nothing if not tight lipped.

He asked a few more questions and said he wanted me in Gaylord for a follow-up as soon as I could arrange it. I went back to stand away from all of them and watch.

"Since I'm the O.I.C.," Dolly said to Brent as he ambled back to stand beside her, "I'm keeping records. I already took the photos … stuff like that. You doing a baseline measurement?"

Brent nodded, then asked one of the officers to get the tape measure from his car.

"Good thing I've been studying crime scene management on-line," Dolly was going on to anybody who would listen. "No damned defense lawyer is gonna catch me out this time if I have to testify."

"Good job, Officer," Brent actually smiled, then ran a hand over his head, coughed a little, and went off with another man to establish the baseline—setting a hundred-foot tape measure from tree to tree: point A to point B to point C, with the woman's body the central focus. From there they took more measurements and recorded them on a drawing of the site—always with the body and its orientation at the center.

I supposed I should be going. I wasn't needed and was actually ignored as the men and women went about their jobs, but it was fascinating to watch how quickly the body wasn't as important as the investigation. Everything was done meticulously. Dolly surprised me, going about recording people at the site, taking her photos, and making notes as to what everyone was doing or finding. Evidently she'd learned a lot since the last couple of bodies we'd found.

The M.E., having finished his work, stepped out of the grid the officers had set up and joined Dolly and Brent, heads down, glancing at the woman, and then at the ground. When their huddle was over, he motioned for the medics to come take the body, packed his bag, and walked off.

I turned away as the dead woman was gone over, hands bagged, then lifted so her head fell back. A thin, white rope around her neck could be seen. I gagged, but not so loud anyone noticed. The body was wrapped and zipped, set on a stretcher—ready for the pathologist. As they wheeled her past me, Dolly must have noticed my face had gone green. She came to where I huddled in on myself and put her hand at my back, patting me awkwardly. "You ok?" she asked, bending her head to mine.

I nodded even though a lonely Special K flake did gymnastics in my stomach.

Dolly leaned closer. "Strangled. Rope. Guess you were right to begin with. Sure is dead. And you know what else? Another thing you were onto before me? I think it's ours: me and Lucky, and you, of course."

She hesitated when I pulled away and gave her my version of a "you've-got-to-be-kidding" look. "I mean, I might know somebody who's hunting for her. We got a missing person called in early today. And it's all about Leetsville. We'll have to take this one on, Emily. It's ours—if it's who I think it is."

"I don't want a body," I moaned as the sturdy little woman moved back, bottom lip determinedly up over her top lip, police hat sitting pertly atop wet-looking, semi-blond hair. Dolly ready for action.

"Doesn't matter what you want," she growled. "We never get what we want, Emily. You, of all people, should know that by now. Didn't sell a book yet, did ya? Didn't get your ex-husband back. Don't have a job. We get what we're given. That's all. We got to handle whatever that is."

After that little philosophical diatribe, I protested no more. All I wanted was to return to my quiet little house on my quiet little beaver-ridden lake, and be left alone. Again I didn't get what I wanted. I had to wait for Dolly to finish and take me back to town to get my car.

FOUR

Still 15 days

A NEAT PILE OF doggie turds waited on the kitchen floor, narrow wafts of steam rising. There was a puddle of water next to Sorrow's bowl. I assumed the water was truly water, dripped from one of Sorrow's long, extensive drinks, and not dog pee. I cleaned up the very neatly coiled pile of shit, wrapped it in a newspaper, and set it out on the side porch to go to the garbage can.

There was another pile to deal with here, a message from Jackson, who was staying in a cabin over on Spider Lake, outside of Traverse City, for what seemed to be an interminable sabbatical year of writing an opus on the work of Geoffrey Chaucer and his Canterbury pilgrims. He was into his second year up here. I wondered if he would ever go back to teaching at the University of Michigan.

"I won't take no for an answer," he was saying. "I haven't seen you in weeks so I'm picking up pasta at Gio's, in Kalkaska, and coming over tomorrow evening. Now, don't bother making faces and thinking up ways to rid yourself of my company, Emily. I'm going to be there. If you are still mad at me for that last … well, indiscretion, which meant nothing, and shouldn't matter anyway since we are no longer married, as you should, by now, have noticed. You will simply have to get over it. See you about six. Oh, and tie that damn dog up. I will be wearing new, and very expensive, slacks and a cashmere sweater. I'd like not to have doggie prints on at least one outfit."

Yuck. I punched the button, erasing Jackson. No use calling him back and pleading the Black Plague. Nothing stopped him when he was on a tear. Like the men and women of the United States Post Office, neither wind nor rain nor sleet nor dark of night deterred Jackson when he wanted something.

I called Bill Corcoran, at the paper. At least I could pretend to be a reporter.

"You found her?" he asked.

"I went out there to do the ghost town thing."

"Oh, yeah."

"I've got photos."

"Of Deward?"

"Yes. And of the body."

"Hmm, I don't think so. Not the body. We're not that kind of newspaper. Tell you what, I'll run with whatever you email me. Save the photos. Keep checking with Lieutenant Brent. Find out who the woman was and what happened to her."

His voice trailed off as he leaned away from the phone. I could visualize him in his cluttered office, large head with longish straight brown hair bent over the phone, his big-framed glasses slowly riding down his wide nose, and his middle finger going up, pushing the glasses, holding them in place.

"Looks like strangulation," I said.

"Um, murder. I'll want you to stay right on it."

"Dolly might know who she is. They got a missing persons report this morning. Dolly thinks the description is close."

"Get back to me when you get the ID, and anything else you've got." He hesitated. "You working with her on this one?"

"You know Dolly. If there's a way she can get herself, and me, involved, she'll do it."

"Hasn't worked out too badly for you," he said, obviously not wanting misery from me. "Got a book from that last one, didn't you? What about that business you two got into with the Indians? You writing that one?"

"Yeah, well, haven't sold the first one yet."

"You will. It's a good book."

"I did hear from an agent, a woman who's interested. I'm hoping…"

"Great!" At last, a friend who wished me well. "Keep me in the loop. Sure hope this works for you. Still looking for more freelancing?"

"Of course. Even if this agent takes me on, there's no money until she sells it. And even then, the advance will be small. I'm not known…"

"I'd like to talk to you when you come to town. There may be a slot here for you… nothing full time."

"Not obits again. That didn't work too well."

"A column."

I thought fast.

"What kind?"

"We could talk about it."

"When? Tomorrow morning Brent wants me in Gaylord to give a formal statement. I could come after that…" Thoughts of calling Jackson with my excuse for not being home when he brought his dinner ran through my head.

"No hurry."

"But…"

"Whatever… oh, and I'd like to have both you guys over for dinner, pay back you and Jackson for your past hospitality. Maybe Friday? Seven o'clock? And Emily, sorry it took me so long. I guess, with Jackson and Ramona—well you know what happened. I've been holding off."

"Sure. That would be great." It had been one dinner at Jackson's, with me a reluctant hostess and Bill bringing a friend, Ramona Sheffield, a small redhead who worked at the Dennos Museum. Ramona and Jackson ended up as… well, not friends so much as… I caught Jackson and Ramona… shall we say *in flagrante delicto*? Translation: while the crime is flaming hot. Water under the bridge. I even thought of Ramona fondly now. She'd saved me from making a huge mistake where Jackson was concerned.

"I'll call Jackson," he said.

"About the column…"

"Whenever." He hung up, dashing any hope I had of telling Jackson I would be away on important journalism business all day tomorrow.

So, no Traverse City. No nailing down more newspaper work, which I needed desperately since the winter gas bills and plowing bills and roof shoveling bills would soon be coming in. There was money left from the divorce and from my dad's life insurance, but it had to last. There wasn't a single penny for anything but the barest of necessities.

No putting Jackson off. I supposed I should vacuum the dog hair off the rug, or at least get that interesting cobweb up near the ceiling. What I did was tell myself I would think about all of that tomorrow—like Scarlett. Thinking was making my brain throb.

It was dusk, but still better to be out at the lake with Sorrow. Though I didn't have as long a history with him as I had with Jackson Rinaldi, it sure was happier. I called my dog, kissed his eager black-and-white head, looked into bright happy eyes, and figured maybe he was the best, and least complicated, friend I had in the world. We headed down to Willow Lake to frustrate the ducks and anger the beaver.

I picked up the sandy, slobbery stick from where Sorrow had dropped it on the wobbly old dock. I gave the stick a long, hard toss, as far as I could get it, out into the evening-still lake. Before the stick hit the water with a mighty splash, Sorrow launched his big black-and-white body off into space, shaking the dock and me. He hit the water, wallowed around for a minute, then struck out for the place where the stick floated, his paws cutting the water, chin up, head focused on nothing but that magnificent prize. Over near the beaver's den, there was a splash as the angry rodent slapped the water with his tail and retreated to his house.

Sorrow had to be part retriever no matter what else our vet, Doc Crimson, claimed for him. Maybe part some kind of English sheepdog, too. Part mastodon. Parts of a lot of things I couldn't, or wouldn't, name. His mother must have been quite the slut, one of a long line of sluts, to have spawned a dog of so many flavors.

I watched him swim full-heartedly after that stick and couldn't remember ever not having him with me. Sorrow might be ugly and ungainly—an animal that did nothing but annoy me most of the time—but when I needed him to come lay his head in my lap, roll his eyes up so that the red rims showed, and give me total and complete love, my heart felt as if it could burst out of my body. No matter how I tried, I couldn't remember ever being affected by Jackson that deeply.

If I could only find a man like Sorrow…

Christ! I thought, standing there on the dock in long shadows, watching my dog and hugging my sweater close, the last thing I needed was a new man in my life. The very thought of picking up someone's dirty underwear and smelly socks, or having to put meals on the table—how quickly experience punctures romance.

A tired sun sprang from behind a bank of surly clouds for just a minute, then it was gone. The air was so crisp you could take a bite out of it. Willow Lake lay quiet in the dying light. The water circles Sorrow made with his arcing leaps from the dock moved off in widening silver rings, catching the lighted clouds in sparkles. Around the lake, the willows had turned a soft yellow, branches hanging into the water. Red maples, golden oaks, tarnished beech and birch— they blended into a hazy, moving, mirrored image of autumn.

Sorrow crawled from the water dropped his stick, and squatted to pee—like a girl dog. Something was delayed in Sorrow. He should have been lifting his leg by now. It was one of my many worries—that he would never develop fully because all he had was me: no guy to show him how to do it right.

When he finished, he retrieved his stick, parted the reeds along the shore, and bounced down the dock to drop the stick next to my foot. He shook. Water flew everywhere. I was drenched, yelling, and cursing a string of fine blue words.

"Emily Kincaid?" a voice behind me called over my manic swearing.

Back up the beach, Crazy Harry Mockerman, my neighbor from across Willow Lake Road, stood giving me a quizzical and distinctly disturbed look.

"You ok, Emily?" Harry asked.

The skinny man in the shiny black funeral suit he wore every day of his life stood tall, surprised by my choice of epithets. He held a bouquet of golden oak leaves in his left hand. His right arm hung rigidly at his side, fist clenched.

My friend, Harry, was once a log skidder with one of the last companies to pull down the virgin pines. That was back in the fifties, way after all the fires had swept across the northern part of the state leaving few tall trees standing. Harry lived alone in a crooked little house, down a thorny, overgrown path across Willow Lake Road from me. He did odd jobs. Some truly odd, like saving me from his own pack of hunting dogs when I'd suspected him of driving his homemade half-car/half-truck into the back of Dolly's patrol car, forcing us into Arnold's Swamp with a bunch of caged birds and a worried old lady somebody was trying to kill.

"Why you mad at the dog?" he asked, frowning. As the proud owner of a pack of nameless and, I imagined, vicious dogs, Harry was an animal lover; except for those he trapped, shot, or picked up from Willow Lake Road—all smashed and very dead. Harry lived off the land. I didn't resent his killing, somehow. It wasn't like the lighted buck poles small towns put up every November. Not like the horror of coming on one of those prize poles at night, when the shadows of the dead animals stretched long and the bodies hung stiff; all the beauty gone.

"He got me all wet." I swiped at my jeans with my hands.

"What'd you expect? See that lake out there," he asked, a smug smile stretching his thin lips. "All water. Case you didn't know."

I counted to a silent twenty.

"Can I do anything for you, Harry?" I asked finally, walking toward him along the dock.

"Sure can." He backed off as I jumped to shore, over the mucky place where Sorrow had to stomp and throw a little mud to add to my damp jeans.

Harry lifted his right hand and slowly opened his fist. A round black button lay there, at the center of the pink and wrinkled palm. I stepped closer, bent over his hand, looked at the button and then up at Harry's grizzled face, into blue eyes so faded they were hardly any color at all.

"Came off my jacket. Can you sew it back on?"

"Well … guess I can try. I'm not much at sewing."

"Me neither. And all's I've got is white thread. That'd look funny, wouldn't it?"

He pointed to the place where a few threads stuck out on his jacket, the place where a button should have been.

I stood back and looked him over. His hair was slicked away from his face with some kind of pomade, maybe lard. A black tie was tied around his yellowed white shirt collar. His old shoes had been given a spit and polish. Harry was definitely more tricked out than I'd ever seen him, except once, at a funeral.

35

"What are you dressed up for?" I asked, not recalling another funeral I'd heard about.

"None of your business," he nodded along with his words. "Got a place I've got to get to and I don't want to go down there looking less than my best."

I smiled, ready to tease the old man as he sometimes teased me—the city girl.

"Come on, Harry. Where are you going? You want that button sewed on? You'd better tell me."

He mumbled a few words under his breath and toed the beach sand with his shoe until he remembered he'd just polished it and bent to wipe the shoe tip clean.

"Courtin'," he said.

"Courting? You mean as in calling on a lady friend?"

He nodded. "Delia Swanson."

I hesitated, trying to sort out the neighbors along Willow Lake Road. I only knew of one Delia. She lived about a mile from me, past where the Survivalists had their fenced-in camp with big "For Sale" signs and no takers. Delia Swanson had to be at least seventy-five but I guessed that was a good age for a man like Harry, in his late sixties. Still, Delia had been single all her life and lived with her mother, Bertha Swanson, who was now close to one hundred. I'd only met the mother once, when Delia brought her into EATS for Thanksgiving dinner last year. Kind of a nasty soul, not a smile or a good word for anyone in EATS, was what I remembered. One of those old people who seemed to melt inward until they had a face as wizened as an apple doll's, or a shrunken head. I remember everyone in the restaurant trying to make Bertha and Delia feel at home, but you could hear Bertha complaining about the stuffing having no oysters and the cranberry sauce straight out of one of those cans until I thought that if I were Eugenia Fuller, the restaurant owner, or Delia, I'd pick the old lady up by the scruff of her neck and toss her out the door.

"I'm inviting Delia into town to see that preacher what's come for the end of the world. Might as well hear the man out, is what Delia says, and I agree with her. She's one smart woman, I'll tell ya. Said that if the world didn't end the way the preacher said, we'd be no worse or better off than right now. But in case it does end, we'll be ready, souls prepared. Don't hurt to play the odds."

I nodded and led Harry up the path through the bronzed and fallen bracken to the house, where I sewed his button on with black thread while he sat formally upright on a stool at the kitchen island. When he was ready to go I offered him my Jeep to take his lady friend to town. His old half-car/half-truck wasn't the kind of vehicle to go a courtin' in and I didn't think it had a valid license. Harry shook his head but thanked me for my kindness. He walked stiffly out the door and back up my drive to where he'd parked his vehicle at the road.

In the house, I searched the cupboards and fridge for wine. Jackson would bring food but he'd forget the wine. And the bread. And dessert. I sighed.

There was a bottle of Valpolicella near the back of the refrigerator. That would do. In fact, I decided it would do so well I opened the bottle, poured myself a glass and went to sit on my sofa, wrapping a Christmas throw around my legs, and wondering if I should find something better than damp jeans and an old tee shirt to wear for my supper of scrambled eggs and two-day-old biscuits.

Sorrow, needing company, joined me, dropping a hard rubber ball in my lap that bounced against my wine glass, tipping it over onto me and the floor as the phone rang. I struggled to my feet, unwrapping the dripping afghan from my legs and pushing Sorrow, who stood barking at me to throw the ball, out of the way.

It was Dolly.

"I'll be there to get you tomorrow afternoon," she said. "Bringing someone with me. The lady who reported a missing person. We've got to get her over to Gaylord. She can identify the body..."

"Can't," I said firmly. "I've got plans."

"Yeah, well, cancel them. This is about the woman you found. You've got to be there. Even Brent said to bring you."

"Well, I've...I don't think..."

"Geez! You're a reporter, ain't you? I'd think you'd want to be there."

"As I said..."

"Yeah, sure. She's getting to town about two o'clock. Should be at your place about two-thirty."

I was left holding the phone in one hand and in the other a coverlet dripping wine. Of all the nerve. That grumpy little person could take herself and whoever she was bringing on over to Gaylord without me. I had better things...

Then came my "AHA" moment. Of course I had to go to Gaylord with Dolly and her friend tomorrow. Probably take all afternoon and evening. Business, after all. Very, very important business. I couldn't let Lieutenant Brent down...

I dropped the winy afghan, did a graceful little twirl in place, picked up the phone, and punched in Jackson's number.

FIVE

Tuesday, October 13
14 days to go

I worked on Dead Dancing Women all the next morning, getting it in shape to send to Madeleine Clark. In some places I took out words; in others I added words. I moved paragraphs around, then put them back. I cleaned up bad punctuation and misspellings even my spell-check missed. It was a daunting job, to get the novel in such good shape it would look perfect to professional eyes. Soon I got tired of the whole thing, went back to the house, and was happy to see Dolly when she drove down my drive at precisely two-thirty.

"Got her in the car." She yanked my screen door open and snapped her head back toward the patrol car. A woman was seated in the front.

"Who is she?" I asked.

"Friend of the dead woman."

"What's Brent saying?"

She shrugged. "No car out there. Helluva walk in without one."

"Think she was carried? Sure looked arranged, there at the bottom of the tree, skirt all neat."

"No deep footprints. No drag marks." Dolly thought a while then shook her head.

"Clothes weren't dirty. No rips that I could see," I said.

"You never know. Brent's assigning an officer from the post to help us, kind of watch over things, make sure nothing's being missed." Dolly's face went a little dark. She wasn't happy with the thought of an overseer. "Hell, as if I need some guy from Gaylord keeping track of me." She shook her head, setting her cop hat to bouncing. "Come on, come on," she complained. "Lady's waiting out there."

True to Dolly's usual state of oblivion, she didn't warn me about the woman in the front seat of her patrol car. You couldn't help but be dazzled—and puzzled. She had to be in her early fifties; dressed in a caftan ranging in color from bright orange to vivid brown, with bronze fringe running down the sleeves and sides. The woman's hair was stop-light red and done up in the messiest top knot I'd ever seen, a fountain of bottle-red hair cascading to her shoulders and hanging in bangs over her wide, green eyes, more red than green at the moment as the woman's long, lush face shone with rivers of flowing tears. Her narrow hand with bright-painted fingernails came out to give me a limp handshake as I leaned in at the open window.

"Glad to meet you," I said, pumping her hand a time or two more.

She was a study in earth tones and misery.

She frowned, tucking her chin into her chest so that a couple of double-chins formed. "Crystalline. From Toledo, Ohio."

"Emily Kincaid."

"You're the reporter who found …" She took a deep breath and let it out, then looked away, toward the lake. She threw her head back, red hair tangling over her shoulders, and let out a deep and mournful sigh.

"Is that your real name?" I couldn't help myself.

She looked up, not understanding at first. "Oh...no. It's the name I was given. I was going to do my Shamanic training with Marjory." She seemed about to burst into sobs again but stopped herself. "Now all I've got is the name. She said I needed that first— to get my head into better places than where I'd been. Crystalline means clear as day. A kind of purity. But of the earth, too. You know, like a gem, a crystal. Marjory said it suited me. Which is kind of funny if you'd known me before. I guess there's a little fire in the crystal. That's what she said. A lot different than who I used to be. She changed my life, I'll tell ya. Marjory. Just changed everything."

"And Marjory is...?"

"Oh crap..." Crystalline was gone, both of her red-knuckled hands at her lips, lacy handkerchief pressed against her mouth.

Dolly leaned over from her seat behind the wheel. "Marjory's the one Crystalline thinks you found out there in Deward. Marjory Otis."

I made a face and nodded. Probably one subject to stay away from for the time being.

Crystalline settled into the seat. I got in back, and slammed the door behind me. The wire screen was between us. I told myself there wasn't much doubt that Crystalline had known the dead woman. If ever there was an identifiable uniform, these two belonged to the same club, sect, group. Whatever it was.

Dolly took off up my drive, through a shower of pebbles and leaves. No siren this time. With un-Dolly-like decorum, or maybe it was respect for the woman's feelings, she contained herself and drove at a normal speed across Sandy Lake Road toward Gaylord, faster than going around through Mancelona but sometimes almost impassable, with deep sink holes and soft, sandy ruts.

We lurched from hole to hole along the dirt road maintained by the oil company with pumps back in the woods. Dolly cursed under her breath, probably at the thought of losing her muffler again.

Crystalline blew her nose into her wilting handkerchief, then half turned to look at me through the wire back of her seat.

"I'm sure it's Marjory," she said. "Oh dear … oh crap."

We let her cry. There was time ahead, after she identified the body, to find out who Marjory was and what she was doing at Deward. Crystalline struggled for control and kept talking, not so much to Dolly and me, as to herself. "Dear, sweet Marjory. I reported her missing early yesterday morning 'cause I didn't hear from her. None of us in our group heard and that's not like Marjory. I kept calling and calling."

Her voice broke. She sniffed hard, blew, and went on talking. "It was like I could feel something immediately. You know, one of those universal warnings—coming at me so fast. I called your chief of police. I told him something had happened to her. There was no need for her to come here alone, the way she did. Any one of us would have been glad … "

She sighed, and turned to look out the window.

"Pretty country … " Her strong voice grew weak. "I can see why she was drawn back … well … not mine to say, I suppose."

We grew quiet as the woods sped past us.

Crystalline stirred. She turned her face halfway toward Dolly. "From your description, Deputy, I know it's Marjory. I know that skirt. She let me wear it. That's how she was. Best in the world."

"This is going to be hard on you," Dolly answered in a, for Dolly, soft voice. "Identification is something nobody wants to face."

"Well, of course not," Crystalline snapped then settled back in her seat. "Better me than the others. They…the women in our group—two more besides me and Marjory—well, they're delicate. You know, they feel things deeper than most people because we're all tuned in to…" She stopped.

"Into what?" Dolly prodded.

"You know, to the world around us. We can zero right in on what people think and feel. That's what Marjory teaches: connection. We can't heal until we can reside inside the body of another. But not power. Oh no. Marjory was so against power—the universal destroyer of civilization, she called it. All that mindless power that kills our babies and…"

It dawned on me what these women were. "You're healers?"

"More than that. Shamans," Crystalline nodded, hair bouncing in a waterfall of red. "Marjory was our teacher. She's done Shamanic studies for years, with some of the best teachers in the country. Oh shit…this world will be such a lonely place without her."

Dolly turned right at the road leading north, to Gaylord. Soon we were in town and at the state police post. Lieutenant Brent came to the lobby to meet us. He was solicitous toward our cringing Crystalline, asking only a few questions, then sending us on our way over to the low gray building used as a morgue, shared by a few of the northern counties.

Crystalline melted between the police post and the morgue. We helped her out of the car and up the indoor-outdoor carpeted steps into the unprepossessing block building. Inside, Dolly went with her to view the body while I sat in a black plastic chair out front.

That word *shaman*—it brought back memories that didn't fit the woman I'd just met. It was back when I was newly out of college. I signed on as an intern at *Mother Jones* magazine and was given the opportunity to go to Oaxaca, Mexico, with a group of journalists to study with shamans of the Zapotec Indians. We lived with the shamans, learned a bit of what they did, and marveled at the healing—with a simple touch, a few herbs, and an intense silent communication. I sat through ceremonies and took part in one where I stood before Roberto, the shaman I covered, and was brushed with branches of a tree or bush as he, trancelike, mumbled words, maybe prayers, over me. Roberto took water into his mouth and spit it out above my head. Not a drop touched me. I don't know what happened to the water, but I felt nothing. I wasn't wet. No water fell on the ground around me. It was gone and I left that ceremony stunned, feeling otherworldly. I was given soaps and herbs to bring home, and had stories to write. I'd felt things there, in Mexico, I'd never felt before. I saw through new eyes. Coming back to the United States had been difficult at first—it was as if the ground still rose and fell above ruins, as it did in Oaxaca. There were things around me I couldn't shake, and couldn't speak about. Those were the stories I didn't write for the magazine.

I was trying to come up with the first line for my new story when a slow moan came from the back of the building. The moan grew to a choking cry and then the "No! No! No!" began.

In a few minutes, Crystalline, holding on to Dolly's arm, stumbled from the back viewing room where Marjory lay. The bright caftan was crumpled in on itself; the woman's head hung. Dolly led her to a chair. After a while, the sobbing stopped, but she kept her head down, hair hanging around her face. Dolly and I looked at each other. We had to get back to the police post. Brent would want a new, signed statement from me—since I was in town—and one from Crystalline. The investigation couldn't begin until we had as much as Crystalline could give us.

"Chris..." Dolly tapped her shoulder.

The woman looked up and frowned. "Crystalline. Please. Marjory gave me the name for a reason."

"Sorry," Dolly said. "It's just that we've got to get back to see Lieutenant Brent before he goes off duty. He'll need whatever you can give him. I'll bet anything you want us to get busy finding whoever did this."

Her head snapped back. "Of course I do. I'm going to tell you stuff...oh, yes...I'll tell you stuff. Whoever did this terrible thing to Marjory...

"It's that place," she went on, sniffing and taking a swipe at her nose with one arm. "That awful ghost town. That's what did it to her. She was afraid of that place. She'd never have gone there alone."

When we walked toward the door we'd come in, there was purpose and strength in Crystalline's step. "Better get moving." She looked back at us and pushed her bright hair over her shoulder with one determined hand. "I'm feeling forces that might kill again. You got people in town...Marjory came here because of them. That's what she said. And a letter..." She gave a shiver. "I think it's Marjory warning us to hurry. She's all around me. She's telling me terrible things are going to happen.

I got the distinct feeling Crystalline, and maybe Marjory, didn't mean because the world was about to end. There was a much deeper evil at work. Even I could feel it.

SIX

14 days to go

"Murder all right," Lieutenant Brent welcomed us in the long hall of the police post.

"Sorry for your loss, Ma'am," he said, noticing Crystalline. He bowed slightly. "We'll need your help."

This time Crystalline didn't cave. If anything, her back locked in straighter. She was on a mission, ready to tell whatever she knew. I squared my shoulders and followed along behind Brent and Dolly and Crystalline, down the hall to his office. Brent stopped me at the door, a large hand in front of my nose.

"Officer Winston needs to talk to you, Emily. Back there." Brent leaned into the hall and pointed down a ways. "You've been a big help, but I'll speak to you later."

"I need information …" I protested, receiving a paternal pat on my back. He nodded that large, bald head and gave me a sympathetic look.

"Realize that. But not now."

"How'd she die? Can you tell me that much?"

"Strangled. Three-cord, white cotton rope. She'll be going down to Grayling, to forensics. They'll fill in the rest."

"Why can't I hear Crystalline's story?"

"Police business. Officer Wakowski will help you later—the best she can."

I stepped back as he shut the dark oak door in my face.

I went to the room he'd indicated where I sat for fifteen minutes, waiting for this Officer Winston to come ask me the same questions I'd answered the day before. By the time the SpongeBob SquarePants man came in, held his square hand out to shake, and took the chair across the table from me, I was livid.

"Officer Winston," he introduced himself, then looked at papers he'd spread out on the desk. "And you are Emily Kincaid?" He glanced up to see if I'd get the answer right.

I nodded.

"With the Traverse City *Northern Statesman*?"

I nodded again.

Officer Winston pulled a pad of paper close, then turned on a tape deck. He settled back in his chair, head upright, his body trying to be military but missing by a chin or two. Everything about the man annoyed me, from his too-well-pressed uniform down to the smirk on his round face. His head was buzz cut so there was only a faint hint of dark hair up there. He looked like a cartoon cop who, like Pinocchio, was trying to be real.

"Sorry if I took too long." He gave me a stretched lip smile. "Had to get an intoxicated individual over to the county jail."

I grunted something.

"What do you write?"

I thought awhile, feeling evil. "Investigative stuff. Stories about police brutality. Official malfeasance—you know what the word means? Things like that."

He shook that almost bald head of his and looked down at the form in front of him. "You won't find any of that in this department," he said with pride.

I pushed myself lower in my chair. "Let's get this over with. I've got a job to do."

"Uh-huh." He made a note in his notebook. "Got the statement you gave to Lieutenant Brent. Gave me a good idea of what happened. Just thought I'd kind of fill in the corners you skirted."

"I don't skirt," I groused, feeling entirely uncooperative and wondering what Crystalline was telling the other two.

"If you would just start at the beginning…" He raised his pen and waited.

I told my story fast. Nothing about mood or why I was out there; and I left out the throwing-up part as none of his business. I didn't mention that damned soup tureen. I liked the sound of what I was saying and thought I came out of it looking pretty good.

"You thought she was sleeping?"

I nodded and noticed the guy's left eye jerked rhythmically. He had a tic. I made him nervous.

"You will have to speak up. The tape doesn't record head motions," he ordered.

"Yes. She looked as if she was sleeping."

He fixed his little round eyes on me, left eye still ticing away.

"On the cold ground?"

"Yes."

"No car anywhere around?"

"I wasn't looking for one."

"And the woman never moved…"

"I didn't stand over her and watch."

Because I was mad and sounded it, the questions came in staccato fashion, without comment.

After a while he nodded and turned off the tape deck. He folded his hands in front of him on the table, and stared hard at me, turning pencil-line eyebrows into doodles.

"Can I go?"

"Think that's all we need. I might be calling you if…"

"I'd rather you didn't." I had no idea why I'd taken such a dislike to this automaton.

"Sorry, but I have a job to do."

"So do I. I'll talk to Lieutenant Brent."

He slipped his pad of paper over to me and asked me to read and sign. I did, then got up to leave. He put out his hand to shake mine. I pretended not to notice and walked from the room.

———

Dolly, Crystalline, and I hurried down the high steps of the police post. Dolly leaned close. "It's ours, Emily. Wait 'til you hear her story. All about Leetsville. We get to find the creep who killed her."

"Good luck," I grumbled, bristling over being separated from the others and interrogated by the little blob of a man. "All I need is a story for the paper. That's it. Everything else is your department."

Dolly looked me in the face. "What if that damn book of yours sells? You think of that? You'll need more. You'll need me. And maybe I won't want to be bothered with you hanging around by then. Two can play that game, Emily."

49

I could have grabbed her by the scraggly hair and tossed her down the steps, but Crystalline had stopped, turned, and watched us with consternation written in her blinking eyes.

"I appreciate it, Emily," Crystalline said, taking a deep breath and pulling her shoulders back. "I'll tell you everything I know. And on that you'll have to trust me. Knowledge comes through different channels. Maybe even Marjory will come back to help us. Whatever it takes—of this world or of a world beyond —we'll find the person who did this to her."

She talked all the way back to my house.

———————

Though it was dark by the time I got home to Willow Lake, Jackson's white Jaguar, parked in my driveway, was unmistakable.

All Dolly said when she saw it was "Un-uh. There stands trouble."

Jackson, long and lanky in his dress-to-impress outfit, leaned against the back of his car with arms crossed, a white restaurant bag dangling from his left wrist. He straightened with a slow, languorous unfolding—sure to wow any woman within one hundred feet. You had to give him a certain grace; an older male model perfection in his black turtleneck under a white cashmere cardigan and his knife-creased slacks. Ah Jackson, I thought, ever the pipe and elbow-patch writer. Crystalline gave an "Umm" of admiration. I muttered something about him being my ex.

He waved at Dolly, and bent forward to see who the redhead, beside her in the car, was, then waved and smiled at her, too. What a charmer. With meanness bubbling straight up from my soul as I crawled out of the car, I thought the charm was wearing a little thin. With bigger meanness, I added, in my head, that the wearing down could be from all those chipper coeds he'd gotten into his bed. "Past sins will out," I mumbled to nobody in particular.

"I called you," I yelled toward him, slowly making my way toward the house as Dolly left. "I told you I wouldn't be here."

Jackson shrugged and opened his arms wide as if I'd go flying to him. The bag from Gio's restaurant swung back and forth from his wrist. "Figured you had to come home sometime. Where on earth is your spare key?" he demanded, walking toward me. "I searched everywhere. There's not a person on this earth who doesn't hide a key under the welcome mat."

I got around him, through the bare rose arbor, to the house, ignoring the arms held out. I felt in my pocket for a key. There was one under the flowerpot near the arbor, but I didn't want him to see where I'd hidden it. "Obviates the hiding, doesn't it?" I said over my shoulder. "To put a key where people expect to find it?"

I pushed my way through the door then turned and smiled up at him. He bent to kiss my cheek and hug me, moving the bag so it slapped hard against my back.

"I needed to see you," he said.

That should have been nice to hear: *I needed to see you . . .*

"I'm sure my pasta has shriveled by this time," he complained.

"Come on in, Jackson. And bring your shriveled pasta with you." I grinned back at him. I felt an old urge to reach up and touch his face where the five o'clock shadow outlined his rugged chin. "I'll make a shriveled salad to go with it."

I didn't add, *and never once think it a metaphor for our shriveled marriage.* I didn't say it, not out loud, but I sure thought it, and then thought what a clever girl I was.

SEVEN

It was so ordinary, sitting at the table, sharing dinner as Jackson talked on and on about Chaucer and how he hadn't finished his book and how his leave of absence had to be extended beyond the time he'd allotted, all the way into next year.

His voice became a familiar buzz working in and around my thoughts. From time to time, I put my hand down to rest on Sorrow's attentive head. Touching my dog gave me a kind of grounding that brought me back to where I was and what lay ahead. When Jackson stopped for a breath, one time, I slipped in the events of my day.

"I found a dead woman out in Deward," I said between two snide observations on the Canterbury pilgrims. Jackson didn't like Chaucer's people all that much, or maybe he didn't like Chaucer, with his raucous sense of humor. But then why the choice to spend a year, and more, writing about him? Ah, the ways of men—ever beyond me.

Jackson's eyebrows shot up. "And where is Deward?"

"Over toward Gaylord."

He nodded, as if picturing the place in his head.

"Another of these quaint small towns?"

"Actually, there's no town anymore."

"Then, what on earth were you doing over there?"

"A story, for Bill. October stuff—ghost towns."

"Ah," he nodded again, then again, as if getting the whole picture. "One of your little …"

"Haven't you missed the point?"

Jackson laid his fork neatly on his plate then crossed it with his knife as if he were in a fine restaurant signaling the server to take his mess away. Sorrow sat up, recognizing a moment when he might get a leftover. "Point?"

"The dead woman."

"My goodness. Actually dead?" He ignored Sorrow, who lay back down under the table across my feet, keeping them warm.

I nodded.

"Unfortunate. Poor soul." He patted at his lips with the paper napkin I'd given him. "So … I've got a few pages I thought I might read to you tonight …"

"And, I almost forgot, an agent asked to see the mystery."

His eyes shifted. He thought a moment, came up with a way to deal with my news, and said, "You don't say. How exciting for you—at last a little interest."

He reached across the table and patted my hand, which I moved to my lap.

I had to grit my teeth. "If she takes it and sells it, I probably will make good money."

His smile was paternal. "Do you realize how unlikely a scenario that is? You must know the odds against publication by a novice … well … an unknown." He clucked a sympathetic cluck that turned my blood into molten lava. Of all the nerve—him and his dry, academic meanderings.

"Better chance than most," I said through tight lips. "People actually look forward to reading what I write …"

He raised his eyebrows. "But mine is scholarship, Emily. You can't mean to equate what you do with what I accomplish …"

I got up to clear the table and cut the leftover linguini into bits for a grateful Sorrow.

Later, I paid for what Jackson had taken as an insult to his work by sitting, curled in a chair, for two hours as he read. His thesis had to do with the pilgrims' lack of piety and their true motives for making the trip. After the first hour I yawned and attempted to get up, only to be waved back to my chair and given an "only a little more" promise. A half an hour later, I fell asleep.

EIGHT

Wednesday, October 14
13 days to go

I WOKE UP CLOSE to three a.m. and found a note saying he'd see me at Bill's party on Friday. I'd forgotten. Something to look forward to. I liked Bill, one of those ardent newsmen who were beginning to seem like dinosaurs. And I looked forward to seeing him later, at the newspaper. I was going into Traverse City to divine what kind of a column he wanted me to write. I was grateful for any job that brought in money. Beggars can't be choosers—unless he wanted a column on geriatrics, or sex. For the one, I wasn't there yet. For the other, my memory was dim.

I went to bed and slept soundly until seven-thirty. I got up as Sorrow did his dance of the new day around me. I had my cereal and tea and walked from front windows to side door and back, uneasy. I'd had enough of Jackson and memories of what should have been. Enough of sad people and inhumane violence. Time to treat Sorrow, who had been neglected and showed it with rolling eyes and big sighs, to a walk.

It was different out in the woods. Sorrow and I were free. No sound, except the rattle of dying trees when the wind blew, and Sorrow's scrambling paws as he dashed off, racing toward whatever he imagined had to be waiting for him.

I watched my dog with pride—his graceful lope, ears back, shining coat of many lengths. Last night I had come home to a pristine house, not a single poop or pee anywhere. Sorrow was growing up. There'd been almost sadness about having nothing to clean. He didn't need me.

One of the reasons for a long walk was Marjory's story, or as much as Crystalline knew of her story. It wasn't a particularly original tale, nor even truly bad, as women's lives went. Still, there was processing to do. If I was going to work on this with Dolly, I had to have all we knew sorted in my mind.

Marjory Otis came from an old family that settled around Leetsville sometime in the late 1800s. Marjory told Crystalline that the Otis family was proud of the great-grandparents who'd worked in the lumbering business, living in the woods all winter, back at a boarding house in Leetsville all summer. By the time her father, Charlie, was grown, the lumbering business was long gone. After high school, Charlie got a job at a manufacturing plant near Mancelona and met Marjory's mom, Winnie Frank; they married and rented a house in Leetsville. Marjory was only a little girl, Crystalline said, when he died, killed in a motorcycle wreck up near Vanderbilt. Later, her mother, Winnie, had what they called "a crisis" and was taken off to the mental hospital in Traverse City for almost a year. When she came back, Marjory said her mother was never the same again. They lived in a run-down little house her Uncle Ralph rented to them, off toward Deward. When her mother disappeared for a day or two, that was where they usually found her—in Deward, camping alone by the side of the river, surprised when they came looking for her.

"I kind of think that was why Marjory hated the place," Crystalline had said. "Maybe because of the way her mother loved it. I don't know. It wasn't that she hated her mother. I don't mean that. It's the memories...I guess going over there to find her mother living in a makeshift tent and seeming happy not to be with her kids, well, the pictures she kept in her head of that place weren't good ones.

"One day Marjory's mother ran off with a guy selling tractors," Crystalline went on to tell us. "She left a note that gave her three kids, Marjory, Arnold, and the youngest boy, Paul, to their Uncle Ralph and Aunt Cecily, their father's brother and sister-in-law, to care for, though they didn't much want children around. All Marjory ever hoped to do after that was get away from Leetsville. She married a soldier who stopped at the Shell station in town and gave her a ride down toward Detroit, which was kind of like what her mother, Winnie, had done. Marjory and the soldier stayed together for four years, until he stopped at another gas station, met a sixteen-year-old girl, and took off again.

"No need for Marjory to come back to Leetsville," Crystalline said. "When I first knew her, just saying the name of the place could make her sad. Bad days for her, when her mother ran off. Marjory always said her mother would never have walked out on her kids, no matter how sick she got, but nobody ever looked for her. Her aunt wanted to think the worst and only said Winnie was getting what she had coming to her. She could still be alive, you know that? Marjory was fifty-two. Her mother could be in her seventies. I wish I could find that old lady. I'd grab her skinny neck and…"

Dolly put up a hand. Crystalline's face twisted into a slit-eyed hate mask. I had gotten an idea what Crystalline was like before Marjory came into her life. She took a couple of deep breaths, closed and opened her eyes, gathered herself back together, then smiled sweetly, and went on.

"Never was easy for Marjory to talk about her past. Then the next thing we know—she's gone. Called from that motel where I'm staying now and said she was up here and would come back when she'd settled things that had to be settled. There was something about having to help somebody, but she never said who."

I'd asked her then if there was anything else she could remember about Marjory's life in Leetsville. She thought awhile. "Only other thing I knew," she said, "was that she, and her brothers, Arnold and Paul, lived with her Aunt Cecily and Uncle Ralph for her teen years 'cause there was nobody else. Otises they were. Brother to Marjory's father. Aunt Cecily, who didn't have any kids of her own, didn't want anybody else's kids, and took care of them only until they turned eighteen when she kicked them out of the house. She might have liked the oldest, Arnold, a little more than the others. It wasn't long after he left the house Marjory heard he was in a junior college down in Flint. You probably heard of Arnold. He's running for state senator here in Michigan. Big deal—Arnold. He almost never contacted Marjory. She said he didn't want people knowing his sister was a shaman. It could hurt him in the upcoming election."

58

Crystalline pursed her lips, took a deep breath, and poked one red-tipped finger into her pile of hair.

"She told you she was coming to help somebody? Did she say who? Or what kind of help she could give?" Dolly asked. "Maybe it had something to do with healing, or something with this Shamanism stuff."

Crystalline frowned. "She didn't tell me who it was. I got the idea it had to do with her brother. I know one thing, it had nothing at all to do with our beliefs. She would have said. I mean, that's what we all do, we share stories, so we're always learning. You know, able to help people better."

"Even when she called to say where she'd gotten to she didn't mention this person she came to help?" Dolly pressed.

Crystalline shook her head. "I asked her but she said she'd tell me everything when she got back to Toledo. She was interested in a Reverend Esau Fritch. You heard of him? I don't know why but she was looking him up online and reading about some kind of stuff. I remember her sitting there in this little office the four of us rent for healings and readings and classes. I remember she was shaking her head and saying somebody was going to have to do something about the whole thing but she didn't say which 'thing.' That's what she said—do something about 'the whole thing.' I hear the guy's here, saying the world's about to end. Maybe that's what she came for."

"Could be one of them's got something to do with her murder. Could be that preacher. Could be her brother. Maybe both," Dolly said, and settled her small, round head—hatless for once—down into her shoulders. She got very quiet.

Crystalline looked sad. "Marjory's was a history of being left and leaving—people and places. But all she ever said to me about Leetsville was that she hoped never to come back here again—until she did. I know one thing, that ghost town gave her the creeps—like all the family trouble started there and the relatives weren't smart enough to know it wasn't pride they should be showing—about being early settlers—but fear."

Before I'd gotten out of the car, the three of us agreed to go hear the Reverend Fritch's evening revival. I wanted a story on the end of the world, the preacher, and his followers. Dolly said not to forget we were investigating a murder and his name had been brought into the investigation. Crystalline wanted to come along, see if she remembered anything else Marjory had said about the man. We planned to meet at EATS at five-thirty and get out to the campground by seven, when the meeting would begin.

That gave me some of the morning to take a walk and work on the manuscript for the agent and then time for a trip to Traverse City to start talking columns with Bill.

I poked under the dying leaves with a stick, looking for wild leeks. They were almost too strong to use at this time of year, but I could throw one into a stew.

Sorrow bounced back and forth through the trees, dancing circles around me, then taking off, black ears flying, pink tongue lolling.

I started back toward Willow Lake. I knew Dolly would have a list of people to talk to when we got together, along with questions. I was going to come up with my own—if I felt like thinking about it. Dolly acted as if she knew everything about investigating a murder now that she was taking crime scene classes online. I was already tired of her preaching forensics and procedure to me.

I'd been a journalist in Ann Arbor for eight years. I'd worked on murder cases before. Even one serial murderer. I always felt Dolly's perspective—being from a small town, rarely going south of Saginaw—might be limited. I wanted to think things over, when I got the time. See if I could connect dots Dolly would never think to bring together and find out what happened to Marjory Otis, and why.

NINE

Later, happily wrapped in a lucky afghan out in my studio behind the house, I poked at the manuscript for a few hours, taking a "the" out here and putting a "the" in there. Nothing moved very far. I couldn't tell if the novel was so bad, or so good, that it didn't need changes. What I really needed was luck, and distance, maybe a new perspective ... maybe a new book.

Over the last four years, since moving up north and trying to make it on my own, I'd learned to say prayers to whoever was listening when things didn't go my way. I said them to the four corners of the earth. I said them toward the heavens and to my dead parents. I burned incense and listened to my lucky music: which could be k.d. lang, or Ani DiFranco. Today it was lavender incense and k.d. lang's *Watershed* album, the album that got me through last winter. Even in early fall, her music translates into hope. "I Dream of Spring..." As if dreaming ever really changed anything.

Sorrow collapsed to the floor with one of those huge groans dogs can give. I was meditating when the phone rang. Usually I don't answer at the studio, but what I was doing wasn't writing. Or much of anything else.

"I got a little more from Brent." It was Dolly. "No defensive wounds beyond a couple of broken nails. Maybe surprised from behind, strangled right there. No drag marks. Anyway, Brent said there was nothing on the back of her skirt. Everything was pretty clean for somebody laid out on the ground. Techs took tire prints. Found a set that probably wasn't from your Jeep. More likely her car since she drove herself up from Toledo. Car has to be somewhere. But how the heck did she get out there? And not liking the place, the question is 'Why?'"

I grabbed a pen and wrote down what she was telling me. "Time of death?"

"Early Monday, maybe late Sunday. Nothing on stomach contents yet but the post mortem lividity, temperature, and rigor point to some time between midnight and seven a.m." Dolly sounded tired.

"Where do we start?" I asked.

"Me and Lucky spent all morning going over things. Seems like the preacher's got to be first—since she came here with some beef about him. Get an alibi and then talk to people in his group. Got to get a hold of this brother of hers, Arnold Otis, the famous one who's running for senator. Whether he likes it or not, that's his sister who was killed out there." She stopped as if reading down a list, "Then the women in her shamanic group—Crystalline thinks they might know something that would help. They'll be here tomorrow morning."

"Wasn't there another brother? Crystalline mentioned three children…"

"Yup, name of Paul. Maybe Arnold Otis can help locate him. Brent's put that Sergeant Winston on it. You know, the one you didn't like much. Seems like a good guy to me," she said, knowing her assessment of that officious cop would enrage me. "Brent said for us to keep going and he'd fill in with whatever forensics came up with. They're taking toxicology samples but he doesn't think she was poisoned. Pretty obvious what happened. He said to tell you to talk to Officer Winston from here on in. He'll have everything you need."

"Yeah, sure," I muttered under my breath, then changed the subject. "How's Crystalline doing?"

"Not bad. Good thing her friends'll be here in the morning. They all want to be with Marjory. Crystalline's meeting us at Eugenia's at five-thirty, then going with us to the revival at the campground."

"Are they all fortune tellers, these women?"

"Ooh, don't say that to Crystalline. They're shamans and healers, not fortune tellers. From what Crystalline said, they take their work serious. Study for years, some of 'em, like Marjory. Crystalline says one of 'em, who's coming up, can get in touch with the dead. They're hoping to talk to Marjory. Wouldn't that make our job a lot easier if they could?"

"I'll see you at EATS. If we can't talk to that preacher, 'cause of his revival, we'll go back in the morning. After that we'll talk to Marjory's two friends, see if she said anything different to them, or if they know why she came here. Maybe even who might want to kill her."

"And then the brother? The one we know of for sure. Lucky called a number he found for him and is waiting for a callback. Somebody's got to break the news."

"What about that aunt and uncle? You ever heard of them?" I asked.

"Nope. I asked Lucky but he said the names didn't ring a bell."

"We'll check phone books and I'll go over and ask Harry. Harry's lived here forever."

"Hmmph," Dolly said. She wasn't a fan of Harry. That car of his didn't have a license and Harry was known (but never proven) to hunt in whichever season he found his freezer empty.

Dolly's call meant stopping the edit and writing a follow-up story for the newspaper. I emailed it to Bill, along with a note that I would be in town later to see him. Writing time was up.

The incense had burned away. The CD stopped. I wasn't going to get the manuscript together today. There would be no cover letter. Tomorrow would be soon enough, I told myself. Or maybe the next day. The longer I put off sending my work to the agent, the longer I put off rejection.

The phone rang as I got ready to leave the studio. Feeling a little psychic myself—expecting Jackson to call—I let it ring. I took Sorrow back to the house, and left an unhappy dog behind me as I drove off to Traverse City and my new part-time job as a local columnist.

TEN

Still only 13 days to go

THE OFFICES OF THE *Northern Statesman* newspaper were down Garfield Road, behind a row of other office buildings. The ivy crawling the red brick walls was dead, bronzed for the year. I went in—perky and pumped—ready to take on whatever Bill came up with, except sports, or recipes, or township meetings, or a lot of other things I didn't know a thing about.

I said "hi" to Belinda, the receptionist, who was busy talking into her headset. She smiled and waved me back to Bill's office.

The office looked like any editor's office I'd ever visited. Newspapers everywhere—not only the *Northern Statesman* but the *Detroit News, New York Times,* and others from around the country. Then there were books and current copy—all in neat piles, or spread across his desk. Every corner of the room was the repository of something. There was one half-dead, potted ivy stuck up on a file cabinet and a sad, stuffed bear sitting on a corner chair, bent over toward his toes, eyes fixed on the floor, one ear up, one ear down, with a striped tie hanging from one foot.

Bill sat in front of his computer, head tipped forward, squinting over his glasses at a story he was editing. His heavy dark glasses hung halfway down his nose. I stood for a minute then "ahemed" and took no offense as he turned toward me, adjusting the glasses with his middle finger.

"Emily Kincaid. Good to see you." He got up, bent forward over his desk, and shook my hand. "You're still coming for dinner Friday, right?"

He nodded and smiled, lighting up one of those almost plain faces that turn handsome when brightened by a smile.

"I'm coming," I answered. "The three of us?"

I got the nod I wanted. He didn't have a date. So, no little red-heads there to surprise me.

"Got the story. Thanks." He pawed through one of the stacks of papers on his desk, came up with my email, and waggled it in the air. "Going in tomorrow's paper."

"I'll keep you up to date."

"Awful thing, poor woman. Any idea who did it?"

I shook my head.

"You working with Deputy Dolly?"

"Looks like it."

"Brent ok with that?"

I shrugged. "The woman was staying in Leetsville. It was something happening there that brought her from Toledo, and then she was murdered. So, sure, Brent wants Dolly on it. And Dolly wants me."

Time to change the conversation. The day ahead was full as it was. "I came about the column."

We talked about things I knew well enough to write about. I told him that could be lonely hearts, how to write a mystery, or maybe about my garden.

"That's it." His face lit up. "Lots of people up here garden. That's what you write about."

"I'm not a master gardener."

"Doesn't matter. Write what you know."

"I'll start with slugs."

"Sure. Good enough. Soon as possible." He looked down at the copy he was editing, dismissing me.

"Can I borrow a desk?"

He pointed to an empty office across the hall and I went off to start my new career as expert on something I thought I knew but learned I didn't every summer when the bugs and slugs and birds and deer got the best of me.

It was a little like being back at the *Ann Arbor Times,* sitting in an office writing with voices around me, phones ringing, people walking by, some stopping to introduce themselves. More company than I'd had in a couple of years. It felt good. There was something about a "real" job—other than staying home and writing books—that made me feel legitimate again.

I took on the slugs, easily turning out 800 words on the slimy, hungry, miserable creatures that plagued my world and had to be removed by hand and dropped into a can of salt where they dissolved, to my extreme glee, which only showed the darkness in my soul.

Bill was still in his office when I finished. As I handed him the copy, he said my pay would be included in the next check. Good enough, I thought, liking the word "check" for its substantial sound. I waved good-bye and was on my way out his office door when a thought struck me.

"That murdered woman? You know, out in Deward. She came from Leetsville originally. It seems her mother disappeared when Marjory was a teenager. Would there be anything in the paper's morgue, you think?"

"How many years ago?"

I shrugged. "Marjory was in her fifties. So, maybe thirty-five years."

"The college's got all the old papers on microfilm. Check there."

I left, agreeing that I looked forward to dinner at his house and asking if I could bring anything. Unlike Jackson, who usually gave me at least half the dinner to provide, Bill said he was all set, even had a menu written out.

I couldn't help but think, as I went out to my car, how being married to a man who planned his own dinner parties, shopped for them, and cooked was the dream every woman writer across the world must dream. Then memories of dirty socks shoved deep in sofa cushions, tops left off toothpaste, and toilet seats left up to snare an unwary woman in the middle of the night tripped through my head, and cooking fell a few notches in my list of attributes a second husband must have.

ELEVEN

Still 13 days to go

I HEADED BACK TOWARD Front Street and the college. Traverse City was always one of my favorite small cities. First driving along Munson Avenue—typical resort town shops: tee shirts (with a big grizzly guarding the entrance), miniature golf with waterfalls and ponds where a galleon sits perpetually half-sunk, and then Old Mission Peninsula, a finger of land jutting into the bay, a place where people lived on little coves and along curving roads. Old Mission was where artists and writers existed among vineyards and expensive, sprawling, waterfront mansions. The artists and writers lived off-water, in charming cottages or falling-down old houses, democratically sharing the spotlight with the wealthy because Old Mission was a little like an Irish town where artists were still respected.

The city had spread out, to the south. There were malls and fast-food shops, but also tiny, family-run specialty shops and quirky restaurants like Eurostop in the old train station where I would go on a summer day to sit beside the tracks, wave to an engineer, and eat a caprese sandwich with fresh basil, fresh mozzarella, and fresh tomato slices. And there was the Dennos Museum; Old Town Playhouse; a symphony orchestra; an ice rink; many, many galleries; the Opera House; and the newest attraction, the State Theatre run by Michael Moore and a host of civic-minded citizens. Traverse City was an eclectic place where, to my surprise when I first got up here, people still smiled and talked to strangers.

Northwestern Michigan College was off Front Street, back in on winding roads lined with big, old trees. Students, wrapped in sweaters, keeping warm against the cold wind sweeping in from the bay, stood in hunched gaggles, laughing and horsing around, the way students do.

I'd done searches in the newspaper's morgue before. This time I struck out. There was nothing in the old issues. No missing Otis. I checked a Winnie Otis from 1967 through 1971, the years I figured Marjory had to be a teenager. Nothing. If Marjory was in her fifties and her mother, Winnie, left when Marjory was anywhere from thirteen to sixteen, those had to be the years when her disappearance would have been reported. I went through page after page, issue after issue, and found nothing. And nothing in the old obits either, not that there would have been, not with her mother running off the way she had, and never coming back. But where did she run to? I sat back in my chair and rubbed my eyes. It was conceivable, even probable, the woman was still alive. Had to be in her seventies. People were easier to find now, with paper trails left every year. Maybe through a social security number, an address, credit, tax IDs—something. If I only knew the name of the man she'd run off with, I'd begin there. One of Marjory's brothers might know his name. Arnold, the famous one, was the eldest. He would have already been in his teens when their mother left them. Surely he'd been told who she ran off with—an area tractor sales-man. We had to talk to Arnold Otis soon.

I made notes. People to contact. Places to search. Maybe even in Antrim County records. A name and address for an Otis who owned property out near Deward. Or Harry—I'd go see him. He had lived right where he was, across Willow Lake Road, all his life. If anyone knew people who lived in or near Leetsville in the last sixty years, it would be Harry. A trip down Harry's treacherous, burr- and picker-lined driveway was in order.

Dusty fall light came in the big library windows. Moving shad-ows fell across the hunched backs of students studying at long tables. Others sat singly, in carrels around the walls. I continued hunting, looking up names and places. I searched for Marjory Otis in the local high school news of thirty-five to forty years ago. I looked up Arnold and Paul Otis. I found two of them under *News from around Traverse City* of 1971. A Marjory Otis from Leetsville High School had been a candy striper. It didn't say which hospital or nursing home she candy striped at, just that she said she found the work rewarding and hoped to be a nurse when she grew up.

Arnold had been president of the debate team. There was noth-ing on Paul. Not a single mention of his name. It seemed Marjory was behind Arnold by two grades, so two years younger than Ar-nold, which would put him at fifty-four. I wished I'd looked for Arnold in more recent papers while I was at the newspaper office. I'd have to Google him at home, though that was always a tedious job since I had only a dial-up connection.

I left the library, checked my watch, and decided to treat myself to lunch at Amical, downtown near Horizon Books and the State

Theatre. It was late for lunch and I was meeting Dolly and Crystal-line for dinner at five-thirty, but I was hungry. I got a table near the fireplace and ordered squash soup plus an endive salad and a glass of chardonnay, spending everything I'd made on my column that morning. I felt I was owed a treat—a kind of celebration for my "columnist" status. And hadn't I recently stumbled over a dead body? Such things could be hard on a woman. I needed soothing and sustenance. Enough of death, and a town full of people claiming the world would end soon. I threw caution to the winds and ordered a crème brûlée for dessert.

As I drove back through town after lunch, I decided that if the Reverend Fritch had real proof the end of the world was coming on October 27, I'd go shopping. I had a feeble line of credit, but Macy's was having a sale. Wouldn't it be fun, if I wasn't going to be around to pay the bill anyway, to buy everything I desperately wanted to own and never could afford? That would be a gorgeous down coverlet with thick down pillows. A lot of books I'd coveted. Maybe some big steaks. I'd invite everybody I knew over and make primavera pasta, grill the steaks, and have bottles and bottles and bottles of wonderful wines from The Blue Goat. And think of the Murdick's fudge I could eat!

I didn't like fur, had no use for jewelry—beyond a pair of gold hoop earrings—and didn't want a new car. Maybe I'd buy a boat to get out on the lake—but I'd never be able to use it, so that was out of the question. As I thought about things I dreamed of having, I realized how pathetic I was. No big wants and must-haves. No big cravings. I wanted my books published and liked. I wanted nice people around me. I wanted plenty to keep my mind busy. As an American consumer, I truly sucked.

Then I got real and thought about what the end of the world might be like. I guessed lots of fire. Brimstone too, but I didn't know what that was. And those four horsemen pounding their way down US131—there would be gnashing of teeth. There would be screaming and lamenting. The storms would be terrible, with wind bending the world in half, lightning streaking the sky; thunder crashing overhead.

One thing I knew for certain, Sorrow wasn't going to like it.

TWELVE

Still 13 days of sunrises and sunsets

FULLER'S EATS, WITH ITS upside-down neon arrow pointing toward the door, was already crowded, the parking lot filled with pickups, rusty Chevys, and new Toyotas. People had their supper early in Leetsville. I parked and went in, pausing in Eugenia Fuller's vestibule to take a quick glance at the latest genealogy sheets she'd pulled from the Internet and hung around the walls, some with big golden stars denoting special people. Since she considered herself an expert in tracing family trees, she'd hung a sign above the doorway into the restaurant: EUGENIA'S GENEALOGY SERVICE: Let Me Find The Lost Sheep For You.

Eugenia used to concentrate on her own relatives, especially those who'd been hanged, until she claimed Billy the Kid and Annie Oakley—people like that. Some of us caught on they weren't really her family, which took the fun out of it for Eugenia. Soon she was researching other people's kinfolk. So far she hadn't zeroed in on me, but there were quite a few in town getting mad at her when they walked in for a quiet meatloaf dinner and came face to face with old Aunt Tilly, who murdered her husband back in 1888, and who the family had been pretending never existed for more than a hundred years. EATS was a lot more interesting since a few of the local families stormed in to register their complaints with Eugenia's "damn fat nose stickin' into business you got no business sticking it into" or "don't you go hangin' no more damn lies about the Abbots, ya hear?"

Angry families boycotted Eugenia's place for a week or two but then, one by one, came back because staying away from EATS meant knowing nothing of what was going on in town. If EATS was the center of the universe for the meatloaf special, it was also the center of Leetsville's gossip patrol and helping hands—if anybody got burned out and needed clothes, if a wife was getting beat up out at a house back in the woods and needed to hide, or if a teen-ager wanted somebody calm to talk to after getting in trouble with Lucky Barnard or Dolly Wakowski, EATS was the place to spread the word. People in Leetsville never turned their backs on each other. There was something so real about the people, I was still fascinated by how the village worked—taking care of their own, chastising their own. Committing a crime meant instant shame. Being a lush meant people trying to help find a cure—all kinds of suggestions from rehab to a copper bracelet. Problems belonged to everybody. A child going wrong wasn't cause for gossip as much as cause for help. Leetsville was a place where troubles were talked about openly. "Things" weren't hidden since those "things" were a part of everybody's life. So many middle-class myths found no place in Leetsville. Life was as it was. Some ran to religion, some to alcohol, some to drugs, some to anger, but most accepted life the way it came. They enjoyed the good days and shared the bad.

Every table in the restaurant was filled. The air was thick with smoke though Eugenia had installed something called a smoke zapper that added to the din with sudden ZAPs and sounds more like flies dying than smoke being eaten. I stood in the open doorway checking out the filled tables until I spotted Dolly and Crystalline in a corner booth. They sat with Eugenia of the big high blond hair and double chins that trembled as she talked earnestly to Dolly. Making my way across the room, threading through chairs stuck out in the aisles, people stopped me a couple of times. Word had spread I'd found a body out at Deward and I'd taken on a kind of macabre sheen of celebrity. Since it was a matter of pride to me that Leetsvillians now allowed me in, a stranger from a strange land—Ann Arbor—I stopped to talk, giving out as much information as I could.

I greeted the women in the corner booth—Dolly and Crystalline on one side, Eugenia on the other. They were deep into something that was making Dolly and Eugenia mad, their chins stuck out toward each other, heads waggling, lips thin. I'd sat through many of these quarrels and figured it might take a minute or two.

Eugenia was in the middle of a sentence, hand curled around the edge of the table, bottom slightly lifted from the seat, preparing to get up and let me sit down though she had things yet to say. I waited patiently, knowing Eugenia could hold her retreating pose for a good long time. She went on with whatever it was she was angry at until Dolly stopped her midway with a pithy thing she'd thought of.

77

I waited, shifting from one foot to the other, hoping Eugenia would soon get over her current snit and leave. When the door to the restaurant opened, I turned to see who it might be. An old woman I'd never seen before stepped tentatively into the room. I figured she had to be with the cult but she was alone, not in a group of three and four as the others were. And she certainly wasn't bald. Nor wearing a sexless robe. If anything, she looked more like Crystalline, or Marjory—kind of blowsy, kind of overdressed, kind of odd.

I watched as the woman came around between chairs and tables, hesitating, searching for someone or something. She looked hard at Eugenia, who was too deep into her argument with Dolly to notice.

The woman, sixty or seventy, wore a long black skirt. Her bright blue sweater was of, what looked like, cashmere. Probably not. Not from the rest of what she wore: a jumble of bright green scarves wrapped around her wrinkled neck; black string-gloves on her blunt, old hands; and worn but still stylish Gucci shoes on pudgy feet in black lisle socks with a hole above one ankle. She had applied almost clown-like makeup around her eyes, mascara seeping through wrinkles down to her cheeks, and lipstick that merged into feathered lines around her mouth. I had no idea what look she was going for, but what she'd achieved wasn't particularly attractive.

The woman stopped and put her hand on a chair back for support. She looked at Eugenia again, frowning. She patted nervously at the white hair piled on her head, caught with a rhinestone-studded comb that threatened to fall off to one side. She took a deep breath, as if for strength. After a few hesitant seconds, she turned to me, her almost opaque blue eyes giving me the once-over and leaving me with the odd feeling I should know her. She stared at my University of Michigan sweatshirt and worked her way down to my paint-stained jeans. With a sniff, and a firm set of her chin in the air, she brushed past me, pulling her calf-length skirt to one side as she made her way to a four-top Gloria, the waitress, was washing off while spraying crumbs into the air behind her.

Another one of Eugenia's indigent souls, I thought as she settled at the table and lost herself in Eugenia's sticky menu.

Eugenia looked up at me, her cheeks a high red with whatever anger was taking her at the moment. "You going out there tonight, to that revival thing, Emily?" she demanded, blowing out a sound of derision. "Woulda thought you were smarter than that. The old man's a crook, you know." She slapped one large hand on the tabletop and lifted her behind up an inch more. "You ask me, he's trying to get everything those folks own. Scarin' them for a reason, I'll bet. I always say, you look where people are putting fear into other people and you'll find a crook."

I shrugged, not wanting to give away too much information. When it came time to have news spread around the town, that's when Eugenia would be useful. Right now no one needed to know why we were going to the meeting that night.

"According to the Reverend Fritch, you'll be caught deader than a doornail if you don't get out there and listen," Dolly, leaning across the table, warned.

Crystalline leaned back and rolled her eyes at me.

Eugenia's ringlets bobbed and the loose flesh under her chin flapped as she laughed. "Yeah. Like dying scares me. You, me, everybody—we've all been dying since the day we was born. You realize that? The guy out there—that Reverend Fritch—he doesn't know any better than me when I'm going to die. And I sure don't have to sign over all my worldly goods to buy me a place to the left of a fiery furnace."

"You don't know anything, Eugenia," Dolly said, a couple of red spots blooming on her cheeks. "And I wouldn't go around slandering anybody until you've got something to go on."

"Heard plenty already. His people come in here bragging about how they gave away all their money and wanting me to feed them for free. Like it's a contest and the biggest fool wins. But that big fool isn't going to be me. Have to be blind not to see what's going on out there. He's doing nothing but breaking the law."

"No proof of anything wrong." Dolly balled her fists and thudded them on the table. One thing she didn't like was people telling her what was and what wasn't against the law.

Eugenia waved an angry hand and stood, turning to give me half the wattage of her usual greeting.

"Who's your new customer?" I nodded to the table the old woman had commandeered, spreading her wide skirt around her and plunking her elbows in the middle of the red Formica.

Eugenia, who'd been too busy talking to notice the woman, looked over at her then back to me. Her mouth opened a little. Her drawn-on eyebrows elevated. I could see she was thinking hard. Finally she shrugged. "Striking woman. Looks like she could use a hot meal, don't it?" She put her shoulders back, straightened the shoulder pads in her white blouse, and made straight for the somewhat familiar-looking woman's table.

Crystalline greeted me when I finally got to sit down across from her. Her face, free of makeup, was drawn and sober; her eyes puffed and tear-washed. The red hair that had seemed so alive before lay flat against her head, the pouf deflated, as if a force had been withdrawn.

I leaned forward to whisper, "That woman over by the wall, at the table by herself, is she part of your group?"

Crystalline squinted, found the woman, and shook her head. "Sure as hell looks like we do, I guess. Could be one of us. But she isn't. Never seen her before."

We studied the menu. I was hoping for shrimp scampi or maybe a tuna steak but realistically considered the salad bar with cheese ball and crackers, or the meatloaf.

"Eugenia puts on quite a feed," Dolly said toward Crystalline.

When Gloria came over, green order pad in hand, Crystalline ordered vegetable beef soup, which sounded good to me so I changed my order. Crystalline had to go to the bathroom then and stood, drawing her long red, silver-edged skirt around her. I watched her walk off, drawing every eye in the restaurant after her.

I leaned toward Dolly, whispering to keep our conversation from the antenna ears beamed our way. "There wasn't a thing about Marjory's mother in the newspaper morgue. I went in this morning. Nothing. Nothing on a Paul Otis either. Old high school stuff on Arnold—debate captain. That's all. Anything new on Marjory?"

Dolly looked around the room, daring people to go on staring at us. "Strangled all right."

I shook my head. "I saw the rope..."

"Compression of the trachea, pathologist said. Died of asphyxia. Rope. Ordinary rope."

"Does that mean no blood?"

"It was there. Very little. Because her chin was down and that hat was over her face, you didn't see it. Mark of the rope wasn't deep, but well defined—bled in places. You missed the cyanosis in the face. Guess you weren't looking for a dead lady with a red face."

"No question then."

Dolly nodded.

"How'd anybody get her out there? Crystalline said she hated Deward, was even afraid of it. Any drugs in her system?"

Dolly shook her head. "Don't know yet. Too soon for toxicology to be back."

"God, this is frustrating," I said. "When will those women from Toledo get here?"

"By morning. We'll go to the revival tonight—see the reverend if we can, then interview her friends. Somebody's gotta know something."

When Crystalline came back, I told her I hadn't found anything about Marjory Otis' mother in the old newspapers. No mention of a missing woman, no death notice. Nothing that might help us.

"I thought—because they were from an old family connected to Deward—that there would be something," I added.

Crystalline shrugged and sniffed back more tears. The food came. We were quiet as we ate. Something about what was ahead stilled any interest in talking. We soon got up to leave, heading to the front counter where Eugenia stood, hand out, ready to take our money.

"Your real name is Delores Flynn, right?" Eugenia asked Dolly after she'd paid and left a dollar on the counter for Gloria.

Dolly narrowed her eyes and took a step away. "I'm not paying for any of this family search stuff you're doin'. Don't have money for crap like that. I had Chet. He was my family. And don't think you can show off by doing it behind my back. Won't get a cent outta me. Not one red cent."

Eugenia smiled and put her hand out for my bill, ignoring Dolly.

On our way to the door, I glanced at the old woman in her fancy clothes. She looked up, but only from the bottoms of her eyes, as if glancing through a lorgnette. Her short nose went into the air as she fixed pale old eyes on us. I saw her lips move, making a comment about me to herself, I imagined. When I looked back again, she frowned and opened her mouth, seeming about to call out something. As the door shut behind me, I told myself I was suffering from a case of nerves. Just an old lady. Maybe a bag lady passing through town. My trouble was that someone was about to tell me how I'd be dead by the end of the month, just when I got a job that I could handle, when an agent was interested in my work, and when there was a dead woman crying out for justice. Sometimes life was complicated enough without looking for another twisted thread.

We got in my car and headed out to the End Timers' camp.

THIRTEEN

PEOPLE IN DARK PLACES become odd silhouettes; elbows at acute angles, noses elongated, chins sharp, bodies taller and skinnier. We walked in a dark place. Those around us—as we made our way up the campground two-track to the place where the End of the Worlders gathered—were silent, except for an occasional whisper. It was eerie to be among a hurrying crowd and hear no laughter, no mumbles of progressive conversation, nothing but the swish of feet in dead leaves as we headed where smoky bright lights filtered through tree limbs and loudspeakers blasted hymns I didn't recognize but knew were hymns by the sometimes martial, sometimes maudlin, sometimes elegiac beat of the music.

A shiver of expectation crept up my spine as I stumbled along behind Dolly and Crystalline. We were as silent as the others, stilled by the single line of blood-red sunset on the horizon to our left and the feeling of being pushed toward death. Whoever this Reverend Fritch was, he knew how to set the stage—this hurrying toward the light. I shook myself again and again, remembering

I was the skeptic here; the pragmatic reporter, and not a believer come to find a way around the endless torment awaiting the great unwashed.

Cars had nosed in everywhere along the narrow lane. Headlights shot beams into the trees, and then flashed off as more and more people pulled in and parked, then joined the parade back to where the reverend would speak.

When we reached the clearing where strings of bare bulbs hung overhead and banks of lights, like those at a night ballgame, surrounded a raised stage, the faces nearby went from silhouette to washed-out and blank. We stumbled into people and over tree roots as Crystalline whispered we wanted to get as close to up front as possible so maybe we could grab the reverend when he finished speaking. "Up front" was lined three rows deep with people in folding chairs set like immovable anchors in the sand. Crystalline, determined to get a good spot to watch the proceedings, elbowed her way forward, with me and Dolly behind her. She stopped behind the last row of lawn chairs, as close to the stage as she could get without having fistfights with the faithful.

With her feet planted firmly in the sand, Crystalline waved me and Dolly to her side. She crossed her arms tightly across her bright green jacket. When people behind us complained, she turned slowly, swishing her long red skirt around her hips and eyeing the hecklers with a look that could have frozen water.

Dolly, in full uniform, had her best "cop" face on, eyes going down to stare straight at the seated people, then up to those standing nearby, then, very slowly, back around to the front. Complaint around us died. Dolly planted her well-shod feet wide, and settled in for the show. I stood between the two women, feeling protected on one side by outrage and the other by officialdom.

By seven o'clock, the crowd stretched back farther than I could see. Here, in the light, I made out the faces of a few people I knew. Harry Mockerman stood off to one side with his lady friend, Delia Swanson, next to him. Harry looked particularly good in his suit (with a full set of buttons) and tie and slicked-back hair. Delia stood a foot taller than Harry, and was as square as a box. Every once in a while I saw her bend to talk to him. He was all attention. The smiles on their faces made me happy for both of them.

There were other Leetsvillians and people from Kalkaska and Mancelona I recognized. Maybe they'd come from all over the north country.

A young kid, in tee shirt and jeans—no coat—came on to the stage and caused an expectant stir in the crowd. He tested microphones that echoed and screeched around the open field. The kid smiled when people yelled that the mics were too loud. He only waved, nodded, and left the stage. Soon a gaggle of men in robes climbed back stairs to stand above us, whispering and looking around, toward where they'd come from. The men leaned close to each other from time to time. One very thin man stood alone. A woman—I thought, though it was hard to tell—came to stand beside him, saying something into his ear. He said nothing back.

After fifteen minutes of expectant waiting, the quiet man, tall, fifty or so, with a pronounced limp, came forward to the standing microphone. He threw the hood of his robe back, exposing his shaved head to glints of reflection from the lights.

His eyes were round and huge, set in an almost emaciated face. Those eyes, reflecting light, turned on everyone—it seemed he could take all of us in at once. The effect was of a man a little shy, but warm and shot full of a kind of awe I'd never seen before. We stood waiting, leaning forward, for what he was about to say.

The man bent to speak into the mic but only guttural sounds came out. Around me people fell silent; some whispered as the man threw back his head and howled as long and loud as a human being can howl. The sound, over that field of people, was grotesque; the kind of sound that reaches down inside and pours out agony. I felt my throat tighten, then a deep pain grab me—as if what the man called to was hidden inside, scratching its way to the surface.

People around me were as frightened as I was. There were sharp intakes of breath, a long silence, and then breath being released in short bursts. A woman somewhere began to moan. Another, farther back, sobbed. The emotion, running from person to person, was of deep and anguished sadness. Maybe the man was bringing on the terrible destruction as that last day approached, embodying the pain to come. It was beyond what I knew as unhappiness. Beyond anything human I had ever felt. I had to cross my arms over my body and hold on before I flew apart.

He bent in two, the bald, mute man, reaching down inside himself, then slowly throwing his arms into the air and wailing a louder, deeper wail. If the sound he made was of all lost souls from all the ages, it couldn't have held more longing or been more unhappy.

When he stopped, it was as if a single note had bound us all together and now was taken away. I had to move my feet wide in order to stand erect. The thing that had held me up, made me a part of the body of people around me, was gone and I was on my own. Deep breaths were taken everywhere. From the back of the crowd came a nervous laugh, soon quieted by shushes.

The man moved back and disappeared from the stage.

Another robed man approached the microphone and asked that we close our eyes and pray until the Reverend Fritch was among us. I pretended to close my eyes but looked from side to side as robed people moved nearby. These were the true believers who, I'd heard, had followed the Reverend Fritch to Leetsville to meet their fate. One by one they took up places amid family groups, behind chairs, or directly next to people standing alone. Slowly they insinuated themselves, like mud oozing into cracks, until I could see more robes than flannel shirts and jean jackets. I felt something brush my arm. One of the robed women, head covered, only her eyes glistening in the light from the bare bulbs, wormed her way between me and Dolly. Another waited at Dolly's other side. I felt someone take my hand. It wasn't Dolly. And it wasn't Crystalline. Both women had been walled away from me now by a third robed person who held on to me even as I pulled hard against her. Crystalline was forced farther along the row where we stood. Increment by increment, Dolly and Crystalline were moved off in different directions.

I didn't like the feeling I was getting, as if I were being pushed out of a circle of friends. It felt creepy to look around a hooded body toward where Dolly stood, eyes closed, oblivious to how she'd been surrounded. And Crystalline, who I would have thought more aware, pushed even farther on, head back, eyes closed, feeling the spirit, or whatever it was moving among us.

There was no place for me to go. I couldn't push the intruders out of the way without causing a commotion. I couldn't step back without running into people pushing from behind. I was boxed in by robes and arms and feet and bodies—row after row of bodies. My breath caught in my throat.

A baby cried far off. There was a long collective sigh when a lightbulb at the back of the stage popped like a gunshot—but no gasps of surprise. No one moved or laughed nervously. We waited. My hand was sweating against the hand that held it. I pulled again but the hand holding mine tightened.

Only the sound of rustling trees disturbed the breathless silence. A single nesting bird gave a gurgle of sleep and fell quiet. We'd become one large body of life—pushed so tightly together I couldn't tell when I breathed or when it was the cloaked figure next to me. With the strange, overly bright light making masks of faces, I had an almost frantic need to be of the mass of people. Not to be near the outskirts where I sensed something waiting, but at the very center, part of that safe heart beating along with mine.

Minutes went by. Anticipation grew. It was hard to breathe. I might have been completely caught up in the silent furor but for that ever-present hand holding on to me. I was caged by warm, long fingers.

Finally, a large man, a seemingly burdened man with head bowed, walked up from the back of the stage. The only thing visible of him at first was that bowed head—a full shaggy head of dark hair—not bald like the others. And then there was the rest of him, a wide torso in voluminous robe, cloth spreading out over a big body, arms lost in folds of course linen, hood hanging down his back, sandals on his bare, spreading feet.

The Reverend Fritch stood before us, looking from staring face to staring face beneath. With slow movements he pulled his sleeves back, one after the other, and threw his arms into the air, greeting the roar that came up from the crowd. The roar swelled and moved around the clearing. The man stood at the very front edge of the stage and slowly lowered his arms; then lowered his head, shook it a few times, and held still under the harsh lights. The roar died in a receding wave. A hush fell over the people.

"How many days now?" the Reverend Fritch cried out, first to his left, then to his right, and then to the center of the crowd, where I stood. With a lavaliere microphone on him, free to walk the stage, he paced quickly back and forth as the crowd called out a resounding, "Thirteen days!"

"How many?" One hand went behind his ear as he feigned not being able to hear.

Again the crowd chanted, "Thirteen days!"

"Are we sad?" he yelled at all of us, a huge smile spreading over his wide face, softening the words.

The crowd screamed, "No."

The preacher stood where he was, bent over, and laughed, the full body under the robe bouncing.

"And you know why, people? You know why there's no sadness in us?" He stopped and straightened. It was a sudden stop. The crowd waited. "Because we're going home!"

The crowd went wild.

When they quieted, he began again, always with a conspiratorial smile splitting his wide, round face. It was as if there was a big secret being shared and I was one of those left out. I felt sad. My eyes welled with tears until I shook myself, and asked, *What the hell, Emily?*

"Like David, I had a dream." He lowered his voice and ran a hand over his cheeks. The portent of the word "dream" drew all of us to lean in closer, waiting for what would come.

"I dreamed … oh, yes I did … I dreamed and the Lord showed me Armageddon. Like David standing there by the river, I saw what I had to see." He paced again, his sandals slapping the floorboards of the stage, the sound making a drumbeat beneath his words. From time to time he stopped, looked into the crowd, bent forward, gave a laugh and called out a person's name to the delight of everyone. I found myself wanting him to look at me, call out my name—though I didn't worry how he would know it. I couldn't have said why I needed to be included, I just did.

"Have I told you this before?" he roared, demanding an answer.

"Yes!" the roar came back.

"Will I be tellin' you this again? Will I be tellin' you about my dreams until the last day, until October 27, when the End will be upon us?"

The "Yes" roar spread around me. People swayed back and forth, bodies synchronized, hands clasped together. When they got to me I had no choice, I was caught up in my small space that wasn't my space at all, but part of this larger group. I swayed, with that hold ing hand moving as I moved.

Reverend Fritch went on. "There was a terrible angel pointing toward what was coming down the river bank at me and I knew, oh yes, I knew right then the END TIME was upon us." He stopped again. "Have I told ya this before? Do we need to hear it again?"

It was point and counterpoint. He had us in a mesmerizing web of words and emotion.

"The Antichrist. That terrible prince. It was Satan, himself, coming straight for me holding up the number: TWENTY-SEVEN. TWENTY-SEVEN. And I knew—oh yes, I knew right then what that number meant."

Little by little I pulled myself back. This wasn't me. This wasn't anything I believed could happen. I could see what was going on. I didn't want my mind taken over by this huge, brightly lighted figure standing above us. I didn't want worms of thoughts I didn't want to think crawling in my head.

I pulled my hand hard against the one holding mine. I pulled and then pinched the hand still fumbling for a hold on me. I got away though someone yanked at my jacket.

"The 'latter days' are here, folks," the Reverend Fritch was falling into his words, moving his body to a beat he'd created as I pushed back through the crowd. "The Apocalypse is upon us as Daniel said in chapter ten, verse fourteen: 'To make thee understand what will befall thy people in latter days...' And that is my burden. Daniel's heavy load is mine."

I looked around but I couldn't find Dolly or Crystalline. I was alone in a sea of robes.

"...to make you understand that if you have not renounced the earth and all its delights, if you have not renounced Satan, if you have not given your soul over to God—the END is coming. The END is near. The END OF DAYS will find you sniveling and crying and begging and pleading but the ear turned your way will be deaf, as yours has been unto Him."

I pushed through the people. They didn't notice me. Their eyes were fixed on the reverend.

"The twenty-seventh day of October, precisely at twelve o'clock, the judgment of the wicked will begin," the man on the stage cried out to answering groans and screams. "There will be fire and blood running in the streets. There will be a great gnashing of teeth as children are torn from their mother's arms; men from their wives. In Gehinnom will the wicked burn forever."

I turned for a moment to watch him. He lowered his head and paced across the stage, stopping finally to turn a terrible, wild face toward the people. "I dream to tell you my visions. 'And the number of the army of the horsemen was two hundred thousand thousand and I heard the number of them …'"

Something dark chased me. That voice rolled up behind …

"…but then there are the saved, the cleansed who will march on to the post tribulation Rapture. There will come the time of Resurrection; the Glorification of the Righteous. That's where you all will be, along with me. The Saved, together!"

There was a cheer, then pandemonium as people cried, then shouted they were with him.

My chest hurt from trying to draw deep breaths. I forced first one and then another of the people out of my way. No one noticed. Their eyes were fixed on the man, their lips moved, they were transfixed. No wonder the man had so many followers, I thought as I pushed between them. No wonder people were prepared to follow him to death. He gave them no choice. They were trapped like flies in the snare his words made.

Face after face. Couples. Children. Old men and women with their arms around each other. I thought I saw the mysterious old woman from EATS, staring up at the stage as intently as the others. I couldn't be sure, Faces melted around me, one into the other. Words blared until I had to cover my ears. All I wanted was to get out to my Jeep, climb in, lock the doors, and shiver.

FOURTEEN

It was another half an hour before people began making their way back from the clearing, past my car where I sat waiting for the other two. There would be no seeing the minister tonight. I couldn't imagine interviewing him after so emotional a service. He had to be exhausted. I knew I was. Exhausted, a little angry, and feeling used. I was mostly angry at myself for getting caught up in what was obviously one man's ego-centered delusion. I couldn't figure out what had come over me. Maybe that hand holding me in place while Dolly and Crystalline were pushed away. It was the kind of thing where you were afraid to hurt anyone's feelings even as you sensed yourself being pulled into a dark place you didn't want to go.

More and more people came out to their cars. After a while, the crowd dwindled, became a couple or two walking by. I waited, wondering if I'd been wrong and Dolly and Crystalline had gotten backstage after all, maybe were talking to him even now, and I'd wimped out.

The door opened, finally, and the overhead light snapped on. Crystalline plopped herself into the back seat with a "Whew! That man is *good*! I sure can see why he's got so many people ready to die." She laughed. "Almost had me with him. I was yelling back I wanted to be among the Righteous and go on to heaven. Ready to follow that man down the long road to Armageddon, until somebody stepped on my skirt, tore it, and made me mad."

"Where's Dolly?"

"I don't know. Last I saw her she was talking to one of those people in the robes. I stood around, waiting. I had no clue but that you'd gone off with them, too. Then I figured I might as well wait in the car."

"Hope she gets out here so …" Just as I was about to complain the door opened again and Dolly got in the front with a shuffle of her boots and a clunk of her hardware against the seat.

"Took you guys long enough," I growled.

"Yeah … well …" Dolly didn't look at me. She took off her hat and set it in her lap. "Let's get going then."

"Are we coming back tomorrow?"

Dolly took in a breath. She hesitated. "I'll let you know in the morning whether you need to come with me."

Her distracted tone put me off.

"What do you mean, 'I'll let you know'? I thought that was the deal. We'd see if Marjory was connected here in any way. There's got to be some reason …"

Dolly nodded her head then let her chin sink to her chest. She was obviously tired. "I have to go easy here. The reverend's got a lot of people following him."

"And I'd stomp all over your questions?"

"Nope." Her shoulders slumped. "Let me think it out, ok? One of the women back there, Sally, invited me to lunch tomorrow. Nice folks, far as I can see. I asked if I could talk to the reverend and she said she didn't see why not. She said he'd be happy to talk to me. Just not tonight."

In the back, Crystalline was silent.

"I'm not invited?" I was mad and hurt. For some reason I didn't understand, Dolly was cutting me out of something important.

"Don't go off crazy, Emily. We don't know anything at this point." In profile, I could see her face was serious. This was a very different Deputy Dolly Flynn Wakowski.

I turned the car around and drove out to US131 saying nothing for a minute or two. When I couldn't contain myself, I asked, "What the heck's wrong with you, Dolly?"

She raised one hand but didn't turn to look at me. "Calm down. Let me think, ok? I'll give you a call in the morning; tell you one way or the other. It's … well … that these are nice, friendly folks. I wouldn't want to hurt them. Sally says they'd really like to have me come around and learn some more."

"Oh no," I groaned. "Tell me it's not that 'family' thing of yours. Please. I'd like to think you're not falling for some line of …"

"Fallin' for nothin'," she snapped back at me. "Plenty for the two of us to do. But I can't get anywhere with you hanging on to the back of my coat, draggin' along."

"Do what you want to do," I snapped back at her. "If the world does end, I can guarantee you won't be among the angels. As I go sailing up, passing you on your way down, just remember who said you're too mean to go to heaven."

She was quiet. Even Crystalline said nothing from the back seat, probably wondering what she'd gotten herself into and how two hopeless fruitcakes could ever find who murdered Marjory Otis.

Sorrow woke me the next morning by landing, four-paws splayed, in the middle of my back. This was no longer a puppy but a full-grown dog, and grown to stupendous proportions. Doc Crimson, Sorrow's vet, said he thought Sorrow was part Afghan and part black lab, with maybe a bit of standard poodle thrown in. Of course, he changed his mind every time I took Sorrow in for a booster shot or to have his long, curving nails cut, or get his hair untangled and the burrs out.

Since I wasn't sure what breed *I* was, I figured we belonged together, me and Sorrow. We didn't quite fit anywhere else.

I let Sorrow out, made a cup of tea, then filled a bowl with Special K and skim milk. I set everything on the table in front of my large front windows. The world had turned a brilliant gold overnight. The maples and oaks between the house and Willow Lake glowed. Mornings like this one, with the sun sneaking blood red over the trees from the east, with every golden leaf reflected in the still water of the lake—I could almost believe the world might come to an end. Outside my windows, it was too lovely to last. Perfection—the kind that philosophers claimed struck ordinary people blind.

I watched the light move and grow as I ate and thought about death: my Mom's, when I was a kid, and how that hurt in a different way from my Dad's death. Dad died after my divorce, after I'd decided to leave Ann Arbor and move to Northwestern Michigan. His death was kind of expected, a heart attack for a man with heart disease. I'd been sad, lonely, but not angry. Mom's, when I was twelve, had been a deep stab inside of me, very personal. What I'd felt most at first had been anger—how dare she do that to me! Then the ache of missing her.

I set my dishes in the sink for my make-believe cleaning woman to take care of and let a woofing Sorrow back in. I filled his dish with dog food and his bowl with water. In the living room I sat at my corner desk to make a list of the things to take care of then called Lieutenant Brent. He'd talked to Dolly already but grudgingly gave me what he had. "Toxicology preliminary," he said. "Nothing except a blood pressure medication."

"So, she was strangled. That means somebody got that close and she didn't fight hard enough to scuff her heels?"

"Looks that way."

"She must've trusted whoever it was."

"Her fingernails got skin under them. She was fighting the rope the killer got around her neck. The skin's going down to forensics for DNA. Probably be hers, the way it looks, with her clawing at her neck to loosen that garrote. Hope she scratched him."

"What about the rope?"

"Ordinary. Cotton. Three strand. Twisted." He coughed away from the phone. "So, what are you two doing today? Dolly says going out to talk to that Reverend Fritch. I hear some friends of the deceased are in town. They might know something. And remember, Emily, don't use anything in the paper that could jeopardize the case. Don't print too many details. I know you're careful. That's why I trust you, but I just want to put in a reminder here. We don't want trouble with the prosecutor when the time comes. Tainted evidence. Things like that."

I promised, yet again, that I would check with him before every story, going over the facts.

"And Emily. Officer Winston—remember? He's the one who took your statement. He knows your special circumstances—you and Dolly—and he's fine with it, as long as you keep him up-to-date on what you're doing and what you find out."

I opened my mouth to object. I remembered Officer Winston too well. Officious little jerk with his eye tic and moony face. I'd leave him to Dolly.

"Almost forgot. Dolly found Marjory's car this morning. Parked behind the IGA there in Leetsville. Locked up, keys gone. Purse inside."

"She talk to people at the store? See if anyone saw anything?" I asked.

"Already took care of it. Nobody saw anything but she left a message on the bulletin board in the store. You might want to put that in the paper. You know, ask if anybody remembers seeing the woman around the car. That kind of thing."

I agreed. It gave me an angle for the story I would get to Bill while pushing down a growing uneasiness—Dolly hadn't called to tell me she found the car.

I took a shower, toweled my hair dry, and secured most of it on top of my head with tortoiseshell combs. I thought of Molly, my hairdresser in Traverse City, and how it was time to visit her before I began looking too much like a hermit, with wild hair and nervous eyes. I brushed my teeth, rolled on deodorant, lipstick, some blush, then dressed in jeans and a fuzzy yellow shirt that dipped maybe a little too much in the front but I figured if you've got it, flaunt it. What little I had needed flaunting. I was feeling old—

maybe that revival last night. All those people thrilled to death that the world would end and so many wouldn't be saved, wouldn't go on to glory, would suffer agonizing deaths. Seemed like that kind of small-souled glee was a big enough sin to throw all the smug of the world into a fiery pit reserved for them alone.

Sorrow and I walked up to the road for the newspaper and yesterday's mail. There was one letter from people inviting me to a financial seminar that would give me a terrific retirement—if I had money to invest. And there was a gas bill from DTE Energy. I opened gas bills with a lot of fear, knowing what can happen by January—how the numbers escalated and I would gasp and hide the bill until I had the money. September's bill would be ok. I didn't have air conditioning to boost use over the summer. Heat came on rarely, as I kept my thermostat set at 60. Poverty was making me live a green life.

I stuck the mail in the back pocket of my jeans and waved to Harry, who stood back in the trees beside his driveway. I got a grunt in greeting.

He shuffled over my way, eyes going back and forth, scanning the road for racing cars. I knew he was scavenging—in case an animal was run over during the night. The only thing I'd never seen him make into a stew was skunk.

Harry nodded politely when he joined me on my side of Willow Lake Road.

"I'd like to talk to you about somethin', when you got a minute," he said, dipping his head at me, setting his long white hair to bobbing.

I checked my watch. "How about in a couple of hours? I've got some work to take care of, then I'll be over."

"Good. You come to my place."

"I'll do that, Harry. I've got some things I'd like to run past you, too."

He nodded a couple of times as if we'd made a deal. "Might have a jar of stew for ya."

"Wonderful. I think I've still got a loaf of my homemade bread in the freezer. I'll bring it with me."

Harry threw both misshapen hands into the air and backed away, shaking his head. I'd taken Harry a loaf of my bread before. I thought it was good, but Harry was a gourmet and they often have tastes above all others.

―――――――

I got down to my studio, dashed off my story for the newspaper, and emailed it to Bill. I expected Dolly to call. She didn't.

I finished the cover letter to the agent and began going over the manuscript one last time. Always so many dumb errors. I found where I'd given someone blue eyes in chapter two and gave them brown eyes in chapter fourteen. There were a few dropped plot twists. Nothing was ever perfect, but I wanted to send off the best manuscript I could put together and not kick myself later for dumb mistakes. After an hour I chucked the whole thing, printed out a fresh copy, stuck the letter and manuscript in an envelope and sealed and addressed it. Done. What would be, would be.

When I turned off the computer, Sorrow got up from the rug beneath my desk and stretched long and hard. I took him back to the house—waiting patiently through a dozen squats and attempts to mark fence posts. I gave him water then spent a little extra time at his side, brushing his hair out of his eyes with my hands and looking deep into those worried doggie eyes. There were days, like this one, when an extra dose of love didn't hurt either of us.

I still had time before going to Harry's, so I called the police station in Leetsville. Lucky answered. "Dolly's just pulling out of the lot. I'll stop her," he said, and put down the phone.

He was back on in a couple of minutes. "Caught her. She's coming in," he said. "By the way, Emily. I got something to clear up with you."

Oh, oh. I wondered what I'd done wrong now.

"In the paper, you put Dolly as Deputy Dolly."

"That's what she's called..."

"But, you see, she's really Officer Dolly. It's the people around here. They started calling her Deputy Dolly sort of after Deputy Dawg—in that cartoon. You know the one I mean. But that's not strictly her title."

"So I shouldn't call her 'deputy' in the newspaper?"

"Don't think so. Just looks wrong. It's officer, ok? Here's Dolly," he said. I heard voices and then Dolly was on the phone, not sounding a bit happy.

"What is it, Emily?"

"Why didn't you call me?" I was mad. First she'd left me out of a big event in the case; then I got brought up short by Lucky for getting her title wrong. Not a good day. "Brent told me you found her car at the IGA."

"Yup."

"Anything else you might want to tell me?"

"Nope. I'm in a hurry."

"I want to go talk to that preacher with you. I thought we were doing this together."

There was a long pause. "We went over all this last night."

"Not to my satisfaction."

"*Satisfaction*," she mimicked. "Jesus—sorry, don't mean to blaspheme—but I told you I was going there for lunch. What I don't want is to go stompin' around makin' enemies. Get what I'm sayin'? Don't need heavy-handed accusations while I'm trying to get the lay of the land."

By that time I was boiling. "You go right ahead and get your 'lay of the land,' but I'm not staying away."

"Can't stop you. I thought we'd be further ahead if you talked to Crystalline's friends from Ohio. She called to say they got in last night and have things to add about why Marjory came here in the first place. Why don't you let me take care of the campground end of things?"

That made me stop boiling and think. A better use of our time. I reluctantly agreed and got Crystalline's number.

I called Crystalline and arranged to meet her and her friends at the Burger King in Kalkaska. Safer there. People wouldn't be speculating and listening in on our conversation the way they would have at EATS. We agreed that four o'clock would be a good time.

Before I could get out of the house with my loaf of frozen bread for Harry, Jackson called to ask if he could run something by me at Bill's dinner party. "You will be surprised," he teased, giving one of those deep chuckles that still stirred my flesh—and other parts, except my brain, which had at long last learned to control my more annoying parts. I told him I could hardly wait.

There are times when I think I'm all grown up. Then I do something dumb like sticking my tongue out at the telephone and I know it is never going to happen. Not really.

The best place to take my childish self was over to Crazy Harry Mockerman's. We'd talk about road-kill stew and puffballs and lions and tigers and bears.

Oh, my…

FIFTEEN

Thursday, October 15
12 days until it all ends

THERE WAS NO WAY I would take Harry's stew if he wouldn't take my bread. I'd wrapped a loaf, fresh out of the freezer, in paper toweling, and carried it under my arm as I made my way up his overgrown drive.

His crooked little house sat alone in its carved-out clearing ringed by golden maples. The rose bush at the front door, which I'd helped him plant in the summer, had one last red blossom on it, drooping and bobbing in the afternoon wind.

Harry answered at my first knock, held the door wide, and invited me in. His suit coat was off. His way-off-white shirt was neat except that the collar gaped around his skinny neck. His wide black tie was perfectly knotted. He waved me to a wooden chair in his tiny living room, a room I'd never sat in before, always being directed to the kitchen since he would have something simmering on the stove and that something always needed watching.

I handed Harry my loaf of bread. He took it from me gingerly, holding it between his two hands. "Thank you, Emily," he said, nodding formally. "If I don't get to it, my dogs will be pleased." He set the bread on a table and took a chair across the room. There we sat, backs straight, smiling at each other over a braided rug and under the watchful eye of a badly mounted eight-point buck. We nodded from time to time but otherwise said nothing. I figured he'd open up sooner or later and waited him out.

"I asked you over here, Emily." He cleared his throat and leaned forward, hands between his bony knees. "To get some advice on … on matters of the heart."

I gave him a look. "Are you sure you want to talk to me? You know I'm not exactly an expert where things like that are involved."

"Well, good enough. You're the only one I trust to talk to. Don't know where else to turn."

"Then I'll do my best, Harry. What's going on?"

"As you know, I've been dating Delia Swanson 'round a week now and I think I'm ready to propose."

I sat back, not sure where this was going and hoping against hope he wasn't asking for the sex talk.

"A little quick, isn't it?"

He shook his head. "Not if what that preacher says is true. Could be all over sooner than we think and here I'd be, dying a single man."

"I'm going out a single woman."

"That's ok, Emily. You was married already. I never been. You believe what that preacher says? I'm kind of leery about it, myself. Seems like too many of that kind I seen come through here during my lifetime." He shook his head. "Still, you don't want to be on the wrong side of things. Just in case."

"Why don't you propose?"

He thought awhile. "I get the feeling that Delia's mother don't like me all that much."

I shook my head at him, hoping this was going to be a short conversation. "You know how she is. She's very old and ..."

"More than that. She told Delia she doesn't want to see me around their house anymore. I take that as kind of being against me."

I thought awhile then admitted I wouldn't look on it as a welcome either.

"What's Delia say?"

He shrugged, "What any good daughter would say, I guess. She says she's got to listen to her mother."

"Delia's in her seventies, Harry."

"Yeah, well ..." He seemed sad. I had the feeling he'd had big plans for him and Delia. At least a week of wild passion before they packed it in for good.

"Did you mention marriage?"

"Yup, but Delia said it didn't appear to be good, not with her mother acting up the way she is."

"What do you want from me?"

"I was thinking. What do you think if I ask Delia to elope with me?"

I would have let my mouth fall open but I didn't want to startle Harry. "Hmm," I hedged. "Again, I think you've got to ask Delia. You don't mean with a ladder anything like that?"

"Nope. Just drive over and bring her back here."

I nodded slowly. "I still think you have to ask Delia what she thinks of the plan. You don't want to throw her over your shoulder. She's got a say in this, you know."

"That's what I figured, with this woman's lib stuff and all. I'll put a note on her door; ask if I can come talk to her." He seemed happy with my advice. Before he could think it over and realize it wasn't much as lovelorn stuff went, I quickly asked him about the tractor salesman I was looking for.

"Tractor salesman? What do you want with a tractor salesman? You don't need no tractor for that small garden of yours."

"No, I don't. You heard about Marjory Otis being murdered out at Deward?"

He nodded. "Simon told me."

Simon, our mailman and boyfriend to Gloria at EATS, delivered a lot more than the mail. I'd gotten Sorrow through Simon and he carried the news from house to house. Simon was an important man back in our woods—for some he was the only touch with the outside world.

I reminded Harry of the time, maybe thirty years or more ago, when Marjory's mother ran off with a man said to be a tractor salesman.

"Yeah, I heard. Never believed a word of it. Woman was unhappy as it was. They even locked her up in a state hospital for a while, just for being unhappy. Back then, they did whatever they wanted. That was no woman looking for a husband to run away with, not Winnie Otis. That was a woman who only wanted to be left alone. But that's what everybody said; she ran off and left her kids."

"She never came back. I'd like to look up that tractor salesman. Do you remember anybody who would fit that description? I mean, a tractor salesman she could have met in Leetsville? Maybe in a gas station?"

He thought that over for a while then shook his head. "I'd try the Feed and Seed in town, if that was me. Old farmers always going in there. They'd know."

He stood. I supposed our afternoon tête-à-tête was finished.

"One more thing." I held up a finger as I stood. "Marjory Otis lived with her aunt and uncle while she was a teenager, along with her brothers."

He nodded. "I remember the boys. Arnold was kind of a blowhard. Paul was a quiet enough kid. You hear, Arnold's running for Michigan state senator? Supposed to be coming to town soon." He frowned. "But I guess that's about Marjory being dead. A brother would have to see to …"

I nodded. "What I wanted to know was about that aunt and uncle."

"Their Aunt Cecily and Uncle Ralph Otis, you mean. Knew 'em some."

"Do they still live around here?"

He shook his head. "Ralph died, oh, maybe twenty years ago. Cecily's up to Bellaire, in a nursing home. Guess you could go give her a visit. Probably doesn't get much company. No kids, you know. And she didn't treat Winnie's kids much good when they was with her. I'd say Cecily might look forward to a visit from just about anybody. Even you, looking for a tractor salesman."

Harry went out to his kitchen, bumbled around for a few minutes, and came back. He had one of his infamous jars of stew in his hands, wiping the lid with the dish towel he carried.

"You don't have to …" I demurred, then took the jar thrust at me. I held it up so I could look in, but it was as dense as ever with carrots and potatoes.

With a sinking feeling, I asked Harry what kind of stew it was this time. "You don't use dead skunk, do you?"

His look was pure disgust. "Can't be choosy, Emily. All the same to the stew pot."

SIXTEEN

Just 12 days left to make plans

IN LEETSVILLE, SY HUETT, our go-getter used car salesman, was out trolling for business, driving his hearse slowly up 131 while yelling to robed people gathered in groups beside the road. "Give ya the deal of a lifetime, folks," he called as he drove along beyond me. "You only have to pay for your new car if the world don't end. Good bet. Like getting a car for free."

I hoped to get by him, pretending to be invisible, but he saw me as I drove into the post office parking lot to mail off the manuscript. I got out of my car, the manuscript package in my hands, still pretending nobody could see me and that I couldn't see anyone either. I was almost to the door when he whipped his hearse in front of me, blocking my way.

"Emily! How ya doing?" He leaned out the driver's window, smiling wide. Sy's comb-over was especially dramatic today, starting somewhere down by his left ear, where he'd made himself a part then flipped the hair up and over a growing bald spot at the top. He'd sprayed his whole head so the hair didn't move, just sat there like a furrowed, and always fallow, spring field.

I nodded in greeting.

"I've been thinking. Isn't it time you replaced that old Jeep of yours?" He smiled.

I shook my head, smiled back, trying to walk around his car. He edged the old hearse forward so I had the choice of talking or having my foot run over.

"Lots of good years left in it, Sy."

He made a sound in his throat, then clucked and wobbled his head from side to side. "Winter's coming. You know what that means. Gotta have a vehicle you can count on when the snow and ice get here."

"Mine's fine." I smirked and started around his car. He rolled backward enough to stop me. "Anyway, Sy, the world's going to end. Maybe I won't need a car at all. Maybe you'll be out of business and we'll all ride around on fluffy clouds."

"Isn't this something? Did you ever...? I've got a deal going with those people..." He nodded to where two of the cultists stood beside the road. A big, broad, yellow-toothed smile spread from ear to ear. "Don't pay me a dime until twelve-o-one, October twenty-seventh. If we're all still here, I get my money. If it's all over—well, they'll have a newer car to drive while they're waiting it out. You know what they say, Emily: *This world and one more; and then come the fireworks.* Give you the same deal I give to all of them."

How could I not laugh at this go-getting, skinny guy in a suit jacket that bunched up around his ears? He sat there, inside his hearse, grinning at me, head back just a little, expecting to make a deal there and then.

"Who says that?"

"What?"

"That fireworks stuff."

"Everybody."

"Never heard it before."

"Trust me. Common saying. Now about the deal…"

"Thanks, Sy, but I'm betting not one of us will get out of paying you."

"Me, too."

I thought a moment, about how Sy was everywhere and heard everything. "By the way, Sy, did you hear anything about Arnold Otis coming to town, the man running for state senator?"

He nodded. "Yeah, he's making a campaign stop in Traverse then heading over here, because of Marjory, you know. I heard you found her out there at Deward. Strange thing. You think she just up and died?"

"I don't think so. If you read the *Northern Statesman* there's news in there about her death."

He waved a hand at me. "Don't need to read any newspapers. I go into Eugenia's place, there," he pointed back toward EATS, "when there's something to learn."

I figured this was one of the reasons newspapers were having such trouble in the country: a non-reading public. Maybe people everywhere were going back to spreading news around a campfire. Maybe the oral tale would take the place of a front-page story. Maybe the tom-tom would come back—Detroit to Saginaw to Grand Rapids to Traverse City and places north. Maybe the hysterics of the Internet would replace who, what, where, when, and how. I sure hoped not.

"Come on, Sy. Break down and buy yourself a newspaper. And, to tell you the truth, I love my Jeep. I'm keeping it. And you know what else, Sy? When it comes time to replace this car I'll be looking on the Internet. Like you getting your news cheap, lots of deals there. I have to watch my money."

Sy wasn't happy. "You don't want to do that, Emily. Who's gonna service it? Who's gonna get you the best financing…?"

I smiled, shrugged, and left Sy sputtering.

Dorothy, behind the counter at the post office, put her hand out for the package I carried. I hesitated. It seemed I was committing an irrevocable act I couldn't call back. She frowned at me, her thick, black brows coming together in the middle of her forehead.

"Well? You wanna mail it or not?" she demanded.

I wrote REQUESTED MATERIAL across the front of the envelope then held it out one more time, delicately, as if it were velvet, with a diamond tiara perched on top. She grabbed it, slapped it on the scale, asked me if it was potentially hazardous—which I had a hard time answering, fearing it could be—asked a few other questions, ran off metered postage to overnight it, then threw my manuscript in the bin behind her. I heard it hit and kept my head down, rooting in my purse for money as I got a hold of myself. It was only a manuscript, not my whole life, falling into that bin.

When I turned to leave, it was like leaving a child behind, in the hands of people who didn't know what a delicate thing I'd given them, nor how they would break my heart if it didn't get directly and safely to New York City.

Next was the IGA. I bought eggs and dog food and a bottle of wine for Bill's party. When I came out, brown paper sack in my arms,

I figured I had time left to get over to the Feed and Seed and ask a few questions before I met Crystalline and her friends in Kalkaska.

I stuck my groceries in the back seat and made my way to the big red Feed and Seed, kitty-corner from the gas station, an ancient building leaning toward the east, waiting for a strong wind to bring it down.

I had no use for pig food or udder cream, so I'd never been in the Feed and Seed before. The smell of the place, when I walked in, surprised me. The smell was good, like old leather and old wood and, maybe, old farmers. The floor, of bare planks, creaked as I walked around stacks of feed and bird seed, looking for someone to ask about a tractor salesman.

Three elderly men stood near the back of the store, talking, laughing, carrying on. They wore overalls and flannel shirts under wide-open jackets. Every one had a billed cap on his head advertising either John Deere or the Detroit Tigers. One of the men saw me walking toward them and frowned, causing the other two men to turn slowly and give me appraising looks.

"Emily Kincaid," I introduced myself, and said I was a reporter with the newspaper. That got their attention.

"Know who you are," one man said. "See you over to EATS. Sometimes in the IGA. Sometimes getting gas." This man was wrinkled but still very good looking, with dark hair sticking from his cap, a wide chest, and a good smile. "Bob Whitfield." He held out his hand.

I didn't recognize Bob Whitfield or either of the other two men. In a small town like Leetsville, it seemed everyone had a knack for recognizing new people who might stay around a while. I didn't have that knack myself, having brought my city obliviousness up north with me.

"With the newspaper?" This man was thin and bent. He wore a checked flannel shirt; said his name was Don Croton. "Well Emily, I guess they're using women in lots of different jobs now. Though I suppose Lois Lane's been around a long time."

I laughed, knowing I was being teased. I took the big, flat paw of a hand he held out to me and shook it.

"Yup, like back in World War II. Let 'em do riveting and stuff," the third man, heavy set, stomach pushing against the front of his stained coveralls, said. "Name's Rowdy."

"I've got a question…"

Rowdy looked to the other two, settled back on the heels of his boots, and raised his eyebrows. He turned to me. "Now what's the question, Ma'am? You want to know how the harvest went this year? You want corn yield per acre?"

They were really having their way with me, these old, and very sharp, men.

"I'd love to know all of that but it's about something different. A woman died out at Deward and…"

"Heard about it. Marjory Otis, wasn't it?" Rowdy turned to the others for confirmation. "Think I heard you was the one found her."

"I did. Now I'm looking into the death with Deputy Dolly Wakowski…"

The thin man, Don, raised his eyebrows. "With Deputy Dolly, eh? Heard our Dolly's been doing some pretty good police work lately."

Bob snickered. "Sure beats busting up patrol cars the way she used to do. Wasn't it Chet Acorn's son, Willard, she chased when he took that candy bar? Ran her car into the corner of the bank when the kid went in?"

"What I want to know," I interrupted before I spent an hour or so trying to get them back on track, "is about her mother, Winnie Otis. I was told she ran away with a tractor salesman back when Marjory was in her early teens."

"Heard that, too," Bob said.

"Do you know who the tractor salesman was?"

All three took the time to look directly into each other's faces, shake their head, and toe the floor. "Never could figure it out." Rowdy, the heavy man, looked at the other two. "You figure out who the guy was? Only tractor salesman I knew back then was Jimmy…eh…what his last name now?"

"Think it was Little." Don, the thin man, took off his cap, scratched the back of his head, then set the cap carefully in place.

"What was 'little'?" Rowdy asked, frowning at his friend.

Don frowned back at him. "His name. What in hell you think I'm talking about?"

"Well Don, to tell ya the truth I'm clueless here."

Before they got off track again, I quickly asked, "His name was Jimmy Little?"

"Could be," Bob said, turning to the others. "Wasn't he the guy would come out to the farm to see how the new tractor was working? Then sometimes, I remember, came out for planting, even for a christening and such? Sure, you remember. Jimmy—big guy, always laughing and carrying on—like he loved what he was doing."

Don asked, "Didn't he get transferred to a different store? Sure he did, down to Kingsley, I think." He turned to me. "Yup, I'd try there. Down to Kingsley. Call 'em first. Make sure before you go. John Deere place, don't remember the guy's name who owns it. They'll know how to find 'im, but he's not involved with any of that business out to Deward, is he, Emily? Wouldn't think so. Must be at least sixty, if he's a day."

"So I might be looking for a man named Jimmy Little in Kingsley?"

"Well now," Bob said. "That was a long time ago. Who knows where the man got to after that."

"Any other tractor salesman you remember around here back then?"

One by one, they shook their head. "None that come to mind," Bob, the good-looking one, said. "But if you find Jimmy, he'll be able to tell you. Jimmy knew everybody. Good businessman."

I thanked the three of them, talked about the weather and what winter was going to be like this year, then shook hands all around and left them to their ruminating and reminiscing about Jimmy and what a good guy he'd been and the winter he'd come out to help plow Rowdy out of a ditch when the snow got over two hundred inches by the first of January.

I was out the door and on my way south, to Kalkaska and the Burger King.

SEVENTEEN

Still 12 days to go

SINCE IT WAS ALMOST four o'clock, most of the tables and booths in Burger King were empty. The three women I looked for wouldn't have been hard to pick out no matter how full the place had been. I smiled, waved to Crystalline, with her wild, red hair, and walked toward them. The two friends were younger. One, with a large soft drink cup and Whopper in front of her, was about twenty-five. Her eyes were ringed with heavy black makeup, long liquid-silver earrings shimmering under the stark overhead lights when she looked up and tossed her straight dark hair back with one hand. She was dressed all in black. Kind of Goth—a gauzy dress far too thin for fall in northern Michigan. Three strands of jet beads hung around her neck. A single gold loop went through one of her dark eyebrows. The hands around her drink cup were thick with silver and gold rings, black-painted fingernails. The Goth girl had the face of a kid dressed up to shock—too much of everything with nothing hiding eyes that begged for something. Under all her stage makeup and dress, the girl seemed sad and needy. I'd met her kind before, and almost always liked them, no matter how they screamed "I'm scary!"

The other woman was in her thirties but maybe that was being too kind. She had one of those long, sad, ageless faces with too much chin and eyes too prominent: big, not in a pretty way, with a lot of white showing. Her neck was too long. Her shoulders too slumped. She wore a flowered sweater that hung halfway down her knuckles. Incongruously, a ring of artificial yellow flowers with yellow streamers sat atop her long and very lank brown hair. I looked at those two and figured Leetsville was in for yet another shock.

"This is Sonia," Crystalline introduced the younger, Goth girl.

"And Felicia." The older one nodded and sent her flowered circlet sliding. She grabbed it, searched her hair for a couple of bobby pins, and jabbed the flower ring back into place. All the while she was smiling a wide, horsey smile, and nodding.

I joined them, sliding in next to Felicia, smiling at each woman a time or two and expressing my sympathy at the loss of their friend.

"One in a million," Felicia said, and sniffed. "I'll never get over it."

"I knew it was going to happen. Saw it coming. Nobody would listen to me." Sonia, shaking her head, sent her silver earrings bobbing. Her voice was harsh, tough. "I told her I saw it, something terrible if she went to Michigan alone. But Marjory said everything would be all right and that it was just my own fear talking. Then..." She waved a hand indicating the ceiling, the windows— everywhere. "You see what happened. If she woulda listened..."

"You did not tell her that," Felicia said, sitting back and giving the girl an incredulous look, her large eyes open and outraged.

"Did too. Right before she left. I was so nervous, pacing back and forth, and I had to tell her what I was picking up. Her aura was off. Way off the charts. I was scared for Marjory and tried to tell her not to go. All she did was say how sometimes in life we have to do things no matter what and hope the universe will protect us." She made a spitting sound off toward her left shoulder. "Yeah, as if …"

"Was that all she said?" I asked. The girl was surprised, maybe at being singled out as special, being the one whose ESP, or whatever they used, worked best. She looked away, reluctant to share her secrets with the likes of me, then shrugged and waved a dismissive hand. "She said it wasn't something she wanted to do, but that somebody needed her help."

"Did she say who that someone was?" I leaned over the table, hoping for a name, something to hang the thread of a story on.

Sonia shook her head. "She told me there are some things that are too private to share."

"Nothing else?"

"Well, she did say that there are times when we have to protect other people—whatever that meant. Then she said this was one of those times for her. I think that's what she said. Something like that. What I understood was that she didn't want to come back here but she didn't have a choice."

I nodded. Felicia, who'd been nervously waiting for a chance to jump in, cleared her throat and put a hand up like a kid in school. I called on her.

"I understand THAT perfectly. She's … well, was … always rushing in to save somebody. The woman was a saint, I'll tell ya. If it wasn't for Marjory I don't know where I'd be. She came to this prison where I was staying and talked to us about worlds beyond this one and how we didn't have to be locked in to what other people thought about us and…"

Crystalline, chin resting on her fist, sighed. "Felicia. Keep it to Marjory, ok? This is important."

Felicia frowned, crumbled her Whopper paper and set it back on her tray. She seemed to rearrange her mind. "Crystalline says she told you most of Marjory's story. What with her father dying, her mother running away with some guy, and having to live from the time she was twelve with people who were mean to her—that awful Aunt Cecily and Uncle Ralph. You can see why there was no reason for her to come here. Who on earth wants to go back into their own past when that past is just too toxic to be believed? I mean, what I teach is to put all that's come before behind us and look to the future. When I do the Tarot, the way Marjory taught me, what I almost always center on is how to heal by getting rid of bad memories and concentrating…"

"Did this have to do with one of her brothers?" I had to break in. The woman barely took a breath, linking her sentences so nobody dared interfere.

"One brother. That's all she had. Only one," she corrected with a quick nod of her head. "And she never saw him. Too important in politics, or something."

"I'd heard there was…" I tried to interrupt but she turned to look over at Sonia and Crystalline. Her face reddened. She was working up to something.

"It was just like Marjory to do something like that. Just had to go help somebody. Like it was an old friend or something. She had to come here and save that person, and see to it that no more evil was going to occur in this terrible place that had claimed her childhood and made her so sad. Even to say the name 'Leetsville,' why she would ..."

Sonia rolled her eyes. Crystalline put a hand on Felicia's arm, stopping her in mid-sentence.

"You said there were two brothers," I said quickly to Crystalline.

She thought a minute before answering. "There are two. I guess I was the only one she told about Paul, the younger one."

"Well! I can't imagine Marjory wouldn't tell me about something as important as a brother and there wouldn't be any reason since Marjory told me everything and I do mean 'everything' and ..." Felicia wasn't happy.

Crystalline nodded, first to turn off Felicia, and then toward me. "She didn't see him either. Not since he was told to leave their aunt and uncle's home. Once she said it made her sad, to think of him out in the world all alone but that she didn't know how to find him. There was some kind of accident. That was the last she ever heard. I guess he was hurt bad, was what Marjory said. She wanted to go see him but didn't know where he was. I think she heard about the accident long after the fact. Maybe that brother, Arnold, told her. I don't know. But I do know she never got another word from him. I think she was afraid Paul was dead."

I understood that there were things Marjory hadn't dared share with the talkative Felicia, and probably other things she hadn't shared with the young and vulnerable Sonia. What I'd pulled from Felicia's diatribe was one word. friend. I hadn't thought about people up here knowing her. There had to be someone who remembered her from high school, or felt sorry for her when her mother disappeared. There had been so little in the old papers about her, or about her brothers. Nothing like what there'd been about other women from Leetsville—parties, trips, engagements, weddings—but that didn't mean she didn't have a friend. Maybe her Aunt Cecily would remember. Dolly and I would have to visit her at that nursing home. If there had been friends, her aunt would surely know.

I went to the counter and ordered a salad and a diet Coke.

Back at the table I mentioned that Arnold Otis was coming to Leetsville. "He's been notified of Marjory's death," I added. "I'm assuming that's what's bringing him here."

"Well, big surprise," Crystalline said. "Never wanted anything to do with her when she was alive."

"Was Marjory ever in touch with him, that you know of?" I asked.

The three looked at each other. Their faces were blank.

"Sure," Crystalline said. "They talked once in a while. And lately she said she saw him in the newspaper, running for office the way he was. I think I told you before how Marjory embarrassed him. Because she was a psychic, and a healer. I saw the letter he wrote asking her to lay low until the election, this November, was over."

"Yeah, like she was going to embarrass him. Like she was shooting people on I-75 or something." Sonia made a face.

"That's pretty insulting. How'd she feel about it?" I asked.

"You never knew with Marjory," Crystalline said. "She didn't want to hurt anybody's feelings so she didn't say much. You know, like it was family so she wasn't going to criticize."

"Anybody mad at her? I mean, like somebody she didn't get along with. Professional jealousy. I understand she was quite well known … in … eh … certain circles."

"Very well known," Crystalline said, nodding emphatically. "There was nobody like her. Not as a teacher. Not as a human being. She was the best healer I've ever seen. Not the laying on of hands stuff, but she could do a healing even over the telephone. Just concentrate, be with the person needing her. Get right inside of them. Use her mind's eye to travel through their body and see what was wrong. I'm telling you, a lot of them came back to tell her how much she'd helped them."

"So," I pressed. "Not a single enemy."

All three shook their head.

"Would anybody gain with Marjory out of the way?"

The women couldn't think of a soul.

I turned to Crystalline. "What was it she said to you about the End Time group? Something like 'somebody's going to have to do something about the whole thing.' You have any idea what that meant? So far we've got two reasons for her to come back here: the Reverend Fritch and helping somebody. Think it might be a person who joined his cult? Maybe this person was giving away all their worldly goods. Maybe it was a client of hers, asking for help."

Crystalline shook her head. "All I know is what I told you. If I'd known she was in danger, believe me I'd have come with her. She never said a word about being afraid of anybody."

So we were back to Leetsville and the past. Back to this mysterious trip of hers that ended in her death. All I knew was that she came to help someone and it had something to do with the Reverend Fritch, or his doomsday gathering. Maybe her aunt was bilked out of her money by the cult, though I couldn't imagine Marjory caring too much about a woman who'd been cruel to her as a kid. Still, you never knew. Family dynamics could be weird.

"Hi, Dolly." Crystalline was smiling and greeting someone standing beside the booth. I turned to see Dolly, with her hat in her hand. Beside her was one of the cult members, robe cinched around her waist with a white, rope belt, hood drawn down so that very little of her face could be seen.

"Dolly!" I twisted around to look up. She nodded at me. There were heavy bags under her almost colorless eyes. Her hair was dirty looking, as if she hadn't showered in a while. I'd never seen her look so tired. She made a noise, expelling a long breath and seeming to deflate, getting shorter and squatter before my eyes.

"Sister Sally," Dolly motioned to the woman standing a little behind her, with her hands tucked up the wide sleeves of her robe. The woman tipped her head toward us but said nothing.

We greeted Sister Sally and made a move to get up, go to another booth where there would be room for everyone, but Dolly motioned us to stay where we were.

Crystalline introduced Felicia and Sonia, who both nodded but gave Sister Sally puzzled looks.

"Only here a minute. I saw your car," Dolly said.

"I was asking Marjory's friends for help in her…"

Dolly put up a hand. "We're not staying. Only dropped in to say hi."

"But we've got to talk…" I insisted.

Dolly nodded. "We will. I'll call you later. Right now Sister Sally and me got to get back out to the campground." She drew a long, loud, breath.

"You have lunch out there?" I asked, worried about her un-Dolly-like exhaustion.

She nodded. "Good food. Nice people. Sally, here, is one of the inner circle, I guess you'd call it. She showed me around the campground. Nothing dangerous I could see. They took care of all the electric connections—things like that. Seems they thought I was some kind of inspector or something. I told them I only wanted a few words with the reverend, but that never happened. I mean, nice lunch and all, but the man's really, really busy."

Sister Sally stood there impassive. She said nothing. As it was, Dolly wasn't saying much either. "You're an officer of the law. You had business with him…" I began.

"It'll happen," Dolly said. "In due time."

"We've got to get back out there, Dolly." I pushed up from the booth. "Can I talk to you a minute? Over there?" I pointed to a far corner, near the pop dispenser.

Dolly wiped a hand across her forehead where beads of sweat had gathered. The room wasn't that warm. "I suppose so. We don't have a lot of time."

She followed me to a place out of the hearing of the other women. Behind us, Sister Sally didn't sit down, only stood where she was, and turned to keep her blank, shaded eyes on Dolly and me.

"What's going on, Dolly? You're not calling. I don't know anything. And now you're carting this… this… Mother Time around with you?"

She glared at me then looked down at her shoes. "You're doing your thing and I'm doing mine."

"We were supposed to work together."

"Be dumb to stay joined at the hip. Too much to cover. I'm taking care of what I think has to be taken care of."

"And I'm not supposed to know what that is?"

"Look, Emily, why don't I give you a call later? Ok? I'd like to know what Marjory's friends have to say…"

"And I'd like to know what's going on out at the campground."

"Pretty sincere people. This end of the world stuff could be real. I've been listening close and they're onto something."

"For God's sakes, Dolly." I was beyond frustration. "You're not getting suckered into this crap, are you?"

She looked me straight in the eye, her face bunched and serious. "I'm looking into things. That's all that's happening."

"Things you need to know for our investigation? Or need to know personally?"

"Maybe both," she said, and turned to look worriedly back at where Sister Sally stood.

I took her arm and held on. "These people aren't your family, Dolly. Don't fall for …"

She gave me a hurt look, pulled her arm away, and went back to the booth, leaving me standing alone where I was. She tapped Sister Sally on the shoulder and led her out of the Burger King.

I wanted to run after her, shake her until the old Dolly came back. I knew I couldn't. What I was going to do was get out to that campground with Marjory's friends and talk to the Reverend Fritch. If he was casting spells on people like Dolly, surely Crystalline or Felicia or Sonia would know.

EIGHTEEN

Friday, October 16
11 days to go

JACKSON'S WHITE JAGUAR WAS already in front of Bill's house when I pulled up and parked behind him. I'd worked all day and was ready to party. I figured I wasn't too late, maybe fifteen minutes—a fashionable time—and that was understandable, since it was raining buckets and I'd slowed down on M72, especially where the rain and wind whipped across the road by the Turtle Creek Casino.

I could see in the large front window of Bill's little house on Eighth Street—a row house from another century with a wraparound porch; a swing; and a huge, very old oak in the front yard.

I could see Jackson inside the house, nodding in answer to something someone was saying. Bill walked past the window, a wine glass in his hand. A thin, young woman accepted the glass from him. I didn't recognize her. No one I knew. Only a girl, really. Twenties at the most. She couldn't be Bill's date. At least I hoped not. Maybe a kid sister. A niece. Or—more than likely—somebody

Jackson found … somewhere. Oh crap, I thought. Here comes another disaster.

I sat in my car for a minute longer, taking a few deep breaths before I went in. There had been so much happening. I couldn't get my head around the changes in Dolly, nor this new friend of hers, Sister Sally, who sure didn't say much but appeared to be occupying an important place in Dolly's life. All I could attribute it to was Dolly's desperate need for family. She'd never had anyone but a series of foster mothers—some who looked the other way as Dolly was abused; others who couldn't handle her and returned her to Social Services as fast as they could get her there. What was left was Delores Flynn, a little girl who needed to carve a warm niche for herself somewhere. That niche had been law enforcement in Leetsville where people had to pay attention to her, where she took on the role handed to her with a desperate seriousness.

But now—family of a different sort. The stuff of cults: live among the alienated, be given pseudo-love, be made important to a cause, just like family, only there was punishment if you tried to leave. The thought of what she could be getting into gave me chills.

Even thinking about this new Dolly Flynn Wakowski made me sad. Poor uptight Dolly whose husband, Chet, had left her six months after they got married. A lot in one fairly short lifetime to get over. I knew Dolly's intense focus on any problem. I knew her honesty. I knew she was a miserable burr at times. I knew she liked to guilt me out to make me help her on cases we worked together. I knew she could be rude, be a pain in the ass, be a bulldog, be opinionated and dictatorial. All of that. But I also knew we were friends. What I didn't know was where the lines got drawn in our kind of friendship.

Time to go in. I couldn't sit there all night trying to understand things that seemed to have no handles on them, no way in, and no hints as to where I might get help.

I hunted for the bottle of wine that had rolled under the seat. It was still in its brown paper bag. I seriously lacked finesse where the social niceties were concerned. Still, I gave myself credit for taking off the $11.99 IGA sticker before putting it back in the bag.

I opened the car door, got out into the pouring rain without covering my head, and ran to the big porch. I rang the bell. Before anyone answered I slipped the wine out of the brown bag and stashed the bag in a flowerpot, among dead geraniums. Bill opened the door as I shook my head to get the water out of my hair. He laughed and stepped back, out of the way, as I did when Sorrow threw raindrops in a circle around me.

Bill took the wine and admired the vineyard and the year, which pleased me since I'd picked the first white I'd come on that I could afford without looking too cheap. He took my jacket and hung it in the front closet while telling me how happy he was that I could make it. I kind of expected a kiss on the cheek, a hug, something to show I was welcomed. Instead, I got a big smile and one hand laid lightly on my back and another hand pointing to the living room where the others stood.

Bill's living room was exactly what you would expect of a guy. No knick-knacks, no matched period pieces. There was a treadmill in a far corner, a few mismatched chairs mostly leather—and a deep, sagging old sofa. On the walls were framed awards for editorial excellence, what must have been family pictures, and a single very good Georgia O'Keeffe.

Jackson, looking his splendid self in turtleneck sweater, well-tailored slacks, and loafers, threw his arms wide and engulfed me in a big hug and a kiss to my forehead. He held me there for longer than necessary, smiling down into my face, stirring old suspicions as to what he was up to.

Bill took my arm, turned me to the girl clutching a wine glass in both her well-manicured fingers and blinking big-lashed, Anne Hathaway eyes at me.

"Regina Oldenburg," he said. "A friend of Jackson's."

Jackson moved over to push her lightly forward, his hand on the small of the young woman's back. "My new assistant, Emily." He beamed at me and at the young woman as if he'd just done the greatest thing.

I held my breath. News to me, that he had an assistant. And if she worked for him, why was I transcribing the Chaucer thing into computer files and burning disks for his editor? I made an unfriendly face—not at Regina Oldenburg, but at Jackson.

He threw his hands in the air. "I know. I know. After all the work you've done…" He snickered and wrapped an arm around the willowy Ms. Oldenburg. "But you've been so busy lately; I thought it was time to let you attend to your own writing. I mean, with this agent interested in your work. So, as a favor to you, I hired Regina, who was available and more than qualified to do the job."

"Is this the surprise you called me about?" I asked, ignoring the hand Regina Oldenburg held out to me. She slowly pulled the hand back and shrugged off Jackson's arm. I noticed the motion and quickly wondered if I was misjudging the girl. Maybe not another one of his floozies after all; the kind who thought "work" meant something you did on your back.

Jackson shook his head. "No, no. Entirely different thing. But it will involve Regina in a lot more intensive labor."

I nodded, then smiled at Regina, looking into a very large pair of confused dark eyes. "I used to be married to Jackson," I explained, assuming from her surprise that Jackson had said nothing. "Sorry if I've been rude. Jackson has a way of springing things on people…"

Behind us, Bill listened quietly. I heard Bill clear his throat.

Regina's face reddened. "I'm sorry if…" She took a deep breath. "I told Mr. Rinaldi I wasn't comfortable coming to a social evening with him. I think our relationship should remain one of business. If I'm not supposed to be here… I mean, if my being here is causing trouble…"

I laughed. "I'm sure you are a lovely girl, Regina. And probably the best thing to happen to me. I've got more than enough writing of my own, let alone keeping Jackson's work up to date. Please, let's forget all of this and start over." I put out my hand. "I'm Emily Kincaid and I'm happy to meet you. Now, can I have a big glass of wine and apologize to everyone for gaffes committed and to come?"

I turned to Bill and shrugged. He put his arm around me and leaned down to whisper, "Jackson didn't say a word about bringing anyone or I would have…"

"Welcome to my world," I whispered back, took the wine he handed me, and offered to help in the kitchen.

Dinner was very good, and so very easy—after that uncomfortable beginning. Bill had prepared braised veal in a white wine sauce, pasta primavera, a spinach salad, and wonderful bruschetta with a homemade spread of tomatoes, olive oil, garlic, and hot peppers. Talk was lively and fun and the more wine we drank, the livelier it got.

Regina, it turned out, was from an old Traverse City family, knew everybody in town. Her father, William Oslow Oldenburg had been mayor at one time and was still active in local politics. I asked if her parents had ever mentioned Arnold Otis, the man running for the state senate from a downstate district.

"He grew up in Leetsville. Kind of a local boy," I said.

Regina screwed her face up, thinking, then shook her head. "I could ask them, if it's important."

"It kind of is," I said. "I'd like to know what his reputation is like. I'm looking into … something." I wrote my phone number on a piece of paper Bill supplied and handed it to her.

She'd taken a chair across from Jackson at the table but paid him little attention. I noticed and decided I could like this young woman and wish her well. I thought maybe a little warning to Jackson might even be in order. I was getting the feeling Regina was more than a match for him and that maybe he'd better watch his Ps and Qs, along with other parts of his anatomy she might break if he got out of line.

"Now, as to my surprise." Jackson demanded the attention of all. He grinned at me and lifted his glass. "As I told you, Emily, I have something big in mind. It comes under the heading of 'if you can't beat 'em, join 'em.'"

I waited, knowing whatever he had in mind wasn't an altruistic gesture to improve the world at large.

"I have been asked repeatedly to expand my horizons." He pushed back his chair and got to his feet, then leaned forward, planting both hands beside his plate and looking at each of us around the table, one after another. "What I'm saying is that this is the announcement that

I am officially leaving teaching at the University of Michigan. I plan to write full time."

I think I gasped. At least I made a noise close to a gasp.

"I know, Emily. But you needn't be afraid I'll starve to death. I have my academic books out there and they sell well. For years people have been telling me that I'm wasting my talents writing only deep tomes based on years of research. I've been told to lighten up, take a less stringent and intellectual view of the world, and begin to write more popular books; more mass market things."

I waited to hear what these "mass market things" were going to be, though I had a suspicion, which drove me to empty my third glass of wine in one huge slug.

"So." He rubbed his hands together and turned a bright smile on everyone at the table. "What I'm planning is a mystery." He bowed and nodded as if there had been wild acclaim. "I have been working on the plot and will soon have a working outline."

I must have said something under my breath, or my face showed my disgust.

"Now, Emily. It's a wide field and I think a male, academic voice is exactly what's needed in the genre, don't you?"

I shook my head but said nothing.

"And, since you will now be working with a very credible agent, I thought..."

"Jackson," I interrupted. "I just sent the manuscript off. She may hate it."

He shrugged. "What I thought was, I might call and have a word with her. What I have to offer is something which has never been attempted before..."

"Do you read mysteries?" I couldn't help but ask.

He made a face and slid back down into his chair. "They aren't exactly ... well ... you understand, the level of intelligence it takes ... "

"My level?"

"No, no. But, you see, that's what I'll bring to my novel. Intelligence. Depth and breadth of knowledge. It will begin in a university town ... "

"You will not call the agent." I slowly rose and laid my napkin properly beside my plate.

Jackson threw back his head and laughed. No one said a word. "Of course, it is simply to feel her out on the academic mystery."

"No," I said again then stood very tall and pushed back my chair. "You will not call the agent."

I walked over to Bill, certain my face was bright red, and thanked him for a wonderful dinner. I stopped at Regina's chair and told her to give me a call if I could explain anything I'd done with Jackson's manuscript in the past, or if she learned anything about Arnold Otis. With a look of relief, Regina said she would ask her parents when she got home that night. She added that she would certainly give me a call if she had any trouble with the manuscript.

At an unhurried pace, I went out to the front hall, retrieved my still damp jacket from the closet, opened the door to the porch where I picked up the brown paper bag I'd stashed, and ran through the pouring rain to my car, a little drunk, a lot mad, and more than all of that, a little embarrassed over the whole damned thing.

NINETEEN

I muttered obscenities as I drove home. I steamed, certain that smoke was coming from my ears as I sped back across M72 despite the slippery roads. Then a turn on to County Road 571—even darker and rainier. A few more turns and I was down my gravel drive. I slammed the car door behind me and made my way through the mud and rain without a raindrop landing on me. I was too fast, and too hot. If rain had hit, it would have sizzled.

Sorrow was the best kind of listener. He sat at my feet as I told him, with expressive epithets, what Jackson had done, yet one more time. Embarrassing me. Making me the bad guy.

"Poor Jackson,"—this said with proper mocking pity, which seemed to please Sorrow; at least his ears stood up—"to think that I, bitch of the universe, wouldn't aid and abet him in his newly chosen career. I wouldn't throw my hopes to the wind in order to place before the world his stupendous talent. Yet another victim of female selfishness."

I sat with my Christmas afghan across my legs and a writing pad on my lap. I wrote letter after letter to Jackson telling him what a boorish, self-centered piece of crap he was; what colossal nerve he had; what a rude son of a bitch he was—bringing that girl, unasked, to Bill's dinner party; and how lucky he was that Bill was a gentleman and never mentioned he had to reset the table since Jackson had presented the problem of Regina. And then to try to pin me down, wanting to contact the woman who might—possibly, maybe, with any luck—be my agent. There were no words...

But I found plenty.

I steamed all night as I gave up the letter writing and simply told Jackson, in my head, to take a flying leap, to never call me again, to stop treading on my life—things like that, until finally I fell asleep and didn't wake up until the next morning when Sorrow leaped onto the sofa, beside me, warning that the phone was ringing.

I got up at what was a very slow and grudging pace. I looked around, hunting for my list of pithy things to say to Jackson, in case it was him, calling to apologize.

It wasn't. Only a very sweet-voiced lady from the phone company wondering if I'd sent my monthly payment in as yet. Late. Of course! Oh dear! Foolish me! I would have smacked my forehead with my palm but the gesture would have been lost on the sweet person who couldn't see me anyway. I agreed I would take care of the payment that afternoon. I'd thought I was safe from sweet-voiced ladies on a Saturday morning but figured even telephone companies were getting desperate. I wrote out a check immediately, fearing that if I didn't get them their money they would soon be out of business.

I went to stand on the deck while Sorrow squatted, peed, and nosed leaves into the air, snapping at them as they fell back to earth. The morning light was a pink gold; the sun, coming over the trees, struck the leftover rain clouds. A rainbow formed directly across the lake. If I were a superstitious person, I thought, I would say that Fate was telling me my gold was right there, in my backyard, in my own lake. But I'm not usually superstitious and I'd given up cheering myself with sugary garbage, so I enjoyed the rainbow until it began to fade.

The rain of the night before hadn't stripped the trees. That would come in a week or so. A heavy wind would take them, swirl them into piles, or send them flying to wherever the wind stopped. I leaned against the deck railing, watching my world waken, and wondered where the wind ended and what was piled in mountains there and what would future archeologists think of us, all our parts in those piles.

That was enough of that. Abstract thought cleansed my mind of flimflam—like anger at Jackson. The phone rang again. I hurried in. It was Bill, wanting to make sure I was all right. "Guess you two don't get along as well as I thought," he said.

I agreed and apologized. "We're kind of friends but Jackson has never had a sense of boundaries ... "

"I don't really think he's the kind of guy I want to get too close to either. Last time it was my friend, Ramona Sheffield. Ramona told me what happened when you showed up and found them together. That stunk. Ramona felt terrible about it but still ... she could have been smarter. Now he brings this woman. She seemed nice enough to me. I guess I didn't realize there was a history. Beyond the divorce, I mean."

"Yeah, Bill. There's a history."

"Why do you bother? You're divorced. Keep him out of your life."

I sighed. Same question I asked myself. "Complicated."

"He's kind of a sad guy. That's not the way he comes across at first. But who am I to judge?"

"Ever been married?" I asked.

"Nope."

"Ah, you wait. What a treat you have in store."

"Cynical," he said.

"You're right. Some marriages stink. Then there are marriages so warm they make me jealous I can't be in that kind of relationship."

"Yeah. Me too."

He asked about the other ghost towns I planned to visit for my article. He seemed a little hesitant, as if afraid I might come up with a dead body everywhere I went. I assured him I'd get at it as soon as possible and keep him up to date on everything I was covering.

"If you want someone to go with you—just to … maybe, the first one. I could do it tomorrow."

"I'll be ok. I know it seems that dead people seek me out, but they don't. And I can handle the rest of the towns alone."

I hung up reluctantly. He'd made me feel better—about myself, about who I was, and about life in general.

What I wanted to do next was find the tractor salesman who'd moved to Kingsley—Jimmy Little. That's what I needed to keep my mind occupied with something other than Jackson. After grabbing a quick breakfast of tea and toast, then walking Sorrow, I sat down with the area phone book and called a John Deere store in Kingsley. The man who answered didn't recognize the name but he called back to a guy name Bob, asking him if he knew what happened to Jimmy Little. Bob came on the line and told me Jimmy Little still lived right outside Kingsley. He looked the number up for me and told me to drop by if I had any tractor needs. I assured him I would, hung up, and dialed the number he'd given me.

"Yeah!" a man's deep voice answered the phone.

"Jimmy Little?" I asked.

There was a hesitation. "Ya know, if yer sellin' something I'm hanging right up."

"No," I said quickly. "I'm not selling anything. My name is Emily Kincaid. I'm with the *Northern Statesman*. It's about a murder that happened out in Leetsville. I understand you used to sell tractors there. This would be years ago now."

"Well, sure, my territory at one time. But what's this about a murder?"

"Your name came up."

"Hope to hell nobody thinks I'd do a thing like ..."

"No, not in that connection. I'm looking for information or some background ..."

"What'd you say yer name was?"

"Emily Kincaid."

"Well, Emily, why don't you come on out here and we'll sit down and I'll see how I can help you. That ok? Me and the missus will be here all day."

"About two o'clock?" I asked. He agreed and gave me directions. A good hour or more to get there but I was intrigued. It was the "missus" I most wanted to meet. I couldn't believe Winnie had lived in the area all these years and never contacted any of her children.

But then I only knew one of them—Marjory. Maybe Arnold and Paul had known about her all along.

Before I could get my tennis shoes on and get out of the house, Crystalline called, wanting to know if they were supposed to sit there in the motel room or if they were going to come help me. I suggested we meet at EATS at six o'clock and we'd plan what to do next.

Then I swallowed my pride and all my hurt feelings and called Dolly at the station. Lucky was on the board and put me through to her in her patrol car.

"I'm going out to Kingsley to talk to that tractor salesman Marjory's mother ran away with."

"How'd you find 'im?"

"Harry told me to go over to the Feed and Seed, see if any of the old farmers remembered him. A few of them did, at least they think he's the one. I talked to him and I'm going there. He mentioned that his wife would be with him. You think it could be her? Winnie Otis?"

"Who knows?" She sounded distracted, not quite interested in what I was telling her.

"You want to go with me? We haven't been putting in much time on this—at least not together."

There was a long pause. "Can't today, Emily. I'm on duty right now. Then I promised Sister Sally I'd get out to the campground and help set up for tomorrow morning's service…"

"Why? What's going on? You're acting…I don't know. You're not getting caught up in this thing, are you?"

"Just looking into…And I'm not as…what do you call it?"

"Cynical? Not as cynical as I am?"

"Yeah, as cynical as you."

"Come on. You know better than that. You're not a scared person who can't take a step unless somebody tells you which way to walk. Dolly, look, I need your help here."

"First I got to go out there with Sister Sally. I told you, I promised her and I keep my promises."

"What about your promise to me?"

"What promise?" her squeaky voice went up an octave. I could tell she wanted me off the phone, and in a hurry.

"You know what I'm talking about. I'm doing all the work and I didn't want to get involved in the first place."

"I know." There was a long hesitation. "I really appreciate it but sometimes there are greater things …"

"I think you've gone nuts."

"No, you don't. You just think you're smarter than everybody else. There's lots of things college don't teach you."

"Yeah, like how not to make a big fat ass of myself."

"Look, you do what you want, ok? I've got to do what I have to do …"

"Did you talk to that Officer Winston? Brent assigned him …"

"No time. Got so much going on …"

"I've never known you to be so lax …"

"Not lax. I got my own way of doing things," was all she said, then seemed to snap her mouth shut.

"Need I remind you—this isn't my job? I thought we were friends, Dolly. I mean, you're scaring me, apart from the murder, there's something going on with you that … "

"Gotta go," she interrupted. "Some kids are teasing a dog on the other end of town. We'll talk later."

I hung up. To make my day complete, I called the nursing home in Bellaire and asked for Cecily Otis. The nurse told me Cecily was under the weather and couldn't see anybody until the beginning of the week. She wanted my name. "Cecily doesn't get any company. It will perk her up to know you'll be coming."

I said I'd call back. I knew my name wouldn't perk Cecily, or anybody else, up. All I could do was get Sorrow out to the car, in case we found a good spot in Kingsley to run, and get on the road.

TWENTY

Saturday, October 17
10 days still to go

KINGSLEY WAS A TYPICAL small Michigan village. Neat little houses. Short streets going nowhere. A block of businesses that had seen better days. You drove through Kingsley to get to Traverse City, going north, or down to southern Michigan. There wasn't much reason to stop as you made the turn at the blinker, except that life there went on just fine without tourists or the flourishes of arugula salads and cappuccino shops.

Jimmy Little's house was a mile out of town, set back under tall blue spruce that had almost overgrown the gravel driveway. The house was yellow, with white trim. A yellow breezeway connected the main part of the small house with a yellow garage. In the front flowerbed, now filled with dying roses, was a bend-over—one of those board rear ends of a female gardener showing off frilly underpants. I hadn't seen a bend-over in years. There was a heart-shaped WELCOME sign next to the front door and a pinecone wreath around the welcome sign. Somebody in the house was either into crafts, or was a devotee of summer craft shows.

I'd left Sorrow scrambling back and forth on the back seat, expecting a walk, not a long sit. I rang the bell. The door was answered almost immediately by a tall, nice-looking older man in a dark blue turtleneck shirt and dark blue pants. He had graying blond hair and the wide, open face that goes with a Nordic type. He nodded, smiled, and pushed the metal storm door open, inviting me in.

The house was comfortable. Two upholstered La-Z-Boy chairs stood before a yellow brick fireplace. There were many little tables around the room with lamps and framed photos. The walls were covered with wedding, baby, graduation, skiing, picnic, and swimming pictures—every kind of family photo you could imagine. A woman sat in one of the rocking La-Z-Boys. I looked at her, wondering if I was seeing Marjory's mother.

"Welcome," Jimmy Little said, a hand on my back, his other hand gesturing me into the living room. "So, you're Emily Kincaid. I think I've seen your byline on stories in the paper."

I laughed, nervous for no reason.

"Cover a lot of murders, do you?" Jimmy asked.

I laughed again, not knowing what the best response to that question might be.

"I'd like you to meet my wife." He guided me farther into the room and up to the tiny woman. I felt my heart skip a couple of beats. It could be her. Age seemed about right. Maybe this was the woman who began all Marjory's misery—by the selfish act of running away.

The woman looked at me with confusion written across her face. Her eyes went to Jimmy's, begging for help.

146

"I told you, Mother. The woman from the newspaper. Remember? She's got questions for me? I told you this morning." He gave me a knowing smile as if expecting me to catch on and say nothing. It was obvious the woman had Alzheimer's or some form of memory loss. I was an anomaly in her very small world and confusing the heck out of her.

"Winnie..." I bent down close to get a look at her face.

She stared back, blue eyes filling with tears. I thought I must be onto something. The name had moved her for some reason.

"No, no," Jimmy said. "Her name is Hilda. She wasn't the one you came to see, was she? I got the idea it was me. Anyway, Hilda is Hilda. If you've made a mistake... well... I don't think I said anything to mislead you."

I stepped away from the poor, confused woman. Not Winnie Otis after all. Not the woman I was learning to detest, for what she had done to her children. This woman had walls of memories. Walls of children. And a good husband taking care of her. I had no right here. That need-to-know thing had driven me to intrude. I wished I could turn and leave without comment; change the thing I'd done out of mistaken hope.

"I'm sorry. I thought you told me your wife's name was Winnie." I looked down at the woman. "Hilda." She looked up, blinking. I said her name again, and got a confident smile in return. The tears were only because I'd rocked her world, taking her own name from her, I felt lousy for even being there.

Jimmy Little asked me to sit, then offered coffee, which I declined, wanting badly to leave and feeling not very good about myself.

"You said this was about a murder." He settled into a recliner across from me.

"A woman was murdered out in Deward, an old lumbering town between Mancelona and Gaylord."

He nodded, hands clasped between his knees. "Used to be my territory—that country out there. Sold tractors and all kinds of farm equipment. Hardscrabble life—farming. Had a lot of good friends."

"This woman—the dead one. She grew up in Leetsville…"

He nodded again, though I thought I saw a hint of suspicion in his eyes.

"A long time ago her mother left her. It seems she ran off with a tractor salesman, thirty-five to thirty-eight years ago. What I'm trying to do is find the woman. There were other children. I'm looking into a connection between the dead woman and the town. Deward. Something that might have brought her back there."

Jimmy sat forward in his chair and fixed me with a look. He wasn't a stupid man. "You thought Hilda, here, was that woman's mother? And I was the tractor salesman she ran off with?" He shook his head.

I opened my mouth, hoping to come up with an easy, comfortable lie. All I had to do was look into his uncomplicated and disgusted face to know no lie was going to work.

"Well, I hate to break it to you," he said. "But Hilda's been my wife since right after high school and I never ran off with anybody."

Jimmy stood and put his shoulders back, rearing away then looking down at me as if smelling something not real good smelling.

I stood too, falling over my own feet. "I didn't think…" Oh hell, I was already standing in a pile of my own making. "I'm sorry," I said instead. "But do you remember something like that happening? It would have been about thirty-five years ago."

Jimmy, his friendly face much less friendly, thought a moment, chewing at the corner of his lower lip. He shook his head. "I'm telling myself you didn't come here hoping to catch sinners living out an old sin. So, what I'm doing is taking your question serious because, as you say, there's a dead woman who must need justice or you wouldn't be going around trying to trick people."

I shook my head, assuring him I wasn't without feeling, without concern (though I felt that way).

"To tell you the truth, Emily. If some man in my business, back then, had done something like that ... I'd say in the whole state of Michigan. I mean, we were like a small town just ourselves—men who sold heavy equipment to the farmers. I knew if one of my clients bought something from Trace Cornfelt down in Grand Rapids, or Wilfred Dawson over to Ludington. Knew everybody in the business. And never once did I hear anything about one of 'em running off with a woman from Leetsville."

He shook his head as he put his hand on my back again, guiding me toward the front door.

I was out of there as fast as I could go. Thank-yous and all of the niceties aren't necessary when you've hurt somebody's feelings.

At a small park on Garfield Road I let Sorrow out of the car to squat and pee then run through the leaves. I trudged along behind him, thinking how I didn't want to get into any of this to begin with and here I was, by myself, no Dolly Flynn Wakowski in sight, And wasn't I making a fine mess of every thing I touched.

What I didn't know about investigating a murder would fill a football stadium. I kicked at the leaves, sending a shower of them into the air for Sorrow to chase and bite. The breeze was warm, but with ice at its heart. Kind of like me.

What I did was get so deep into self-pity I forgot what I'd been told by Jimmy Little. There'd been no running off with a tractor salesman. Winnie Otis had disappeared, but not the way everyone was told. What I had to do was find Arnold Otis or Aunt Cecily and clear up the confusion. Maybe the guy hadn't sold tractors. Maybe he'd sold brushes, or pots and pans. Or maybe he'd never existed and one mystery had just become two.

TWENTY-ONE

It was only five-thirty when I got back to Leetsville. I was meeting Crystalline and the others at six. They wanted to help, but I wasn't coming up with anything for them to do. All the paths to an answer were so tortuous—one thing in one direction, something else in another. It wasn't as if there were easy pieces here, all fitting together. I wished it would be more like writing a novel—things falling right into place, no hesitations, no gaping holes you could fly an airplane through.

I sat in my Jeep in front of EATS, grousing at life in general, at Dolly Wakowski, and at my own stupidity for letting her talk me into an involvement I didn't want or need. I noticed the old lady, the string-gloved one, looking out one of the front, fly-specked windows. She didn't notice me but sat looking north, delicately lifting a white coffee cup to her lips, one stiff pinky finger shot into the air.

I watched the overly made-up old woman and wondered again about her. She didn't seem to be with the End Timers, nor anybody else. And why was Eugenia putting up with her in the restaurant day after day?

With her black lace, no-finger gloves, a hat with cherries on it sitting on top of her mass of unruly gray hair, and the round spots of rouge on her withered cheeks, she reminded me of an over-the-hill Mary Poppins. I watched the hand and coffee cup come up to her mouth. She took a sip, then put the cup down. Arm went up, then down. What the heck was she doing in Leetsville? None of my business, but since when did that stop me from asking questions?

As I sat there waiting, my imagination worked overtime. I gave the woman a checkered past, a history that crossed continents, a tragic life. I figured you didn't end up in Leetsville unless you really wanted to. But then again, that was true of any place in the world. I finally got out of the car, ready to take on Crystalline and her friends, yet still wondering why I was doing this if Deputy Dolly was no longer interested.

My stomach went into spasms when I saw the sheet of paper flapping over the cigarette machine in EATS' lobby. I might not be psychic, and sure had no shamanic powers, but I knew what this was about and knew that World War III was about to begin. At a time when I doubted everything about Deputy Dolly, I knew this was still going to send her over whatever fine edge she teetered along.

FLYNN FAMILY TREE, the paper said in a very large font. The drawing beneath the heading was crude. It had to be a tree, but one with lopsided branches stuck on a skinny stick-figure of a tree with a couple of roots shooting straight into the earth. Dolly's family tree was really a short bush that looked as if it had grown against a wall, in deep shade.

Evidently, Eugenia hadn't loaded up on genealogy stock yet. Or she was in such a big hurry to drum up business for her new venture she didn't mind putting up kindergarten drawings.

I stood on tiptoe to see what Eugenia had found. The only names filled in were on the mother's side, explaining the lopsided look. There was a grandmother and a grandfather: Catherine and Ricardo Thomas. I'd seen the rest a while ago, when Eugenia had displayed Dolly's birth certificate.

Mother: Audrey Alice Thomas, 17 years old in 1974
Father: Harold Flynn. 31 years old in 1974
Sired: Delores Flynn, October 17, 1974. Women's Hospital,
*   Detroit.*

October 17! That was today. Dolly's birthday. I'd never thought to ask. She seemed so ... birthdayless, like somebody hatched from an egg.

I went in, lifting my nose, hoping for fresh baked bread, and took a seat near Eugenia's front counter, where she busily polished the glass, blew at it, and then polished it again. The old bag lady sat at her usual window table, a plate of meatloaf untouched in front of her. I nodded. She nodded stiffly back. A few of the other tables were occupied by families of pilgrims. At others, Leetsvillians sat together whispering, their heads nodding. A lot going on in town for people who were used to solitude.

Eugenia glanced up as I ordered hot tea from Gloria. She grinned.

"So? Whadda ya think?" she called over.

"About that?" I nodded toward the vestibule.

"'Course. Told her I'd find something."

I shook my head. "She's going to be pissed off at you."

Eugenia waved a hand. "Eh, she'll get over it. Did you notice? Today's her birthday."

"I saw," I said.

"Should we throw a party?"

"I'd wait until she sees what you've got up. Maybe fireworks enough right there."

"Phooey. Dolly's too sensitive. She's always moaning about having no relatives and now I found her some. If she don't like that I'm hanging her tree for everybody to see, that's too bad. I got my career in genealogy to think of. I'm doing hers for nothing. Won't be that way with other folks."

I had a few other things to add but the door opened and Crystalline, along with her friends, walked in. Obviously the women didn't mind the spotlight. Every head turned to watch them make their way to where I sat. Every pair of eyes in the place turned to the person next to them and rolled. Sonia looked particularly Goth with black eye makeup and a black headscarf drawn around her forehead. Felicia was done up with flowers and bows. Crystalline was her bigger-than-life self with red hair puffed and bunched into a cascading waterfall.

"We spent the day over at Seven Bridges on Valley Road," Felicia said, leaning in close to me after ordering a diet Coke.

"It's the water," Sonia added. "Marjory always told us—when you're upset, go stand by running water. That's the thing that will make everything clear."

"We all felt it," Crystalline said. "There is the deepest reverence in rushing waters. Always cleansing, you know? That's why this north country's got the forces it's got."

"'*You can never step in the same river twice,*'" I misquoted, wanting to be in the loop on our mystical, magical country.

"Anyway," Crystalline sighed and went on. "Standing there, on those bridges, and watching that water run beneath our feet. I can't tell you..."

Felicia broke in, excited, "I sensed something special is going to happen. And pretty soon now. Like truth being discovered."

"Me too," Sonia, not to be left out, said. "But what I felt... well... there will be death."

Crystalline nodded, hair flopping into her eyes and having to be pulled back into place then pinned with a huge green barrette.

"This whole area is in store for something," Crystalline went on. "Don't know if it's death or change, but you can feel it in the air. Maybe Marjory set all this in motion."

"Reverend Fritch says the world's going to end," I reminded them, feeling chilled. "That's pretty big."

"Bull shit." Sonia rapped the table with her knuckles, making her silver bell earrings give a small tinkle.

"Let's not get carried away," Crystalline clucked, then turned to me. Across from us, Sonia and Felicia argued in whispers. "If you ask me, Emily, I think we'd better get out to that campground soon and meet this Reverend Fritch. I'll be able to tell you right away if the man is genuine or not. I know these things. And maybe we can figure out what Marjory meant by having to take care of something with him."

"Those were her Words? That she had to 'take care of something with him'?"

Crystalline frowned, thinking. "Something like that. She was talking about him. I know that much because she had his website

155

up. Seems she said…" Crystalline frowned hard as she thought, giving me a glimpse of a younger, more innocent woman. "What I remember was 'somebody is going to have to do something about the whole thing.'"

"So, Emily," Sonia leaned over and put her hand on mine. "I want to see this guy. I was thinking, maybe we should have a séance. You know, contact Marjory."

Crystalline shook her head. "We don't do parlor tricks, Sonia. You know what Marjory always said. What we do is honorable. We help and heal. Help and heal. No foot tapping and taking money for contacting passed love ones."

"There's a service tomorrow morning," I said. "How about after that? Maybe in the early afternoon? I need to talk to him too."

"Are we sayin' the truth, about why we're out there?" Sonia asked. "Or should we come up with a story…?"

"Truth, Sonia," Crystalline said. "We've got nothing to hide. Let's go see what the man's about, pick up on the scam and how he's working it—if there is one—and find out if he knew Marjory."

I agreed. We ordered meatloaf, ate, and made our plans. We said good-bye out front, agreeing to meet about noon to go to the campground. I stood, waving, as they drove off, then turned to find the old lady's eyes on me through the window. She sat where she'd been sitting for hours. She lifted her coffee cup to her lips in a quick, pinky-pointing movement. I waved at her. I thought her eyes were on me but she didn't wave back. The delicate, lace-covered hand took the cup to her lips, then down. Up, then down.

I was free to go home and write my next garden column, about the garden in winter, which would make it a short column since my garden would be under five feet of snow by January. But I was nothing if not resourceful. I'd come up with something—maybe a vole's eye view of wintering tulip bulbs. But I didn't have any tulip bulbs. The deer had already done away with them. Crocus, then. Or a worm's eye view of rose bush roots. I drove home trying not to think about mysterious old ladies, or weird women who picked up their information from the air, or people who could be mean to little girls like Marjory and Dolly, or voles eyeing tulip bulbs, or mice drooling over the few rose bushes I had left.

I got home, found a quarter bottle of Pinot Grigio in the fridge, and went to bed with the bottle and P. D. James.

TWENTY-TWO

Sunday, October 18
9 days to go

ALL I WANTED TO do Sunday morning was stay home, nurse my wine headache, and read the funnies to Sorrow, who lay on his back beside me on the bed, all four feet stuck up in the air.

When I'd gotten home the night before there'd been a call from Jackson, very apologetic about Bill's party and telling me that Regina had explained to him how it was intrusive of him to ask to call an agent who was considering my work. At that point he gave a nervous laugh. "She also said I should never have invited her to the party without checking with Bill. She said I am a rude person but, of course, she doesn't know me very well, yet." There was a pause. "She reminds me of you, Emily. I rather like that particular kind of feistiness. Perhaps I've been missing it in my life. Would you say you were the rudder I needed to keep me on a straight course?" He made a thinking, kind of clucking, sound. "Wouldn't that be something? I mean, if now I learn that what we had together was what I needed all along?"

My stomach was too tender for that much sugared pap so early in the day. I would not call him back. I would not call Dolly either. Let her call me. I was going to make a list of everything I'd learned about Marjory Otis so far and another list of what we still needed to know. I sat with my first cup of tea of the day—making it a chai, which warmed my soul. I started my lists. When I'd finished I found I knew a lot about the woman, and just as much I didn't know:

Who had she come to Leetsville to help?

How was the Reverend Fritch involved?

Who had she taken out to Deward with her?

What did Arnold know about their mother?

Where was the other brother—Paul?

And the biggest questions of all: What was Marjory doing at Deward to begin with? What would make her go there, to a place she'd said she feared? And why did she fear it?

I made a list of people I needed to talk to, beginning with the Reverend Fritch, Arnold Otis, and Aunt Cecily. Most of all I had to sit down with Dolly and find out what was going on. Maybe I even needed to talk to Lucky, see what he was picking up from her. And, God help me, that Officer Winston from the Gaylord state police office, I had to get in touch with him. He was expecting results from me and Dolly. I didn't know how he would feel about a reporter doing what a police officer should have been doing.

Bill called a little after nine to see if I wanted him to go with me to the next of the ghost towns on my list. I had this tug at my conscience. What I really wanted to do was go out to a ghost town with Bill, walk in the woods, enjoy what was promising to be a fine fall day, and get really happy. I wanted to be free of my obligation to a group of women I barely knew, going with them to a place where I'd been uncomfortable, and talking to people I thought were truly nuts.

"Can't, Bill," I said, letting my voice show the deep disappointment I felt. "I promised to go out to see the Reverend Fritch. It's about Marjory Otis' murder."

He hung up reluctantly. Probably didn't trust me not to turn up a dead body every story I went out on. I could see that, after a while, an editor might get suspicious. And—after a while—a thing like that might make any reporter nervous.

Sorrow and I took a long walk to clear our heads and check out the chipmunk population. I wanted to go up to Willow Lake Road and over to Harry's to see how the courtship was going, but I didn't like to take Sorrow there with me. Harry's dogs went crazy at the sight of another animal. Anyway, with Harry, I never knew where the fine line between busybodyness and concern lay. He could get testy if I asked too many questions. What I would have to do was wait until he came to me, maybe with his new bride on his arm. Or mad as hell, and swearing off women for the rest of his life.

At my studio, I tried to work on the new book, Dead something or other, but it grew elusive, wouldn't fall into a nice straight line I could follow from beginning to end. I figured I'd just name all my books starting with Dead. That way they'd be in a straight line—if they ever got published—in bookstores and libraries.

There was something there—to this new story I was writing. Dolly and I had lived it but I couldn't get it to sit still on the com-

160

puter. A young Indian woman kept jumping in and out of my vision. Lovely. Young. But scarred. I brought her forward in my head but she didn't want to be trapped in words. Not yet. I would have to coax her, work with her, let her get to know me before I asked that she put her life in my hands. I made a few notes—on my part and on Dolly's part in the story. Nothing more happened. I sat staring at the screen, let my finger rest on J, and watched a funny line of dancing j's run across the screen. Time to get out of there.

I walked around Willow Lake, tip-toeing through wet places where the tag-alder and lake met. At one of the beaver's slides, Sorrow ran in circles, nose to the ground, sniffing the six-inch lengths of wood the beaver had readied for transport down to his den where he would live off the cellulose all winter. The beaver, swimming around his conical house, wasn't happy when he caught us at his slide. He paddled back and forth, slapping his tail on the water, trying to get a big enough wave going to scare us away. Sorrow watched him, trying to decide if it was worth the swim out to visit or not. Being the smartest dog on earth, Sorrow said the heck with a cold swim and the chillier welcome, and came bounding back to me. We moved on, making a bouquet of perfect red and gold and multi-colored leaves to take home with us, to put in my garage sale crystal vase and set where the sun would hit them, in front of the big front windows.

That was the good part of the day.

I stopped at the Green Trees Motel just after noon, figuring we didn't need to take two cars out to the campsite. The women were ready, chattering among themselves, and coming up with questions to ask the reverend. All three were deeply into discovering what had happened to Marjory in that terrible place she had been afraid to go.

As we drove back through Leetsville, Crystalline wondered if she could see any of the photographs the police took of Marjory, there at Deward. Dead under the tree.

"Not that I want to see her...like that." She made a face. "I mean, I can imagine how awful it was..."

I shook my head. "Not awful at all. She looked as if she was asleep. That's what I thought..."

"What we were talking about was that maybe, by how she was sitting or something around her, we could figure out what happened." Felicia leaned over the seat to join the conversation.

"I pick up things by holding a picture in my hand," Sonia, her voice whispery for a change, offered from the other side of the back seat.

"I took photographs," I said, only then remembering. "I'll put them on my computer when I get home tonight and run off the best for you."

"Could you run off all of what you have?" Crystalline asked, turning tear-filled eyes my way. "If there's any chance...We want to help."

I agreed, kicking myself for not remembering I had my own photos of the scene. If Dolly had been doing her job and realized what I'd done she would have asked for them before now or shown Crystalline the photos she'd taken. It was her fault I wasn't doing

162

the best work I could be doing. This was her department, damn it. I was only supposed to write the stories, not be at their center. I should have been Boswell to Dr. Johnson. Dr. Watson to Sherlock Holmes. Not this damned girl detective without a clue to her name.

By the time we pulled into the two-track leading to the campsite and the End Timers, I was fuming at Dolly all over again and deciding she could take over her own investigation or give it back to Gaylord. Officer Winston seemed like the kind of guy who would be glad to get us out of the way and hog glory to himself.

Well... not glory so much as aggravation and fear and feeling stupid and abandoned.

Damn Dolly. After this visit to the Reverend Fritch, I was going to hunt her down, make her tell me what was going on, or give her a knock on the head to bring her back to her senses.

Then I would wish her a happy birthday.

TWENTY-THREE

Still 9 days to go

THE CAMPGROUND, WHICH HAD intimidated me with shadows in the dark, looked shabby and ordinary in daylight. Tents, cars, and beat-up campers were pulled in at odd angles, nosed under trees, lined around the perimeter of the meeting space, or drawn up beside one of the blackened fire pits dotting the brown grass. The pits looked greasy and cold despite all the people who must have cooked a meal or two over them. Clotheslines hung listlessly from tree to tree, drooping under scallops of pinned shirts and yellowed underwear. The whole place had a crazy Steinbeck feel to it. Like the Joads and other Depression-era families had taken up residence, waiting for a dust storm to clear.

Around the edges of the campground, people sat huddled at crooked picnic tables, leaning forward in their heavy jackets though the day wasn't cold, only chilly. Some looked up as we passed, staring with lifeless eyes. Many were bald clones of one another—men and women in their heavy robes. They looked like Martians, with their knobby, misshapen heads. Others, maybe new to the group, wore nondescript sweatpants and sweatshirts with football logos on the chest, or stained black-and-white sweatshirts with THE END IS COMING emblazoned across the back. The strain of what they waited for was showing. I guess seriously contemplating one's own demise can bring up some pretty dire thoughts. Even the children, leaning into parents for warmth, were unnaturally quiet.

Crystalline asked one man, who stood and nodded as she greeted him, where we could find the Reverend Fritch. He pointed to the back of the campground, behind the stage where a circle of tall pines formed a separate clearing.

At the edge of this clearing, just before the place where the forest began again, a huge RV was parked, taking up all of the space between two tall oak trees. In front of the RV, a circle of picnic tables surrounded a deep fire pit; the pit smoldering with large, stacked logs giving off ribbons of smoke. Men in robes covered by heavy jackets sat at picnic tables or in low folding chairs, reading Bibles. A few, I noticed, read that morning's *Northern Statesman*. One by one, the men looked up as we drew close, then stood, their faces taking on wary smiles. Two ambled toward us.

"Good day to you, sisters." A tall, middle-aged man got to us first and put out his hands, taking one of mine and then one of Crystalline's in his. He moved to Felicia and Sonia, taking their hands but dropping them quickly, looking down at his palms in surprise, as if he'd received a shock

"Welcome! Welcome!" He turned, indicating the RV, their clearing, and the other men. His voice resonated around the open space. "I'm Brother Samuel. May I be of service?"

"We're here to see Reverend Fritch." My voice cracked halfway through the reverend's name. I was feeling confined, or maybe trapped was a better word, by these men. Crystalline's face had gone an odd shade of puce, that strange color between red and brown. Felicia frowned and stood with her back straight, her head rearing away from the man. Sonia made a face and hung behind Crystalline.

"The reverend is resting. What was it you needed to see him about?" Brother Samuel smiled benevolently as his dark eyebrows went up.

"I'm with the *Northern Statesman*." I nodded to the Sunday newspaper one man held in his hands. "I'd rather discuss it with Reverend Fritch. I'm ... eh ... writing a story on your group and what you're doing here."

"Of course." Brother Samuel clasped his hands together across his narrow chest.

"And there's been a murder."

He frowned at me. "What's that got to do with any of us?"

"A woman's been killed. She told her friends here," I indicated the women around me, "it had something to do with Reverend Fritch, or what's going on ..."

He tilted forward, then back on the balls of his feet, like watching a pole about to fall.

"And you are ...?"

"Emily Kincaid," I said, then introduced the women behind me.

He nodded, sighed, thought awhile, then motioned to one of the other men, who headed up the steps of the RV. The man returned, standing in the open doorway. He nodded to Brother Samuel. He stepped back, indicating we were to go on in.

The Reverend Fritch stood with a great deal of trouble as we stepped up inside the RV. He moved to take our hands—one by one—and welcome us.

"Bless you all." The reverend pulled me close to him. I was hugged hard against a wide, soft body and then released. He hugged the others, whispering something in their ear. I was uncomfortable, and dying to find out what he'd said to them he hadn't found fit to say to me. I imagined we would laugh later. It was that normal inclination—toward nervous laughter—forcing me to stay where I was though I felt exceedingly creeped out and ill at ease.

The reverend pointed to a sofa, then settled himself in a low and wide captain's chair with a grunt. He tented his thick hands at his chest and began to nod his head. He nodded at nothing. He said nothing. The nodding became a rocking motion of his whole body. He closed his eyes and rocked faster and faster, until he snapped his eyes open and leaned forward.

"You're not saved." This was directed toward me. The words were said with gravity, and pointed accusation. The small, dark eyes had me pinned where I sat.

I nodded my head, agreeing. Nope, not that I knew of.

"What will you do on October 27? Where will you be?"

I shrugged, feeling dumb, the way I had in third grade when Miss Shirley made fun of girls and punished boys by putting them under her desk to look up her skirt.

Probably waiting for the end of the world with the rest of you, I wanted to say but decided that might sound flippant.

He nodded. "Are you aware that you will die a terrible death?" I thought he would go on, maybe with a graphic description of what I didn't like to think about. He only waited, expectantly.

"Sister Sally told me about you," he said, surprising both of us. "She and Dolly Wakowski have been worried."

"Really?" There was a needle of aggravation growing somewhere around my shoulders. If anybody should be worrying about her soul, it should be Dolly, I thought.

The reverend turned to a very thin man who had joined us from the back of the RV, the mute man of the revival. He turned anxious eyes on the preacher. "Brother Righteous, why don't you invite Sister Sally to join us?"

The incredibly thin man looked hard at the reverend's face, then at us, one by one. His face was beardless, dotted with acne scars. There was agony in his eyes. His lips began to move, to push out as if needing to form words, then work from side to side. All that came from the effort was a single sound that frustrated him even more. He stopped, panted hard a time or two as if he'd been running, took a deep breath, and left the room the way he'd come.

Crystalline, impatient, spoke up. "Our dear friend was murdered out near Deward. Before she came to Leetsville she told me there was something she had to take care of here. It had something to do with you. She didn't say your name, only that it had to do with what was going on here. Maybe it's somebody in your ... group. We need to know in order to find out who killed her ... "

The reverend watched Crystalline's face as if reading her lips rather than listening. The look was intense. "Many people come," he finally said, leaning far back in his chair. "Not all have the faith ... "

"It wasn't about faith." Felicia leaned forward, her narrow face tight with a mix of fear and belligerence. "She came here to help somebody."

"You think it's one of our followers? A lot of people mistakenly think they have to save a loved one from our group. As if the End can be avoided. If there was someone here … do you have a name? We could talk with that person. Perhaps they don't even know the woman met an unfortunate end. The ways of the world are harsh, you know. Evil is loose …"

I'd had enough of whatever was going on. The reverend seemed to find us irrelevant, a way to launch into one of his canned speeches.

"Would you ask among your followers? Her name was Marjory Otis." I stepped into the middle of his rhetoric just as he described the hoof of a mighty horse falling on the neck of an unrepentant sinner.

He turned his big body my way and blinked slowly a few times—getting me into focus. "Very sad. Maybe, because we're all strangers here, you've decided the murder must have been committed by one of us. Is that what you have in your mind?"

"No," I shook my head. "The woman lived in Leetsville at one time. She was here to help someone, and it had something to do with you. That's all we know."

He raised his eyebrows and moved his wide, red lips over his teeth as if tasting something bad.

"What she said was that she had to do something about 'the whole thing.'"

"What 'whole thing'? That hardly describes our mission here, at the end of all time. And there is nothing here for an individual to stop. The wheels are in motion. The end is near. Perhaps what the woman meant was that she was coming to join us, put a stop to the way she had been living her life. People from around the world are coming, you know. They see that the time of terrible sin and greed is over. They gather with me to save themselves from the eternal fires."

"I don't..." I was about to protest that wasn't Marjory Otis' mission.

"Marjory Otis, you said? Was that her name?" He fell deep into thought, ruminating like a camel, cheeks moving from side to side. Finally he looked up. "I'll ask among the faithful. Maybe someone knows her or has information. I wouldn't, however..." He gave me a conspiratorial smile as Sister Sally came from the back of the motor home and stood with her hands up either sleeve of her robe, hood halfway off her bald head. I couldn't imagine how she kept that hood in place. No hair to stick a bobby pin or clip to. Maybe double-stick tape, I thought. Or maybe magic.

Her small, dark eyes went from me to Crystalline to Felicia to Sonia. She said nothing, simply narrowed her eyes more and stood very still.

"But please understand..." He went on talking without acknowledging Sister Sally's presence. The emaciated man entered the room and took a seat behind the Reverend Fritch. The preacher reached around and put his hand on the man's shoulder. Brother Righteous bowed his head, tucking his chin into the button holding his robe closed at the neck. He stayed that way.

"There isn't anything to worry about," the reverend said. "You see, the woman will be back among us on the 27 of this month. She'll walk the earth and point to her murderer. If she is saved, and clear with God, she will be helping all to that place of salvation. I'll ask for prayers for her soul. We'll pray her into heaven. Then she will do the same for us. Amen..." He bowed his head as his plump lips moved in silent prayer.

There was a quiet knock at the outer door. The reverend, startled from his reverie, called out, "Come in and be welcomed." He pulled himself up straight with a mighty lunge of his big body.

A small woman, lost in one of the cult's archaic robes, hood drawn forward over her face, walked up the three steps, then turned to close the door behind her. When she looked up, saying nothing, her misty blue eyes went to Sister Sally, then to Brother Righteous, then to the preacher. She stood straighter. Her hood fell back from her face. It was an odd face, under the slick bald head. A kind of bunched-up face with small eyes lost behind puffed cheeks.

I held my breath. There was no way...

The woman turned to look at me at last. The right eye veered nervously off, away from mine.

She pushed the hood completely from her head. A strange blank canvas of a face. A head of many knots and slopes, the cranium bulging out behind.

I didn't know the bald head. I'd never seen it before and hoped never to see it again. It was the face I knew. The small face that could draw itself up in distaste. Could be wide open with a broad smile. Could frown hard enough to scare any lawbreaker.

Dolly Wakowski.

TWENTY-FOUR

CRYSTALLINE TRIED TO SAY something on the way home but I shook my head. This was beyond anything I could believe in. Not cranky, sad, needy, overly officious Dolly. Not my good friend—probably one of the best, and most frustrating, I'd ever had—caught up in this mass delusion. And after the 27 of October? Would she go on believing if given another date?

The sight of that vulnerable head with enough dips and valleys to compete with the moon made my stomach ache. Walking out, leaving her behind, was like walking away when your sister is about to face a firing squad.

I had to get the women, who had finally fallen into a respectful silence, back to their motel. Then I had to find somebody who could make sense of this whole thing. It didn't feel like being caught up in a nightmare as much as being trapped in a space warp where nothing was as it should be and there was nothing solid to hold on to. Part of me wanted to go home, sit down, and cry. I couldn't figure out what part of that was childish jealousy—my friend had turned her back on me—what part was fear for Dolly's sanity, and what part was total, flaming anger.

I went back into Leetsville, to the police station—which was locked, with a number to call in case of emergency on a card pasted to the door glass. I drove over to The Skunk Saloon, parted the clouds of cigarette smoke, and found the pay phone on the wall by the men's room.

I dialed the number. Lucky Barnard answered immediately. Because I was choking with everything I had bottled inside, all I could do was tell Lucky who I was and that I had to talk to him about Dolly. He was at home, just finishing Sunday supper, he said, and invited me to come right over.

Lucky lived a few blocks from the police station, on a dead-street of small white houses set under big trees, with plenty of space between houses. He met me at the door and said his wife had taken their son to her mother's house so we could talk. I figured it must be all over town—that Dolly had joined the cult. Something this big wouldn't have gotten by Leetsvillians, who seemed to pick news out of the air, as if it were pollen.

"What's going on?" I asked as soon as I got in the door and sat on the nearest chair in their small living room with fall floral bouquets on every table. He sat and put his hands between his knees. He shook his head, taking a long, deep sigh before looking up. "I haven't got a clue, Emily. All I can tell you is she came in yesterday and said she was taking the rest of the month off work. She's got a lot of vacation coming to her but I asked if this was a good time—what with all the people in town and her on this murder case with you."

"What'd she say?"

"That it was something she had to do. She started to say more then stopped, like she couldn't bring herself to admit she'd joined the cult or there was something she didn't dare tell me. I don't know. I've never seen Dolly act like this before. She's always been a responsible police officer. Oh, maybe she's smashed a few of our patrol cars, but that's because of trying too hard to do her duty. This . . . well . . . I don't get it."

He looked at me, face serious. "Maybe the two of us could work together. With Dolly out I won't be much help. I mean, somebody's got to take care of town business, and with this group here things are going crazy." He hesitated. "It's up to you."

I looked at him hard. I wasn't in law enforcement. Lucky was putting a lot of faith in me. Maybe more faith than I had in myself. He looked tired. The crowd in town had to be getting to him. There was a lot of worry on his face, as if he couldn't figure what was going on with Dolly any better than I could. He was a good man, a good police chief, and probably the best friend Dolly had— other than me. With his help and with Lieutenant Brent or Officer Winston feeding me the forensics data as they got it from Lansing, I asked myself, why couldn't I do this alone? What was holding me back?

Maybe a lack of training? Maybe a lack of experience dealing with murderers? This was scary stuff I was into. My instincts told me to run, let the state police, the sheriff, anybody but me, handle it. Then, from another part of my brain, came a resounding yell: *Hell no, Emily. Something's wrong. That's not the Dolly you know. She's in trouble. More going on here than you can imagine. Is this the kind of friend you are?*

I looked at Lucky and skewed my face into a wince. "If I've got you, and all of Marjory's friends, I'll keep at it, Lucky. I won't get in trouble—at least I hope not—and if I think I'm in way too deep, I'll turn everything over to you and get out."

He looked relieved. "Want to talk about what you've got so far? Maybe a fresh eye looking at things will help."

"Hasn't Dolly kept you up to date?"

"She's been…well…I'd call it preoccupied. She told me the friends were in town and that you both talked to them, but that's about as far as it got."

I caught Lucky up to date—what the women had said about Marjory and her reason for coming to town; about looking into the Otis' background in Leetsville; about seeing the tractor salesman and now having doubts that the mother had ever left town on her own.

"So, maybe two murders. Is that what you're saying? You think Marjory got onto it? That's why she came here? Murderer probably still in town, then. Must be a local. Probably the one who met her out at Deward—or went with her."

"Had to be they went out together, in his car. Dolly found her car at the IGA."

He thought awhile. "Yeah, there's that. And the tire tracks at Deward didn't match Marjory's tires. You think maybe it could be a woman? Somebody she trusted? Seems kind of logical."

"What about strangling her? You think a woman could do that without Marjory fighting back? She would have had to be overpowered."

He nodded. "Probably right. So a man."

"What I'm thinking," I went on, "is that this whole thing goes back to when the mother disappeared. I don't know what really happened, or when, but it seems like the pivotal point. The place where everything began."

I went on to tell him I was going to Bellaire to see the aunt as soon as she was well enough.

"And that brother of hers, the guy running for the Michigan senate from downstate somewhere. I talked to him," Lucky said.

I nodded.

"He's coming to address the Young Republicans in Traverse City this Thursday. He'll be over here right after that. See what he can do to help. I have to tell ya, he did ask me to keep it quiet. Because the election's so close, he doesn't want any of this getting out."

"Yeah, like his sister getting murdered won't hit the papers. You know I'm putting him in my next story—I mean, being her brother and all. Won't take more than a few hours to be everywhere after that."

He shook his head. "I told him you worked for the local paper and knew all about the case. He asked me to request you keep his connection to Marjory out of the paper until he has a chance to talk to you."

"As if that's going to happen," I scoffed.

"The guy knows a lot of people in high places. Somebody will be onto your editor pretty quick."

I had to smile. Anybody telling Bill Corcoran not to publish a legitimate story was in for a surprise. If anything, Bill would run the story sooner.

Lucky stood. We were finished. He showed me to the door. "I'll call Winston. Let's plan to meet with him on Wednesday. That all right? When I hear from Arnold Otis I'll set up a time with him, too."

I agreed and walked to the door. "And about Dolly? I'm going to do everything I can to get her out of that group ..."

"Wish you luck, Emily. You know Dolly when she gets something in her head."

"Yeah, well, you don't know me when I get on a story. If I have to follow her to get her alone, without that awful Sister Sally around, that's what I'll do. She's done dumb things before. This is just one of her dumber efforts."

Lucky nodded, smiled, and walked me out onto his leaf-littered porch.

———

Home and no phone call from Dolly. I thought sure there would be. I could hear her strained little voice: *Emily, it's all a joke. You know how I am. Thought I'd get involved and see what they're all about. A joke, Emily. Don't get pissed off at me ... we got a lot of work to do ...*

One call. Regina Oldenburg, Jackson's assistant, asking me to call her. I dialed her number, wondering if I was going to get an earful about what a terrible letch Jackson was, or maybe a threat to sue him for sexual harassment. But no, such things wouldn't come to me. It would give me too much joy. I let all of that waddle around in my brain for a while before realizing trouble for Jackson didn't really make me happy after all. I'd just feel sorry for him again; a brilliant man who hadn't caught on how to be a good human being. He tried—I'd give him that. But the actual knowing was beyond him. Some people didn't always get it, what being human meant. By the time I called Regina I was hoping the call was to tell me how much she enjoyed meeting me and how she hoped we could be friends… and all that other stuff everybody hopes for but rarely gets.

This time I got what I wished for.

Regina answered. There were voices in the background. She turned away from the phone to ask her dad to be a little quieter. That was followed by laughter, then quiet.

"Hi, Emily. Sorry about the party the other night. Your Jackson can be a little dense, I'm finding."

I had to laugh. "Once in a while," I agreed.

"Well, I'm still working for him, but we have very strict rules, and one is that I'm not going anywhere with him as a date. Only business."

"Good rule," I said, hoping I hid my skepticism.

"Anyway, the reason I called was because you asked me to find out if Daddy knew anything about Arnold Otis, remember?"

I agreed that I did remember, though I hadn't until she called.

"Well, Daddy said Mr. Otis is coming to town this week. Did you know that?"

I said I'd heard.

"Daddy said that he remembered something involving Mr. Otis from way, way back. He thinks it was when he was in college—I mean Mr. Otis. It was a story he told at a Young Republican party back then, about his mother dying when he was a young boy."

I thought fast. The woman didn't die when Arnold was young. She ran off. Why would he change the story? To make himself look better? After all, a mother running off with a tractor salesman might not have played as well with the party, or with the public. I hoped to meet Arnold Otis soon so I could ask him. Here was the wedge I needed. The small fact that might throw him off.

I thanked Regina and wished her luck with Jackson. We talked for a minute about my computer system versus hers but decided there would be no problem with my files since we both used Microsoft and had virtually the same program. I hung up after telling her to call if she needed help—and meaning it. I liked her and thought maybe she was the right person to handle Jackson's need to dominate every woman in his life, and maybe the right person to keep him off my back for a while.

TWENTY-FIVE

Monday, October 19
8 days 'til the end

DOLLY'S LITTLE WHITE HOUSE with no porch and a red door, three concrete steps up from the street, looked abandoned. Newspapers leaned against the door and a UPS sticker was stuck to the window. Her concrete planter, at the foot of the steps, held two very dead geraniums bending over each other. The planter had been her pride all summer long, with the pink geraniums blooming wildly and Dolly bragging about her secret fertilizer, about which I was afraid to ask.

Dolly's patrol car wasn't in the drive but that didn't stop me from parking and going up the broken concrete walk between small patches of weedy brown lawn, then standing on the second step and pounding at her door. "Dolly!" I called again and again, knowing I was reaching no one because there was no one in there to reach.

That was it for me, I told myself. Let her do whatever dumb thing she wanted to—look like a coconut or a casaba melon if that's what made her happy. I would be damned if I was going to get myself worked up, caring about some little runt of a woman who didn't care about any of her friends, about her job, which she'd always said was the most important thing in her life; and was letting all of us down—especially me. I stomped down the steps to my car, leaving a string of mumbles behind me.

Who needed a billiard ball for a friend? I asked myself as I drove over to EATS to get a fried egg and a stack of pancakes and fried potatoes and white toast—throwing caution and my arteries to the wind. Who needed a person who went flying off in all directions when you most needed her to keep her feet on the ground and concentrate?

It had to be Dolly's "family" thing, I told myself as I parked in the EATS lot. She had nobody. Her string of foster homes hadn't been warm and fuzzy. I heard about a couple of abusive boyfriends she'd had to put in the hospital, and then there was her husband, Chet Wakowski, who didn't stay around long enough to let the ink on the marriage license dry. She'd already spent money to bury the unfaithful Chet, after he was found dead, his bones floating out in Sandy Lake. She'd looked on his uncaring family as her own, until they stiffed her on the funeral, and left town early. Now she'd found a group that, like all cults, reached out and sucked her in with smiles and pats on the back and talk of being together, right up to the end of all time. Which wasn't long now. Maybe she'd already given them money, maybe signed the deed to her house over to the reverend. If the world was going to end, what good were any of those things to the cult leaders? I had no doubt that the Reverend Fritch was no different from others who came before him, all greed and power-lust and ego under the guise of religion. If God ever got into smiting again, I would happily provide him with a list of smite-ees.

I found a booth in one corner of the restaurant and sat on the side facing away from everybody. I didn't want to be bothered. What I needed was to be left alone to nurse my steaming anger and take in enough calories to blow up my rear end to a size I could blame on Dolly. Gloria came over fast. I think my narrow eyes, hunched back, and fast walk warned everyone else away. She looked down at me nervously as I told her what I wanted and added that I didn't want the eggs hard—as Eugenia usually cooked them; and I didn't want my toast burned; and I didn't want the potatoes floating in lard.

Gloria got the idea, wrote out my long order, and turned on her toe to get away.

"Has Dolly been in yet?" I think I growled, catching her mid-turn. Whatever I did, Gloria's eyes got huge. She blinked a few times then looked around for reinforcements, in case I attacked.

"Did you hear?" She dared to take a step closer. "She joined those pilgrims out to the campground."

"Pilgrims?"

"You know, those folks who're waiting for the world to end. Shaved her head and everything. Eugenia saw her yesterday at the service."

"What's Eugenia doing out there at a service?" Now I was truly tripping through Never Never Land.

"She doesn't believe in any of it. Not Eugenia. She only goes to see what's happening. Cheap theatre, she calls it. Wants to keep count of who's the most gullible in Leetsville. I'll tell you, Dolly really surprised her."

"Yeah, me too. But that's her choice. Anybody that dumb..."

I didn't want to get into a rant before breakfast so I smiled and sent Gloria on her way.

I settled back against the booth, ran my hand over the red Formica table, picking at hardened egg someone left behind as a souvenir. I glanced around the restaurant to see who I'd snubbed in my snit and who would be mad at me for a week or two.

The bag lady was there, watching. She was a vision, in all her finery. Today it was a torn designer skirt and her down-at-the-heels Gucci shoes. A rhinestone butterfly was pinned at the very top of her white pouf of hair. Every time I'd come in lately there she'd been, sitting with a cup of tea or coffee or a mostly uneaten plate of food in front of her. If she wasn't a relative of Eugenia's, I couldn't imagine why she let her kill so much time, taking up a seat or a stool and lingering for hours. Eugenia had claimed not to know the woman. Said she thought she was famous. Maybe infamous, I thought, wondering again if this was one of Eugenia's outlaw relatives come to life.

The woman stared at me. I was in too belligerent a mood to be stared down. I frowned but didn't nod or acknowledge her. Let's see who gives up staring first, I told myself, and settled my elbows on the table, chin in my hands.

The woman rose slowly from her table at the center of the restaurant. It took a little time for her to rearrange the green scarves she wore around her neck, then to pull her skirt down over her terribly uncomfortable-looking shoes. She never took her eyes from mine as she straightened her rhinestone butterfly, wings standing straight up at the top of her hair. With shoulders settled back, she took step after step toward me. No smile. No expression at all. Just this little old lady coming around tables and chairs with me clearly in her sights.

I moved back into the corner of the booth, hoping she would make a right turn toward the bathrooms. She stopped beside me, gave me a long, hard look, then slid into the booth without being invited.

"You are Emily Kincaid," she said in a surprisingly strong voice.

I couldn't disagree. "And you are …?"

"Call me Cate. That's what I'm known as."

"I've seen you in here a lot lately. Did you recently move to town?"

She shook her head, the butterfly dancing.

"Are you related to Eugenia?"

Again she shook her head then looked over toward where Eugenia stood at her counter, keeping an eye on us.

I watched the old woman from the sides of my eyes, suspicious. Maybe I was in for a sales pitch, or about to be hit up for a loan. There'd once been another old lady, with red cherries on her hat, who accosted me in Grand Central Station in New York City. She'd pleaded that her purse had been stolen and could I lend her enough money to get home. It turned out the trip would cost her twenty dollars and I couldn't resist an old lady asking for money. She wrote down my address, to send my money to me. I never got it. Not again, I told myself. Not this time. I wasn't a kid anymore. Nobody could fool me.

"I want to tell you a story," Cate said, sighed, and gathered her wrinkled hands together before her on the table.

Gloria brought my platter of food and set it in front of me. She filled my tin tea pot with hot water, brushed crumbs from the table, then—finding no other reason to hang around—attended to the crumbs on the table next to ours.

Cate waited while Gloria tidied every table around us then brought a broom to pick up the crumbs she'd dropped to the linoleum. I ate the fried eggs, poured syrup on the pancakes and ate them, then nibbled at a piece of toast while the woman sat across from me in silence.

"Can I get you tea or coffee?" I'd already been less than hospitable. Tea or coffee wouldn't cost me much. Cate shook her head and turned to smile at Eugenia, who nodded slightly and went out to the kitchen.

I finished my toast and pushed the empty platter away. I wiped my fingers on a paper napkin from the holder on the table, finding I was stickier than I'd thought. I tipped the water glass over my fingers, got another napkin, and cleaned up as Cate watched me. When I was finally finished with all my ablutions, she leaned forward.

"A story," she said again and cleared her throat. "Once upon a time I had a daughter..."

Never Never Land...

"She grew up to do destructive things to herself. I thought I had the power to stop her, but I never could. She ran away with a man and had a baby. The man left her... such an old, sad story... and she gave her baby away. When I asked about the child, she told me she'd found a loving home for the girl and it was all for the best. After that she found a group of people she said were helping her to straighten out her life; they were treating her like family and she was seeing the error of her previous ways. I was happy for her."

Cate drew a deep breath.

"The next thing I knew, her group didn't want her coming home again. They moved to a village in France. I tried to tell her it wasn't right, what they were asking of her. All I could think of were terrible stories I'd heard of cults and how they stole the minds of their followers. She said she'd be fine, she was happy with her friends, and she would write to me. I was disgusted and swore I'd never ever have a thing to do with her again as long as I lived."

I couldn't help myself. "Who are you?" I asked.

She shook her head. "Let me finish."

Light was dawning. This was going to be a Dolly thing. Everyone in town must know how mad I was at Dolly and were using this poor soul as a way to tug at my heart strings, this woman with a daughter who'd given away her kid, like Dolly's mother had. It wasn't going to work.

"I went to France to find her. I searched everywhere. For a while, I stayed in Paris and put ads in all the newspapers, asking her to contact me. I never heard. I should have acted sooner. Anger didn't help either one of us. Maybe I could have rescued her…"

I sat back and smiled. "Eugenia sent you over to tell me this story, right?"

The woman nodded. "She thought you should know because you're so mad at your friend. Like my daughter, she needs your help. Don't wait…"

Her words deflated me. Like a balloon, curling down flat, I sank into myself. "It's her choice." I sounded like a miserable little kid.

"Maybe not. Maybe there's more we don't know."

I raised one hand. "Excuse me…eh…Cate, but what are you doing here? Who the hell are you? And what's this all about?"

"I overheard people talking and I thought I could help."

"But…"

She moved to get up.

"Do you go from town to town, righting wrongs and battling evil-doers?"

Cate's look was withering, and I deserved it. "I'm not staying in Leetsville long. I have a few weeks left, until this End Time thing is finished. Then I'll be gone. I've followed cults before. Something I'm compelled to do. Often, when the disappointment sets in, people need help, someone to talk to, a way to get back to their real lives."

"Sorry," I said, and meant it. "But what can I do? I mean, about my friend, Deputy Dolly?"

"Go out there and find her. Talk to her. Let her know how worried you are and then offer her an easy way back to her real life. She may be sorry already, about what she's done. You could be a lifeline."

She reached over the table and put one of her knobby hands in tough black lace on mine. "You could be a friend."

TWENTY-SIX

Still 8 days to the end

I LEFT THE RESTAURANT with my jeans tight and my mind in tatters. Walking in circles around my car while I tried to decide where to go next didn't help. Nor did I feel better when Crystalline, Felicia, and Sonia drove up and parked beside me.

They waved, getting out of their car, all dressed in wild colors or basic black. If it hadn't been for the reverend and his followers, Leetsvillians would have been titillated. Women like these three didn't come along very often.

"We're going to pass out business cards," Felicia said, putting one in my hand. "Might as well do some healings and some readings while we're staying here. Crystalline said we should fill our time, and help with the expenses."

I looked at the card. Tarot Readings. Psychic Healings. Past Life Regressions.

"If you're interested," Sonia moved up next to me, "I'll give you a discount."

I shook my head. "A little busy…"

"The motel owner gave us Marjory's things," Crystalline said as she eyed an older couple going into the restaurant.

"Is he allowed to do that?"

"He said Deputy Dolly went through everything already. He guessed that if he was supposed to keep them she would have said."

News to me. I hadn't heard a thing about Dolly going through Marjory's effects. "I wonder if she found anything," I said.

"As far as he knows, she took nothing. Wouldn't she have had to give him a receipt or something?"

I nodded.

"I'm glad we've got Marjory's books, and her notes. She was looking into effecting world peace through joint visualization. People everywhere creating mind pictures of a world without war." Crystalline looked away, off over the ridge of hills to the east.

"Will you keep up her research?" I asked.

"We'd like to," Felicia said. "There's a bigger group, out of Boston. They've asked to see the notes Marjory left behind. This is a worldwide project…"

"I needed her Tarot cards anyway," Crystalline turned back to me. "I left mine at home. Such a big hurry to get up here. You know, Emily, it wouldn't be a bad idea to read the Tarot for you. Your question could be who did this to Marjory."

"Maybe later. Right now I've got so much on my plate…"

"Be a good idea if you came out and looked through what we've got. I'd hate to think we missed something important."

I can't right now. I want to get back to that campground. What Dolly's done is really bothering me."

"Don't blame you," Sonia said, pushing her dark hair out of her eyes. "She looked like a turnip with that bald head."

"How about later? When I get to town? Will you be there, at the motel?"

"What time?" Felicia asked. "We might get readings."

"Twelve-thirty? I can't imagine taking longer than that. I just want to sit down and have her explain what she's doing."

We agreed to meet at the Green Trees Motel and go through everything Marjory left behind. What we were looking for, I had no clue. If Dolly found anything, she sure hadn't shared the information. What I felt was like being on a slick branch hanging over a furious waterfall and feeling my fingers sliding off, one by one.

There weren't many people around the campers and pickups parked in and among the trees at the spiritualist campsite. I saw almost no one and, of the few I came upon, I recognized no one. I didn't have a clue how to find Dolly. Especially not with her in that robe. She could be any one of the anonymous men and women who looked alike and walked alike. I had an empty, lonely feeling, as if she'd been swallowed by a whale. I went back around to the reverend's RV, where I knocked. No one answered. All I could do was sit at one of the picnic tables where the men had been sitting yesterday and wait until someone came along who would help me.

The bench was cold. A damp wind came through the pines behind me, slurring the branches, making a ghostly sound. A few robed people passed by but didn't look my way. No one stopped to help. I tried to get one woman's attention, hurrying over to her only to be elbowed abruptly aside. I went back to the table to wait some more, sitting hunched in my corduroy jacket over a black turtleneck, as fingers of cold worked up and down my spine. If I'd been invisible I couldn't have been more ignored. I figured they knew who I was by now and, like people in Leetsville, sensed when there was danger among them, someone come to upset the order of things.

Despite the breakfast I'd eaten—and there'd been more than I'd admitted to—I was getting hungry. Or, I was finding an excuse to get up and leave. Watching people take wide circles in order to avoid me did nothing for my self-esteem. I was about to go when one of the robed figures, hood far down over his face, came to where I waited. He worked his long, skinny legs over the bench, then pulled his robe around his body, and said nothing. Finally he turned and lifted his head. Brother Righteous, the man who couldn't, or wouldn't, speak; the one who had roused the crowd the other night simply with his sounds. The pale gray eyes I looked into were a sensory shock. There were things there I would never be able to name. Questions shot out at me, and pity, and gentleness, and a form of life I'd never seen before. There was light, as if Godly light inhabited him. The man, this close, was an assault to my system. I pulled back. He looked at me wordlessly, in a language I had no key to. There was, in me, a feeling of being inadequate, that I couldn't, or wouldn't, understand what he was trying to say. After a few minutes he moved his lips, but not into words I could make out. When he saw there was no communication between us, he held his mouth still. He looked directly into my eyes, until mine watered and I turned away. I was moved, and so sorry I was letting him down. He shook his head sadly. He laid one of his thin hands on top of mine and left it there, cool and encompassing.

"Do you know where she is?" I whispered toward him, hoping to get through, to make him understand that Dolly wasn't really like the rest of them. What she wanted was to have a family, not a religion, not a mission to end all life on earth. Dolly needed people who cared if she lived or died.

He nodded slowly, removed his hand from mine, and got up. Without a sign or a gesture to follow, he walked off, the tall, bent, thin man, turning only once to make sure I wasn't behind him.

I watched him go, wondering if I was supposed to have been reassured, warned, invited—there was no knowing. What I was left with was embarrassment. I looked around to see who had been watching. No one. I got up, clumsily lifting my legs back over the bench, and went out to my car.

———

While on my way back through Leetsville, I stopped to see Lucky. I told him about Dolly taking a look through Marjory's things at the motel.

"Didn't know she'd been out there." He shook his head as if these were facts about his officer he wished he didn't have to know. I didn't own up to going out to the campsite to talk to her. For all I knew, he'd been out there too. I couldn't see him turning his back on her, nor Eugenia, nor Gloria, nor anyone else in Leetsville. She might make herself unpopular with her speed traps at either end of town but when it came to caring for their own, Leetsville people had their priorities straight.

Lucky told me that Sergeant Winston would be at the station Wednesday and wanted to talk to me and Lucky together. I promised I'd show up, mentally planning to get my ghost story for Bill done by then. Lucky let me use his phone to call the nursing home in Bellaire to see if I could visit Cecily Otis any time soon. The nurse thought her cold might be about over by the next day, if that would be all right with my schedule. She asked for my name but I hung up after mumbling something like Apple Tart. I didn't want my name preceding me, nor any other reason for Cecily Otis to refuse to see me.

On the way out to the Green Trees Motel, I came up with excuses to get out of having Crystalline read the Tarot for me. I was too superstitious to allow anyone to tell me what my future was. What if that made it happen, by saying it aloud? Dumb. Irrational. I just didn't want to sit down and pretend to take a Tarot reading seriously.

Sonia opened the door and invited me in. The room was a typical up-north motel room—generic bedspreads and drapes and fake mahogany headboards and suspicious-looking indoor carpeting. They'd spread Marjory's thing out on one of the double beds—mostly a pile of long skirts and a couple of bright sweaters. There was a stack of underwear, which we all ignored because there is something so sad about old underwear, something so raggedy looking. Her black purse was on the bed beside the other things.

Crystalline upended the purse on top of a pair of paisley print pajamas. "I've been through everything," she said, separating the tampons from the Kleenex and a rubber-banded stack of business cards with one finger. I went through Marjory's wallet—the usual: driver's license, money, Sears and Citibank credit cards. There was a Toledo library card, car insurance, and registration. There were a couple of folded utility bills she had probably meant to take care of while she was gone, and the usual round brush, lipstick—bright red—and blush.

There were a couple pairs of shoes on the floor beside the bed and a pair of not-too-clean white slippers. From a beige bag with the word HOPE emblazoned on one side and the name of a bookstore on the other, Crystalline pulled a pack of Tarot cards and several pink quartz stones. There was a package of stick incense— lavender. There were three books on shamanism. I picked up one after the other and ruffled the pages while holding them upside down. Nothing fell out.

There was a notebook, but Crystalline said there were only notes of expenses, appointments—business things. There was a card folder filled with business cards from other shamans and psychics and readers, as well as cards from customers. Marjory had quite an upscale clientele: lawyers and doctors and one Episcopalian priest. She must have been good at what she did. I sighed, sticking the cards back into their folder and thinking how I could certainly use Marjory's psychic talents in the mess I was currently in.

As I looked through things, Sonia put her hand on mine, stopping me. "I have to tell you something, Emily." Something important was caught in the hush of her voice.

The other two women shot glances at me and then at each other. The room went still.

"It's about that reverend."

I waited, wondering what was coming at me now.

"His aura's white."

I waited for more. "I . . . don't know what that means."

Sonia looked at the others, then back to me. "Death," she said, shaking her head with a soft tinkle of her earrings, like far-off wind chimes. "Bright white. It means he's going to die, and soon. The man's not kidding, Emily. He might be right. The world could end."

I took a deep breath. Insanity was growing all around me. If only I knew the words to stop it. Even in this nondescript room I could feel the fear—a child's fear of the unknown.

I looked at Crystalline as she held the pack of Marjory's Tarot cards in her taut hands, turning it between her fingers, averting her eyes. I didn't know what I could say to challenge something I knew nothing about: white aura. Probably as good as misreading Scripture to frighten the masses.

After a few silent moments, Crystalline opened the Tarot pack and let the cards slide out into her right hand. For a minute she simply held them, then fingered them, running one of her long, bright nails across the back of the top card. She felt the card again, then flipped the deck so it lay face up in her hand. On top now was a piece of white paper. It looked as if it had been torn from a book of lined notepaper.

Crystalline looked at me, then set the deck on the bed, taking up the torn paper and opening it. She read:

> *Marjory—I am a friend of your brother. He is in terrible danger and afraid of what might happen. Please come to Leetsville. Everything began here. He will know when you get to town, or someone will contact him. Above all, he says he is very sorry ... but he needs your help. There are things that happened in this town. They have to be exposed. He needs you now as he's never needed you before.*

TWENTY-SEVEN

Still only 8 days to go

Now I HAD AN answer to one part of the puzzle: what had brought Marjory to Leetsville. Not what had taken her out to Deward; I didn't know that piece yet. But at least we knew for certain it had something to do with her brother, Arnold Otis, and with the End Time cult. I had to talk to Mr. Otis. So many questions—about Marjory, about their mother and what had really happened to her. And about the reason she had to meet him in Leetsville, the thing that had put him in so much danger. Then, what I needed most to know was, why hadn't he been here? If he was afraid for his own life, didn't he care that his sister had put herself in danger?

All I wanted was to get home. I'd had more than enough of people and problems for one day. I took the note with me, tucked into my jacket pocket. I would turn it over to Lucky and Officer Winston on Wednesday. Maybe they'd know what it meant or at least could force the wannabe senator to come to Leetsville, sit down, and fill in the empty places in Marjory's story.

My stomach growled as I turned onto Willow Lake Road, then down my driveway, stopping only to get the newspaper from the box beside the road. I was already visualizing a Swiss cheese omelet with a slice of thick peasant bread from the freezer. Maybe I had half a bottle of Pinot Grigio. I thought so. And it would be cold. And, if I could work up the ambition, I'd throw together a bread pudding. I'd learned to make one pretty close to Emeril's while covering Mardi Gras in New Orleans one year, but I nixed the bread pudding pretty quick. Not the kind of thing you fussed over for yourself. Then I nixed the nixing. I was worth a little bread pudding.

Like visions of sugar plums exploding into bright pieces in my head, my omelet, my glass of wine, and my bread pudding went off like firecrackers lost in an endless sky. Harry waited on the side porch. Sorrow, getting his ears scratched, sat upright beside Harry's poky old knees.

He stood slowly when I got to my door and pushed a joyous Sorrow down. I invited Harry in. He usually preferred outdoors for talks but this time he followed and took a seat on the sofa while I made us both a cup of Earl Grey tea, though after one attempt to get his bent finger through the delicate cup handle he gave up and ignored the tea.

"Ya see, Emily," he started, skinny legs together. "What I'm here to ask you is to go down to Delia's house with me. We're having trouble. Delia's agreed to marry me but her mother's acting up something awful."

"Maybe she doesn't like the thought of living alone after all these years."

He shook his head. "Got a son down in Atlanta, Georgia, she could go live with. Or I could move into their house there down the road. But she says that's never going to happen."

"Could it be your dogs, do you think?"

He gave me an odd look, as if a thing like that had never entered his head.

"So, what I thought you might do," he went on, ignoring me, "if yer willin', that is, is to go down there with me, tell Bertha I'm a good provider and how I'm so handy you couldn't live here without me."

"You mean now?" There was no hiding my reluctance.

"Yes, now. We can't just sit around waiting for the old woman to change her mind. I've got to do something…" This was as excited as I'd ever seen Harry get. "If that reverend's right, well, I'm not gonna spend these last days living all alone."

I sighed and agreed. We drove over to Delia's in my car because I wouldn't go in his.

The Swanson house was like all the others along the road, set back in the woods, an old farm house with a steep pitched roof so the snow would slide off, two stories—all the bedrooms upstairs—and a small porch that had obviously been put on years after the house was built. All the houses up here had been built for utility. Maybe the Swansons had actually tried farming in what locals called our Kalkaska sands. Maybe that was the way everybody built their houses back sixty years or so ago. People up here didn't look for frills.

Delia was expecting us and led us to what she called "the back parlor." I sat uncomfortably on an upright chair while Harry took a chair across from me. Delia excused herself, bowing her curly gray head and going off to get her mother, Bertha, who was taking a nap. The rousing of Bertha and getting her down the stairs took at least fifteen minutes, during which time Harry sat rolling his eyes at me. An unhappy Bertha came in from the hall with Delia holding her elbow and directing her to the nearest chair. Bertha sat and frowned at Harry and then at me.

"You're that woman from down the road," she said. "The one who's trying to write stories or something."

I nodded that the description fit me so I must be that woman.

"Nice of you to call." The old lady dripped sarcasm. "Finally."

She eyed Harry and said nothing to him. Harry's face reddened. He looked hard at the floor.

"You come with a reason in mind?" she went on. "Or just being neighborly?"

Delia cut in, before her mother got too testy. "Miz Kincaid came over to put in a good word for Harry. We know you've got yourself set firmly against us getting married ..."

"Bah," the old woman spit out. "Married! At your age? You've gone straight out of your mind. And Harry Mockerman, of all people. Couldn't you find yourself a man so you could marry up in the world instead of down?"

The woman made a face and looked toward the door she'd come in, as if planning her escape.

"Harry's a fine man ..." Delia said, defending him as he sat on the edge of his chair with his hands working at each other in his lap.

"Harry's a good friend of mine," I said. "He's a wonderful cook and if I ever need anything done around my house, why, I wouldn't call anybody else. He's honest ..."

"Phooey, you say. He's a handyman. To think I'd live to see the day my daughter goes off with a handyman ... well ..."

The thought was beyond words for Bertha.

"Don't you think your daughter's old enough to make her own choices?" I asked, not meaning to set off a civil war. But I did.

Bertha narrowed her eyes. "Get that person out of my house. I want her outta here!"

She coughed, then put a hand to her chest and thumped a few times. She fell back in her chair, mouth open, eyes rolling. Something very serious was going on. I hoped I hadn't brought on a heart attack—the woman was in her nineties, after all.

Delia went to her mother, then turned to Harry and me. "Maybe you'd better go. She gets like this from time to time."

I got up as fast as Harry did. At the front door I turned to try to say I was sorry but Delia, bending over her mother and whispering quietly to her, looked up and nodded. She mouthed "thanks" at me. We were out of there as fast as Harry's old legs could pump their way to my car.

I stopped to let him out at the head of his drive, trying to say I was sorry if I'd brought on a heart attack. Harry only waved a hand in the air and grunted something that sounded like "That one don't have a heart to begin with" before he was off and hidden among the overgrown trees.

———————

The omelet tasted flat. I'd already had eggs that day, two more seemed to cement the fact I was alone and had nobody to cook for but myself. I decided it was definitely a night calling for Emeril's bread pudding and put everything into the bowl—the hard bread cut into squares, more eggs—everything. I got out the cinnamon can and tapped it over the bowl. Nothing. No cinnamon. What was bread pudding without cinnamon? I couldn't waste the other ingredients so I tried more sugar and some nutmeg, but after it was baked it tasted bad. Just bad. I scraped the pudding onto a paper plate to put out for the birds and decided to get my mind off murders and sisters and brothers and everything I'd been thinking about—like Dolly Wakowski having lost her mind.

I went on the Internet and looked up ghost towns in Kalkaska, Antrim, and Grand Traverse counties. There were plenty. I chose two to do the next day: Rugg and South Boardman. I stumbled on a site that listed all the ghosts in Kalkaska County, and decided to broaden my article. Not just ghost towns, but actual ghosts. Now I was having fun. This was something I might enjoy, without too much running around, or going to places such as Deward.

I dug my notebook out of my purse, wrote down directions and what I might find at Rugg Pond and South Boardman, then went out to my car for the camera I'd left on the back seat.

When I was doing stories, features like this one, I always made sure I had spare batteries in the camera case. Being out in the woods with the light dying and the batteries gone was an event I didn't want to have happen to me again.

And an extra film disk. I slid the disk door open and removed the disk I had in there. It could be full. Better to delete the photos I didn't need.

It hit me. What I had on the cartridge were photos from Deward. Not just the pictures I took for my story, but pictures I took of Marjory, laid out under the tree. Maybe it wouldn't make a difference—

nothing in the pictures the cops didn't already have—but I wanted to see for myself. Maybe give the photos to Crystalline.

At my desk, I slipped the disk into the printer and turned everything on. It took a while, as it always does, but eventually the computer recognized the printer and they agreed to bring up my photos. I couldn't tell much from the small snapshot size of the photos, so I made them full screen and set it to a slide show.

One by one, all the pictures I'd taken that day—of the river, of the foundations of houses, of the trees, the railroad grade—everything moved past me at ten-second intervals.

Then Marjory. Just as serene. Just as colorful. Hands in her lap. I felt that she wasn't a stranger now that I knew what her life had been. She lay with her hat off to the side, eyes staring out. The jack pine cast shadows even at noon, so some of the photos were dark. Others were crisp and clear. The images went by and the show came to an end. I pushed the button, starting at the beginning again. There'd been something...

I ran the slide show three more times before I chose the photos I wanted to copy.

Something near Marjory's body that I hadn't noticed when I was out there. It was caught in the way the sun had moved overhead, or in the shadow of the tree. Something about the ground—a shape. I had to show this to Lucky. I'd show this to Officer Winston. Maybe I was crazy, looking for answers where there was nothing. Or maybe I was so frustrated with how slow this murder investigation was going that I was seeing things. Or, even if what I saw was there, maybe it meant nothing.

TWENTY-EIGHT

Tuesday, October 20
7 days 'til the end

IT WASN'T SIMPLY BECAUSE of the story I was working on that I went to Rugg Pond. Nor just because I was worried about Dolly, though I was certainly worried. Rugg Pond was a place to go, like Seven Bridges, when you need to get in touch with nature. You could stand at the dam, water rushing hard, falling to a riverbed below, or you could stop on the other side where the pond was tranquil, flat, and quiet until it slowly seeped over a catch basin that fed the water to the dam.

I stood for a while looking down as the noisy water cascaded over rocks, swirled in worn places, then fell again, then again, the sound deafening, mist rising as the water moved, hit the bubbling Rapid River, and coursed faster downstream. A root-exposed maple leaned out, colorful leaves rattling in the clouds of mist for the last season—the brightest fall of a tree's life, just before it died. By winter, the lower branches would be encased in ice, frozen in place, roots pulled from the ground, and next spring the tree would be dead.

Too much about death in my head, as if it was the most important part of living. It wasn't. I leaned my elbows on the metal railing and watched the water do what water was meant to do. *All the world's a stage, and all the men and women merely players; they have their exits and their entrances...*

A cliché, even in Shakespeare's time, but like most clichés, worthy of a revisit.

Exits and entrances. In between a story is told. I wondered about Marjory's story, the scenes that led her back to Deward. Was it about her mother, Winnie Otis? Winnie Otis, in her madness, had always returned to Deward when she needed to be alone. There was a family history that drew her there—back into pioneering times. Then that same history drew Marjory. Buried within families there were often secrets. In mine it was my grandfather who went crazy and tried to murder my grandmother one January night. My father told me once he thought it was that shameful secret that killed my mother. She'd carried the knowledge deep but had to be nice to my grandfather. Mother never said a word to me, burying first her mother—with her father leaning in to kiss his dead wife's cheek as if he'd been the finest, most loving man, all through their lives together—and then burying her father, in a cheap pine box going into an unmarked grave.

That was anger.

And Marjory? What brought her back to Deward? A letter from a brother—we knew that now. But what part did the ghost town play in the thing that happened to her? She wouldn't have come back to a place when she was afraid of it. She must have trusted the person she was with. So, trusting … who is it that women most trust? Friends? Relatives? Strangers?

Anyone?

I shook my head and went to stand on the tranquil side of the dam. A few late swans cruised the far shore. Starlings, in groups, swooped and soared across the water's surface, chattering and carrying on before flocking to fly off south. There were a few geese up on the grass. Every year, as the geese got into formation, honked orders, and flew away, I thought of rats leaving a sinking ship. But in the spring, when I heard their honking overhead, I'd get tears in my eyes. They were back and I'd made it through another winter—by myself, with only a few nice guys to help me, like Harry Mockerman and my snowplow man.

I took photographs to go with my story, but there wasn't much left of the town that had, at one time, been called Mossback. In 1902 fire wiped out the buildings. In 1916, while a Waldo Yoemans was helping to search for Fred Hill, presumed drowned while fishing in the Rapid River, Yocmans' store, too, burned to the ground. Nothing of the stores or post office or people left. They'd had their time on stage. That act was finished. I couldn't even see the railroad grade that brought the train to town back then. I'd have to make the past live through words.

There was one stately home I wanted to photograph. The beginnings of the place went back to the Civil War and Rolando F. Rugg, once the sheriff of Kalkaska County. He enlisted with Company D, Fiftieth New York Engineers, served until July 1865, then learned carpentry after the war and came to Michigan. Mr. Rugg, one day, rode his horse into town to cash a $12 check, his pension for being in the war, and dropped dead in the store.

Odd to think of people who thought it a good idea, like me, to make a life where winters went on forever, where the ground was like quicksand—hard to farm, the distances between towns wide. It seemed that the biggest connection between people, over all of time, was their need to be away from crowds and better their lot in life. Made me wonder, was that what I was doing? And how was I better off? Certainly no crowds. Certainly a lot of new and interesting and individual friends. Certainly a life that wasn't counted off in clock ticks with me salivating to get moving, like one of Pavlov's dogs answering a bell. Starvation could loom. Maybe I would be found one spring—like an old couple at a nearby place still called Starvation Lake—stiff and cold and very skinny.

I went back to my notes, trying to get a handle on my inability to concentrate for very long.

I tucked my notebook into my jacket pocket and pulled out the envelope with the photographs I'd run off the night before. One by one, as I stood there far from Deward, I looked at them and let myself go back to that morning, and the woman laid out beneath the jack pine. I looked closely at her chin, dipping down into her chest. There was nothing to see. I couldn't have known.

There were photos of the tree behind her. I'd taken a picture while turned toward the path leading in from the approach road. I'd taken pictures while squatting on my haunches, down at her level, close to the ground. There were two of these, dead-on photos with her eyes looking past me, over my shoulder, as if someone knelt back there.

And the last two, the ones I couldn't get out of my head. Something there. I wished I could ring my head like a gong, make everything I knew settle into place. What I needed was Dolly's pragmatic brain. I needed her telling me to "get real" or "try to make some sense, ok?" I needed her bringing me down to earth.

I told myself I didn't want to find anything. It was probably the way the sun fell—an odd shadow because it had been close to noon when the sun is directly overhead and the light is flat; not a good time to take photos. I would have to go back there and prove to myself that what I saw outlined on my photo didn't exist. Shadows in a photo were only shadows—they might take forms and hint at more, but they were only shadows.

Why didn't I believe it? I looked closer at those two photos then put them away. Something there. It meant going back to Deward.

I put off driving to South Boardman, because I'd heard there wasn't much left of the old town which once stood along US131. There were other towns to find—near Grawn, Keystone Pond. Maybe Old Mission. I wanted to talk to Jim at the country store out there. And then I would fill in with ghosts I'd found: a ghostly plumber mailing a letter at the Kalkaska Post Office; a Civil War soldier reading while sitting on the shore of Log Lake; a headless woman in Advent Swamp; a child in an upstairs room of a building that had once been the local funeral parlor.

I drove back to my house because I needed Sorrow. If I was going to Deward alone, at least my happy-go-lucky dog could go with me. Now that I was deeply into ghosts and hauntings and places with histories, I'd spooked myself to the point where if Sorrow didn't go, neither did I

At Deward Sorrow took off running, ears laid back, as soon as I parked to the side of the sandy two-track and let him out of the car. The day was overcast, chilly; the trees had either dropped all of their leaves or the leaves were that bloody end-of-season color that wasn't pretty any longer, only burned looking.

Because I'd gotten myself so involved with ghosts, I was convinced Marjory would be there again. She would tip her head up this time, greet me, smile, and wish me a good day. As I walked around the last bend before Deward, I stopped a minute, confusing Sorrow into a sliding halt in the sand. He came bounding back to see what I'd found that he'd missed, sniffing around my feet, forgetting himself and jumping up against me. Content that I was still me, and ok, he ran off, down the path toward the town.

Huge questions bothered me. If a brother wanted her help, what did it have to do with Deward? And which brother was it? Arnold, the brother running for state senator, a very visible figure, probably powerful? Paul—who might not even be alive?

There was nothing under the tree, just scuffed dirt and disturbed grasses where Marjory had lain and the police had walked. I stopped on the trail. The tree was absent of crows now. I knelt in the exact place where I'd shot the photos of Marjory and the ground around her—before the police got there, before anything was disturbed. What I'd seen in the photo was a faint depression in the ground, a large rectangle filled with gnarled weeds and disturbed earth, but sunken—like the foundations of the houses. I walked around the depression, bending to brush leaves away as I moved. About the size of a grave. But not mounded. Or, if once mounded, not now.

I looked at the picture. The photo showed the dimensions of the rectangle better than I could make out in front of me. There was something there, not far from where Marjory had lain. I sat at the head of the rectangle, putting my hand down on the sunken earth. I closed my eyes as I sat there, trying to see what Marjory could see; maybe visualize what Crystalline or Felicia or even Sonia might see. I got nothing. I moved to the other end of the rectangle, carefully brushing away dead leaves. Both my hands were within the rectangle; my head was bowed. I closed my eyes and wrapped my fingers around sticks lying on top of the dirt. I held on to the sticks, feeling them, seeing them as parts of the jack pine, or maybe bits of underbrush. I lifted one, hoping there was something in it that could help me. Wishing I could find answers to questions I couldn't form.

Something stuck into my thumb. I threw the stick down and looked at my hand where blood pulsed out in a slow ooze around a thorn—a curved, triangular thorn lodged firmly in my flesh.

TWENTY-NINE

I PUT MY THUMB to my mouth and bit out the thorn, spitting it off beside me. As my thumb bled, I wiped it along the side of my jeans, upset because it seemed everywhere I turned something worked against me.

I looked down at the stick I'd been holding, then lifted it up from among others, where it lay. Not a piece of underbrush or a dead twig from the jack pine. About six inches long with more thorns along the stem, and at the top a flower head twisted down, the flower brown and brittle.

A dead rose.

I lifted one and then another—six dead roses. Sorrow snuffled at what I held until I pushed his damp nose away and he went flying off. Roses. Maybe Crystalline and the others had brought them to lay where Marjory died. But the roses would never be this dead. These had been here a long time. And they weren't under the jack pine but where the ground had sunken in and an almost perfect rectangle had formed.

I picked up the dead flowers. I knew I might be disturbing evidence, but I didn't dare leave them there to disappear, or be carried off.

As I gathered the dead roses, one by one, Sorrow barked his welcoming bark somewhere down the path. I hurried, though I had no place to carry the dead flowers other than in my hands. I looked around, expecting Sorrow at my side, and was startled by a pair of legs standing behind me. I followed the legs up to the reddened face of a big man in his fifties watching me, frowning down through wire-framed glasses. The man was broad, stomach pushing hard at the belt of his chino pants. He wore one of those leather vests fishermen wore, stuck with hooks and flies. Sorrow jumped into wild, black-and-white circles behind where the man stood. It had taken me months to teach him not to jump on people. For a few seconds, as I knelt on the ground grasping a bunch of dead roses to my chest, I thought maybe I'd made a mistake. I could have used a good jumper about then.

"Are you in trouble?" the man, with graying hair sticking out from under a fishing hat replete with different colored flies, asked.

I shook my head. "Just looking into something…" I began then stopped, sighed, and sat back on my knees. I smiled up at the man, who took a few steps away from me.

"Isn't this where they found that dead woman? I mean, right in here somewhere?" He pointed to the tree. "I read about it in the paper."

I nodded.

He made a face. "Should you be doing…" He looked down at the ground.

"I'm the one who found her. I…eh…just came out on a hunch…"

"About what?" The man studied me. He had the face of a college professor, or a bank president saying no to a loan. It was one of those male faces that made you feel small: the principal chiding you for kissing a boy in the hall; the editor who wanted to know why your story was late.

"I took photographs when I was out here. There was something…" I reached for the photos on the ground, picked them up, but didn't offer them to the man standing over me. He seemed about to ask.

"You're fly fishing," I said, turning the subject away from Marjory and from me.

He nodded. "May I have your name? This seems…well…odd, what you're doing."

"Emily Kincaid. With the *Northern Statesman* newspaper, out of Traverse City."

"A reporter. Doing a story, are you?" His thick eyebrows shot up behind the rim of his glasses.

"I've been following the murder since she was found…"

"What do you mean, 'murder'?"

"The woman I found out here, Marjory Otis, was murdered."

"Yes," he nodded, then nodded again as if thinking hard.

I picked up the roses. He only watched as I struggled to get off my knees, stand, then brush dirt from my jeans.

"Nice to meet you. Emily Kincaid, is it? You live around here?"

"Outside Leetsville," I answered, nervous, feeling his presence as too massive. I was suddenly aware of the emptiness between the trees and the silence around us.

He nodded a few times. "Well, it's back to fishing for me." He didn't turn, only stood staring at the ground where I'd been crawling.

"Me too. Gotta get going." I whistled for Sorrow to get away from a hole where he frantically dug at a chipmunk.

On the way back to the Jeep, I turned from time to time to look over my shoulder. The man hadn't gone back to the river, but followed me, keeping a short distance away. When I got to the road, I noticed there wasn't another car along the sand trail I'd followed in. The man must have started upriver somewhere and walked down to Deward, or the other way, from outside Grayling. Here was another person in the woods with no visible means of transportation. I was uneasy, and happy I had Sorrow with me. Maybe he wasn't a little female cop with a pistol tucked into her belt, but he was noisy and obnoxious enough to keep away all but the most dedicated murderer.

I dug my keys from the pocket of my jeans and glanced over my shoulder at the woods. He stood there, watching me.

I got in and locked the car doors immediately. I wedged the roses against the seat so they wouldn't fly off, and I glanced up at Sorrow's eager face in the rearview mirror. I was upset with him. He'd been such a welcoming committee. But that was Sorrow. You either got one that growled and made life hell, or a dog with bright button eyes, a shaggy black-and-white coat of all lengths, and big, splayed feet, who loved everybody.

A fisherman, the man had said. Only then did it register that he'd carried no fishing pole. What fly fisherman would have left his pole wedged under a rock along the river, hoping for a strike he wouldn't be there to land? What about waders?

And what about a name? I'd never asked. He knew mine.

THIRTY

Still 7 days 'til the end

I TOOK SORROW HOME, drove to Mancelona, and then over to Bellaire, to the nursing home where Marjory's aunt stayed. It was north of town, up a winding road, nestled into rolling hills—a long, low red brick building under tall oaks and fir trees.

Inside the outer double doors, the walls of the facility were covered with flowered wallpaper in muted lilacs and soft pinks. The woodwork and doors were a natural oak. Photos of wildflowers decorated the long corridors. It was a cheerful place. Much better than many I'd visited.

The young woman seated behind a front desk was dressed in a white uniform with a blue sweater draped across her shoulders. She smiled and asked if she could help me.

When I asked to see Cecily Otis, she looked back at another woman in the office, behind a big glass window, then turned and smiled up at me.

"Cecily doesn't get much company. You must be the woman who called last week."

There was no denying who I was, nor reason to.

"She'll be pleased that you came to see her. Were you a neighbor?"

I shook my head.

"A relative…?"

I shook my head again and she gave up trying to get information from me. She laid a map on the counter and drew a blue line leading to Cecily Otis' room: 178. As her last gesture of help, she leaned forward to point me in the right direction.

Room 178 was at the back of the building. I passed windows that looked out to the woods, and to a grassy lawn, now covered with leaves, where Adirondack chairs sat in friendly clusters. There were picnic tables, even an in-the-ground grill, the kind state parks provided. Not a bad place. It seemed more a hotel than grim home for the elderly, except for the long halls with wheelchairs standing at angles, and the bins of dirty linens, a stack of bed pans, and the faint odor of medications.

The sign outside room 178 said: Bed 1: Cecily Otis. The sign beneath it read: Bed 2: Wanda Harcourt. So, a double room. Cecily had a roommate. It might be best to talk to Cecily somewhere else, if the roommate was there. I'd had interviews, in the past, with people in nursing homes—one for a local history story in Ann Arbor, where the roommate wanted to join in and take the conversation wherever he wanted it to go, causing me a wasted hour of time and coming away with little of value from the shyer man I'd gone to interview.

Cecily Otis of Bed 1 sat hunched in a wheelchair next to the rumpled bed. Her head was almost pink, scalp showing through fuzzy, white hair. She wore a pretty rose-covered robe with a frilly collar over what looked like a hospital nightgown. I guessed Cecily didn't have a lot of things of her own, and no one to bring them to her. Her back was bent so her head jutted out, turtle-like. She wore wire-framed glasses too small for her face.

I stood near the end of her bed, smiling and waiting to be noticed. She looked over at me, then turned her turtle head back to a glassine envelope she was trying to open, with what looked like sewing needles inside.

"Damn thing," she swore and threw the envelope at a rolling tray near the wall. She sat slouched and angry for a few very long minutes, ignoring me.

"Can I help you?" I asked.

"Need the god-damned nurse," was all she muttered. "Get me a nurse. That's how you can help me." She turned her head. "What in hell you doing here anyway, standing there like that? You think I'm some kind of bug on a windshield? What do you want with me?"

Behind the curtain surrounding Bed 2 came a weak, disgruntled "Shh."

"Shh, yourself." Cecily raised her voice and shushed back. "How'd you like having some idiot standing over your bed staring at you?"

"I didn't mean to stare," I said, gathering my dignity about me, and readying myself to take on a true harridan.

"What do you call it then?"

"Not staring. I came to talk to you."

She glared at me, suspicious. "About what? Not Medicaid. Better not be any more shenanigans about that issue. I'm as entitled as the next person and nobody's kicking me out of ..."

I shook my head and shuffled my feet, calling on patience. A thing I wasn't long on.

I introduced myself and told her I was there about the death of Marjory Otis.

She leaned back and gave me an incredulous look. "Marjory? You mean to tell me Marjory's dead? Why, the girl can't be more than fifty-three or four ..."

"Fifty-two," I corrected.

"Whatever. She's got no reason to die. If anybody should be dying, it's me. Look at how I have to live now, and my gallbladder gone—they grabbed that when I got my first green stool. Then they took a lot of other things, telling me I had to have them out but I'll tell you ..." She raised one bony finger and shook it toward me. "They better not be selling off my organs or I'm gonna get a lawyer and sue everybody I can find."

I nodded, hoping to steer the conversation back around to Marjory.

"Could we go someplace where we could talk privately?" I finally asked.

Cecily, who had the kind of face you see on old women who haunt backwoods bars—with heavy lines, mean eyes behind tiny glasses, squashed nose, and thin lips—shrugged and wheeled her chair past me without a word. She rolled into the hall, down a few doors, and into an open room with a TV high on the wall, tuned to a soap opera no one was watching. Only an old, nodding gentleman lounged in a far corner chair. He paid attention to nothing.

Cecily Otis motioned me to a chair, then wheeled around to face me. "What do you want to know about Marjory? And how in hell did she die, anyway? Probably something to do with that stupid witch stuff she got herself into. I heard all about it. Reading cards and telling fortunes."

"She was murdered."

The old woman's mouth dropped open. "Murdered! Oh, my good lord. That's what the world's coming to. Just as well I'm on my way out. Good riddance to all of this." She gestured around at nothing in particular.

"She was found in Deward."

"Nope. Nope. Nope." Again she reared back. This time she shook her head hard. "Oh, no you don't. This is some kind of trick you're playing. Marjory hated that place. Probably because of Winnie, her mother. Winnie liked going out there. Got so bad she left her kids alone for days and camped out in Deward. Got it in her head, when she went 'round the bend, that she had to be close to her ancestors. Just 'cause some of her people used to be in loggin' out there. Like that made her special. Crazy woman."

"Winnie's kind of what I wanted to ask you about. And about Marjory's brothers."

"And who in hell are you again?"

"Emily Kincaid. I'm with the *Northern Statesman* newspaper ..."

She waved at me then put her hands on her wheels to get away. "No damned reporter. You can't fool me. You'll get me to say things that'll make me look bad, then I'll have those pappa ... rats ... whatever, chasing me around."

I reached out and stopped the woman, determined to get something from this weird struggle.

"I'm also working with the local police to find out who killed Marjory," I said, using every trick I knew.

She frowned hard then slowly turned the chair back to face me. "You with both of 'em? Never heard that one before."

I hurried on before I lost her.

"First of all. About Winnie. Marjory thought her mother ran off with a tractor salesman."

Cecily nodded. "She did. Left her kids behind for me and Ralph to finish raising, as if I didn't have enough of my own stuff to take care of."

I let the "stuff" bit go. "I've looked into the allegations—about the tractor salesman—and it doesn't seem to be true."

She frowned. "Then where in hell'd she get to?"

"Who told you it was a tractor salesman? And who first told you she was gone?"

She thought awhile. "I think the kids told us she was gone. They'd been out to Deward hunting because that's where she usually was, but they didn't find her. Went back day after day for a couple of weeks before coming to us. Don't know who said she ran off. All's I remember was a tractor salesman she met at a gas station and then just up and left. Can't remember beyond that. I know I called the police. Maybe it was the police said it? Or maybe even one of the kids. I can't remember now, too long ago. You can't expect a woman my age to be holding on to all that old stuff. Didn't change the fact that me and Ralph had to pay for everything for her kids. Told 'em, when you're eighteen you are out of here. Only one worth anything was Arnold. That boy's makin' something of himself. You hear? Runnin' for state senator. Arnold got to college. Always was my favorite. Arnold…"

She took a swipe at her nose, then glared hard through those too tiny glasses that made her eyes look pulled together and huge. "If you want to know the truth about Marjory, well, let me tell you a few things about that girl. Nothing good there. Not a damned single thing. After all I did, she ran off just like her crazy mother. Always thought she'd end up in a mental hospital. The way Winnie did."

I took a long breath and promised myself I'd be gone soon.

"Not that I ever wished her a bad end—like she must've got. It was just the way they all were. Ungrateful. Even Arnold, I helped him out with some college money but you think I ever hear from him?" She shook her head and made a face. "Not a word. Not a thank-you. Not a kiss my ass. Nothing."

"What about Paul?"

She made a disparaging noise. "Don't mention that one to me. Only thing I ever heard was he got himself almost killed in some accident."

"But," I prodded. "… he lived?"

"Far as I know."

"Do you know where he is now?"

"How in hell would I? Not one of those little bastards ever come to see me. Left my house and that was that. Ralph always said we should've turned 'em over to the state and be damned to them. I was the one kept sayin' 'Oh Ralph, but it's your family.' See what family gets you? Ralph's gone and those three could be a comfort, but you think they'd call me or drop by to visit?" She shook her head, answering yet another of her own questions.

"Did Marjory have friends in the area?"

"Friends? Nobody she brought home. I had enough to do without having a bunch of kids mess up my house." She looked at me hard and shook her head. "Friends. Nobody special I remember. One girl she talked about, when she did some kind of volunteer work at the hospital. But that one went off to college and never came back." She thought a little longer. "Nope. No friends. Marjory wasn't that kind—you know, popular. Kept to herself."

I was out of questions. The tractor salesman was at least blown out of the water. No evidence he ever existed. I thought now that Paul was still alive, or had been the last Cecily heard. I knew poor Cecily had a whole bunch of ungrateful relatives and was assailed by doctors selling her off, piece by piece—which made me wonder what a dirty mouth might be worth on the black market. It had been an instructive half hour and I couldn't wait to get out of there.

I offered to push her back to her room, promising myself not to run her hard into a wall. She turned me down. I got the idea she had people to see and brag to about the woman who just came to see her, and maybe get a few pity clucks over losing her beloved niece to murder. I hoped that was all Cecily Otis would be able to wring from our meeting. It didn't cheer me any to know I'd just spoken with the woman who'd made Marjory's life hell.

I got in my car and threw my purse to the floor on the other side. Something was wrong. I looked for the things I'd laid on the seat next to me: the roses, my camera, and photos. The seat was empty. I bent down, turned my purse to see if they had fallen to the floor. Nothing. I searched the back seat. Maybe I'd moved everything and forgotten. I did that often enough. Too much on my mind.

Nothing. My camera was gone, along with the photos, and every one of the dead roses.

THIRTY-ONE

THE NICE WOMAN BEHIND the desk inside the nursing home offered to call the police for me. She was all apologies but "No," she
said, no one had come in to report anyone taking things from a car
in the parking lot. Probably because who would think it suspicious,
someone taking their own camera and a half dozen dead roses? I
turned down the police. It was no use. Whoever had done it was
far away. I could see stealing the camera—my fault, I never locked
my car. Who would want the photos? And the dead flowers? The
man at Deward kept flashing into my head. No one but that man
could have known what I had with me. But why would he care
about photos and dead roses? And he certainly couldn't have followed me. His car had been elsewhere, upstream or downstream.
He might have gotten my license number—still, what good would
that do him? Could he have called someone? Nothing was probable and nothing improbable. It was all one huge scrambled mess.

I started my car, wondering who knew I was coming out to see
Aunt Cecily. Dolly—would she tell anyone at the camp? Was Dolly

my enemy now? I had to shake my head, driving south out of the parking lot. The thought of Dolly turning against me made me sick. There was no stopping what I had to do. I had to find out what had happened to my good friend, and then what had been done to Marjory Otis. Crystalline and the other women depended on me. I depended on me. I even had the feeling that Marjory depended on me.

The cost of a new camera hit me right in the gut. I'd paid five hundred for the one I'd just lost; probably well depreciated in the four years I'd been using it. I wondered if my homeowner's policy would cover the cost of a new camera. Maybe, but if I remembered right I'd just upped my deductible to something like five hundred, to save money.

I'd buy used. Plenty of cameras on the Internet. I'd talk to Bill. Maybe there was a camera at the paper I could use, or buy. Nothing was insurmountable. No loss too great—I kept telling myself this as I thought about selling something I owned to cover a new camera, and not letting my shrinking bank account parade, like a TV crawl, through my head.

On the way home I stopped at EATS for coffee. I wanted to see if Dolly had been in and seen her family tree. If the paper was torn from the wall, I'd know Dolly had been around. But first, I wanted to drive by her house, see if she was there—though I didn't know what she would be driving with no access to a patrol car. Dolly didn't own a car of her own.

I drove past her house twice, going slow, seeing if I could spot anyone through the front windows. A car was parked in front, at the curb. An old white Oldsmobile with a rusted trunk. I figured maybe someone from the End Time cult was staying there, one of them who'd resisted Sy's persuasive car "deals." Many hadn't resisted and newer cars bloomed along 131. Sy, the used car dealer, was banking on getting his money on October 27 precisely at twelve-o-one. He was betting against the cult. I guessed I was too; though, even if I considered myself a fairly intelligent and over-educated person, I was feeling the same unspoken fear I sensed creeping through town: *What if they're right and I'm wrong? Won't I have egg on my face when the fire balls start shooting?*

With a sinking feeling, the thought hit me that Dolly might have signed over her house to the Reverend Fritch. Eugenia had said people did this kind of thing—a token of faith. There was never talk of what would happen if the world didn't end on the twenty-seventh, I'd been told. I wondered if the reverend would be long gone before then or, like others before him, he'd simply announce a new date for destruction.

I had nothing to lose. I got out of my car, walked up the steep cement steps to her door, and knocked. Inside, a voice called out, "Dolly, someone's here." I heard footsteps crossing the living room. The door opened and Dolly stood there wrapped in her robe with the wide sleeves rolled back and the hood off her very bald head. Dolly's little eyes, lost in all that pale skin, made her face look as if it were melting. This wasn't an attractive look for Dolly, who needed all the help she could muster.

She nodded but said nothing. I stepped up and pushed her aside, since she wasn't asking me in. While she took a few steps back, looking none too happy to see me, I got far enough into the living room so she wouldn't be able to throw me out without help.

That help was standing in the arch leading to a small hallway going back to Dolly's bedroom on one side and the kitchen on the other. Sister Sally, her robe more in order, looked from Dolly to me and then back. She folded her arms and waited to see what Dolly was going to do. There would be no conversation with Sally. I detested the smirky woman who, simply by her smug smile, made me feel like a lesser being.

I looked hard at Dolly. "So? What's going on? You give your house to the cult yet?"

"It's not a cult. The reverend doesn't take houses or money."

"Bull shit!" I wasn't there to play games or listen to excuses.

Dolly shook her head and closed the door—since it seemed I wasn't leaving immediately—then walked around me, brushing so close I felt the hard material of the robe against the back of my hand.

"Listen, Dolly. I think I'm owed an explanation here. I don't get what's going on. Officer Winston is coming to see Lucky tomorrow, probably to take the investigation away from us. Lucky can't see to town business and be working on Marjory Otis' death too, not all by himself. I've got no official standing. I think there's something out at Deward that has to be looked into. I took photos—remember when we were there the day I found her? Now somebody out at the nursing home in Bellaire, where the aunt is living, stole my camera, the photos, and ... ." I looked at Sister Sally, who stood behind me, listening. "Something else. When I was out there I found ..." I was just too uncomfortable, standing between them. I couldn't finish what I wanted Dolly to know.

I changed tactics. "You'd better get over to the station tomorrow afternoon, be there to talk to Winston. If you don't, well, I guess that's all I need to know." I took one step away, uncomfortable to be the sandwich filling between these two.

"What'd you find?" Dolly leaned back on the heels of her shoes and lifted her chin, challenging me—to what I couldn't fathom.

"Come to the meeting and you'll know. Only don't bring her." I pointed at Sister Sally. It was rude but I didn't care. Dolly had turned against everything in her life because of this woman. I owed her nothing, except maybe a damned good fight for Dolly's soul. Which side I was on—angel or devil—didn't matter. I might not be the most religious person on earth, but I knew good from evil and had seen plenty of both in my life. Sally and the reverend and Brother Righteous—they weren't on the side of the angels. So I guessed that would have to be me. I stood straighter and faced Sally.

"I don't know what the hell you've been feeding Dolly. She's always been a vulnerable person—needing family. You're not it. None of you. I'll tell you one thing: I can't wait until the twenty-seventh and the twenty-eighth when the bunch of you slink out of town, dragging your forked tails…"

"Emily," Dolly demanded, "leave Sally out of this. She's only trying to help…"

"Like you need help. What about the law? You're willing to let a murderer get away?"

Dolly slowly shook her head. "There will be a time soon…"

"Yeah," I scoffed, and pushed past her. "Yeah, after the world ends and you'll be sitting up there on a cloud laughing at all the writhing bodies being tortured down below. Nice group you've joined, Dolly."

I got to the door and opened it, seething. I wanted to slam the damned door so hard the whole house would shake, and maybe shake some sense into Dolly's head.

"You better be at the station for that meeting. I don't know if it will be a help or not, Officer Winston seeing you like this." I indicated the robe and bald head. "But you'd better be ready to go to work, or we've lost it. And I've worked hard. I know a lot more than we did, even might be close to the murderer. I'll tell you one thing: I'm not saying a word in front of her." I indicated Sally. "What you do with the information afterwards is up to you. You'll probably tell her. That's how much I don't trust you, Dolly. And that's how sad I am that you used to be my friend."

I slammed the door, but there was weather stripping or something in the way. The effect was weak.

The next afternoon I stopped at EATS for a pot of tea before going to see Lucky and Officer Winston. I was still fuming at Dolly. I even welcomed Cate, the old lady in the string gloves and open knit sweater over a green silk blouse, to come sit with me.

She slid into the booth.

"I think she's already signed over her house," I said.

She frowned and clucked. Eugenia brought a cup of fresh coffee to the table for her, bowing as she slid it into place. She offered to fill the creamer. Cate shook her head.

"I'd like to talk to her," she said to me.

"Dolly? Why would she listen to you? You mean because of what happened to your daughter? I think Dolly's too far gone for cautionary tales at this point."

"Still, somebody's got to do something."

I agreed with that. Somebody should be doing something. But what I had no illusion that Dolly would show up at the police station. And no illusion that we were still friends. That last thought made me sadder than the first. We'd always argued and complained about each other, but beneath that had been respect—me for her doggedness and ability to ferret out criminals, and I think she respected me because I had the education and experience she would like to have, but never had the opportunity to go after. Whatever it was, our friendship had been fun. Now, here was this bald, anonymous person I didn't know, and didn't want to know.

I looked over at the old woman with silly makeup running every which way on her face, and decided to trust her.

"Why don't you come with me to the police station, just in case Dolly shows up?"

The woman nodded.

"If she doesn't come, you can wait in the lobby and I'll bring you back here when we're done."

"And if she does?"

"I'll leave that up to you."

We had an agreement. I gave up trying to drink my tea and we left. Eugenia gave me a thumbs-up as I paid. "You'll be surprised what that woman can do for you," she whispered toward me.

I leaned in over the counter. "She never pays. She's here all the time. What's going on, Eugenia?"

Eugenia looked at the woman, then shook her head at me. "I'll let you know soon. It was ... well ... her idea to do things this way."

"She's probably scamming all of us, you realize that?"

Eugenia moved her head until her blond hair bounced and fell in tight tendrils across her forehead. "No. It's just ... well ... some day you'll understand."

"Yeah." I nodded, wondering what had happened to all these people I knew in Leetsville. Everyone was changed. They were on edge. It had to be the end of the world coming. I supposed that would make anyone bite a few nails until the threat was over.

"You hear?" Eugenia leaned back then forth, hugging herself with news. "I'm having a big 'clean out your refrigerator' dinner the night of the twenty-sixth. We're gonna get together and I'll cook whatever people bring in. No use letting all that food go to waste." She threw back her head and laughed, gathered herself together, and went on. "The night of the twenty-seventh I'm planning a big 'Whew, we made it' celebration. You got anything to donate to either dinner, bring it on in, but don't wait until the last minute. I gotta plan the menu."

THIRTY-TWO

Wednesday, October 21
6 days left

WHEN I CALLED LUCKY's name he yelled from back in his office. I took Cate with me to meet him and told him why she was there. He stood and bent forward over his desk, offering Cate his hand. They shook and she pulled her long skirt around her, then took a chair.

Lucky looked at me. "She's not staying for our discussion with Officer Winston, is she?" He turned back to Cate. "Sorry, Ma'am, but this is police business."

"She'll wait in the lobby. I'm not sure Dolly's coming…"

Lucky gave me a forlorn look.

"But if she does, Cate would like to speak to her. Her daughter got caught in a cult, over in France. Cate thinks maybe Dolly will listen."

Lucky nodded. "Hope it works. This Dolly I'm dealing with isn't anybody I ever knew. The law used to be the most important thing in her life. You ever know Dolly to make a move that wasn't right up to the oath she took as a law enforcement officer?"

I shook my head.

"You ever know her not to follow through on a case?"

I didn't bother shaking my head.

"Me either," he said, then looked beyond me.

There was a throat-clearing from the doorway. Officer Winston stood there, waiting to be acknowledged. Here was my spit-and-polish guy with the buzzed head, hat tucked under his arm, back straight. The little square-bodied officer was the picture of officialdom; the consummate cop.

He walked to the desk, introduced himself to Lucky, and bent, with a military snap of his heels, to shake hands. He nodded at me and glanced toward Cate, his eyes narrowing a little.

"This a good time …?" He looked back at Lucky.

Cate rose, knowing her part in the plan. I walked her to the lobby and saw that she was comfortable. "Might be all for nothing," I warned. "I don't think she'll come."

"I'll be here," was all Cate said as she settled her Gucci-shod feet beneath the old oak chair and thumped her hands in her lap.

First we had to deal with the Dolly thing. Lucky told Winston Dolly had taken some time off, but that he was still on the case.

"Can you handle it, Chief? You've got the rest of town business to take care of."

Lucky shook his head. "Leetsville people don't break the law. And if somebody does, everybody knows it and the shame's worse than anything I can do to them. What we mostly have trouble with here, is people passing through. Tourists ripping off the gas station, leaving EATS without paying—that kind of thing. Some teenagers—

always got them acting up. You know: smashing mailboxes, ringing the doorbell and leaving a bag of burning shit on the porch so the homeowner comes out and stomps out the flames, drinking over to Sandy Lake, open liquor in a car, speeding through town."

Winston nodded. "That's what I meant. You've got your hands full as it is."

"What's Lieutenant Brent say? He think Gaylord should take it back?"

Winston sniffed. "Brent's impressed with the progress you've made."

"That's all Emily," the chief said, nodding toward me. "She's been working on this. First it was with Dolly but since Dolly…eh…got sick, Emily's been looking into things. She's a reporter, but she's reporting everything she finds to me first."

Winston turned his tight, square body my way. He didn't seem able to turn his head without turning everything. When he blinked I noticed the tic in his left eye was back. Tic. Tic. Tic. I smiled as if waiting to be congratulated.

He turned to Lucky. "This officer, Dolly Wakowski, she's done some really good work in the past, I've heard."

Lucky nodded.

"And her reason for taking time off right now is…?"

"Personal reasons. Maybe not feeling up to par."

Winston nodded and was about to say something when we heard voices from the lobby. The chief listened, thinking he had to get out there and take care of whoever had come in. I listened too, recognizing Cate's voice, and then Dolly's mumble as she made her way past Cate.

Seeing Dolly there, in her old surroundings where she'd been so much in charge of herself and so much an upholder of the law, was like a kick in the stomach. She had her hood back and her hands up the sleeves of her robe. She looked like a gay monk—womanly but stripped down to nothing.

Winston jumped to his feet, turned, and snapped off a head-bow in her direction.

Dolly kind of bowed back but seemed confused. She looked Winston up and down—from the perfectly polished black shoes to the buzz-cut head. I could hear her draw in a sharp breath and hold it, then open her mouth to speak. She stopped. A look came over Dolly's face I'd never seen before. Maybe I would call it consternation. Maybe—since I liked words and relished what I was watching—I'd call it chagrin. Whatever it was, Dolly reached up and ran a hand over her shaved head, then pulled the hood of her robe forward. Red crept across Dolly's cheeks—chin to forehead. She nodded again at Officer Winston and took a chair next to Lucky's desk. Winston's eyes were on her, his flat face maybe astonished or—let's see: confused? I enjoyed the heck out of this encounter, thinking maybe I was in on the one thing that would bring Dolly back to her senses.

I nodded at Dolly who nodded back at me, face blank. Her hood slipped and she grabbed it before it slid off and showed her bald head again. I got the idea that at some time or other Dolly had passed a mirror and know what a cue ball she looked like.

I launched into what I'd discovered so far—touching on the two brothers: Arnold and Paul. I pulled the note from Marjory's Tarot cards and passed it around.

"Came to see her brother?" Officer Winston said, and passed the note to Dolly.

Lucky broke in to say Arnold Otis would be there the next day, after the meeting in Traverse City. "He's coming to talk to us. From the looks of this note, he might clear up a lot of things. Said he wants to see his sister's friends, too. Something about the funeral, I think. Seems a nice enough fellow. Willing to talk about the family history, he said. Just as long as it's relevant to his sister's murder. I guess, being in the public eye and up for election, he's got to be careful."

I went on about Marjory's friends and why they were in town. I got to the tractor salesman—how that theory was blown out of the water, unless whoever had spread the rumor got the job wrong and it was a fertilizer salesman or a pots-and-pans salesman.

I told them about the photos I'd taken, getting a stern frown from Winston, who opened his mouth but snapped it shut without talking.

Next came my gathering dead roses out at Deward, while there to check something I'd seen in my photos. Then, though I didn't like to admit leaving my car unlocked, I told them about the theft of my camera, the photos, and the roses while I was inside the Bellaire nursing home.

"Who'd know you had them with you? Think somebody from that cult's keeping an eye on you?"

I shuddered at the thought. "I've got no idea."

I ticked off other things I'd learned, like Paul Otis still being alive despite a bad accident a few years back. I told them what Marjory had told her friends; about her coming here having something to do with the End Timers in town, and helping someone.

234

"What was in the photograph?" Dolly asked, leaning forward.

"It looked like something there, close to where I found Marjory."

"Like what?"

"Yes, what?" Winston echoed Dolly's question and tone. He drew his faint eyebrows together. "I looked at our photos. I didn't see anything. You mean something we overlooked? Didn't collect? I find it hard to believe that we..."

I shook my head at Dolly and at Winston. "The shadows were different in my pictures. Shadows outlined something. It's a sunken rectangle. All filled in with gnarled dirt—like...I don't know. Just gnarled-up clumps of earth. And leaves. And bits of underbrush. The shape is a rectangle. Maybe I'm nuts, but it looks like a grave to me. You know, the kind you see in old cemeteries."

Dolly moved uncomfortably back and forth, as if she was having trouble sitting still. Two halves of Dolly were at war right in front of us. For just a second, I got a glimpse of the old Dolly, wanting to fire off questions and cut through the crap, straight into the heart of what we were talking about. She snapped her lips shut. I could see she was in pain, wanting more information, maybe even to take on Winston. She squirmed in her hard chair while we watched, then eventually hung her head, shook it, and stood to leave.

This was beyond me. I got up and grabbed her arm, getting her to face me. I made her look me in the eye and tell me why she was turning her back on the law and her whole life.

"What's this about, Dolly?" I gave up and yelled directly into her face, so close I could see the tiny veins in her pale blue eyes, the one eye wandering slowly off to look at something else. "What in hell's going on? Is this some split personality thing? Are there a couple of other Dollies in there?"

Lucky was up and around the desk, pulling me away from her. She looked at him sadly, then hurried from the room. All I could hope, watching her flee, was that Cate would grab her on the way out and wrestle her to the floor.

Winston sat up straight and tight, eyes away from me, and on Lucky.

"So that's what your officer's doing," he said.

Lucky nodded.

"It has something to do with this end of the world business I've heard about?"

Lucky nodded again.

"Hmm." Winston leaned back, tented his fingers at his squared-off chest, and considered. "From what I've heard, Dolly Wakowski is a fine officer. Someone to admire. Has it occurred to you this might be part of her investigation?"

"You mean Dolly undercover?" I asked, grabbing on to the hope.

He nodded, then shrugged. "No doubt Lucky, here, would be in on it. Now, about that thing you saw in your photos . . ."

Winston got us directly back to the rectangle at Deward and off the spectacle that was Dolly. I mentioned the dead roses again, and how they'd been stolen, too. I brought up the fisherman.

"You get his name?" Winston asked.

I had to shake my head. No name.

"Lots of people fish out there. Manistee's good fly fishing," Lucky said, seconded by Winston. Then they were off, the way northern men could take right off when hunting or fishing came up.

"Fish the Au Sable?" Lucky wanted to know.

Winston's eyes lit up. "Yeah. You try the pheasant tail? Good strikes on that one."

Lucky, smiling and nodding now, "Used the peacock. How 'bout the hare's ear … ?"

"Should we meet out at Deward?" I spoke up, figuring I'd be up to my eyeballs in fly fishing soon. "So you can take a look at what I found? I could pull more photos off my computer …"

The men looked at me as if I'd hit them in the head. Lucky, the first to recover from their trip into the fantasy land of fly fishing, blinked. "Not necessary. We'll go see. Right, Officer Winston? Let's meet out there—tomorrow morning, before Arnold Otis comes to town. Sound good?"

Winston agreed but was bothered by something. His bland face, with blue eyes set a little too close, his nose a little too squashed, twisted up with a question.

"What do you think's the deal with the roses?"

"I've got an idea," I said. "But … I'd rather wait until we get out there …"

He nodded. "Roses don't grow in Deward?"

I shook my head.

"Maybe somebody put them in the place where Marjory Otis died, then an animal got them and …"

I shook my head harder. "Odd animal, that would pick up flowers and carry them a couple of yards away to drop. More like they were put there on purpose—on this place in the ground."

"How about those friends of hers? The ones you said came to town? Think they might have gone there, maybe didn't know the exact … ?"

"These were old roses, Officer. Dried. They'd been there a lot longer than a week or two."

We agreed on a time to meet the next morning and I went out to rescue Cate, who said she'd tried to hold on to Dolly, but that Dolly ran out before she could stop her.

The question of who was in charge of the investigation hadn't come up. I guessed it would be the three of us. Winston might be officious, he might be unbending, he might be cranky, he might be rude—but I was used to all of that.

THIRTY-THREE

Thursday, October 22
5 days to go

No one questioned what had to be done. The rectangular imprint on the ground not far from where I'd found Marjory was evident to everyone. Maybe I'd outlined it, or cleared it completely; now it stood out so no one could miss the place that had obviously been dug over. The three of us—me, Lucky, and Officer Winston—took only a minute or two and everything was decided. Lucky called the DNR, which monitored the Deward property. There was no permit required, he was told, not if the police were looking for a connection to a murder out there. Only the presence of one of their men was necessary. Everything fell into place for the next morning: DNR man, Lucky, Officer Winston, me, and some diggers from the Gaylord post. Before we left Deward, I asked if I could invite Marjory's friends out, too. They needed to be there. I couldn't have said why, exactly, but something about this whole business made me pity Marjory—and whatever had been buried near her. It just seemed right for her friends to be present for this next step in her story.

———————

After another trip to Deward, home was a good place to be. Sorrow and I went chasing leaves and crows—especially one crow that had taken a dislike to Sorrow early last spring and made Sorrow's summer miserable with surprise dive-bomb attacks. In my garden, the pumpkins were ready for picking, big orange lumps on dying vines. The zucchini was already stored in a place Harry made down in my crawl space. He suggested that I not leave them there long but get busy on my zucchini breads and zucchini spreads right away, which I solemnly promised I would do, as soon as I figured out what a zucchini spread was, and as soon as I could figure out what I'd do with fourteen breads.

The morning at Deward had been overcast. Fitting for our task out there. I think we all had some awful dread in our mind, but nobody said it aloud. Morning would be soon enough. And though I wasn't looking forward to being there with the men digging into that place, I wasn't sure what it was I most feared finding.

After I picked the pumpkins and set them on the porch, Sorrow and I went for a long walk, checking out the late toadstools—orange, mostly—and the wildflowers sporting red berries on unbelievably white branches. Sorrow squatted along the way, missing the toadstools but making me wonder, yet again, when the heck he'd learn to lift his leg. I found patches of wild leeks, but they were too strong to pick at this time of year. In spring they'd be young and mildly flavored. Late-season leeks overpowered the taste of soups and stews. Much too oniony for me. I made a mental note of where new patches of leeks were growing—for my next year's inventory of comestibles. After only four years, I had my own secret patch of morels, my places where purslane grew, my puffball clearing, my milkweed patches, and my places of the leek. Plus recipes to go with them. Most came from Harry, so the recipe was easy: wash 'em, dip 'em, fry 'em up in butter.

Only after we got back to the house—after Sorrow stepped in his water bowl, which I cleaned up as he nuzzled me with his wet nose, needing to see what I was doing down there at his level, on his floor—did I pay any attention to the flashing message light on my answering machine.

I put my finger out to hit the playback button, then pulled it away. There was just too much going on in my head right then. At times, I went days without a single phone call. On those days I moaned about how unpopular I was and why didn't I just go back to Ann Arbor—where I had friends, and a good job, and nice clothes, and frequent trips to a hair dresser, and my nails weren't chipped, my fingers stained from digging around in the dirt or chopping the logs into kindling-sized pieces—getting ready for winter, when my little fireplace would back up the furnace if the electricity went out and the cold crept under the doors.

No time for phone messages.

I dug out Crystalline's number at the motel. When she answered, I explained what we were doing at Deward in the morning and asked if they'd like to be there.

"What do you think it is?" Crystalline asked, after explaining to the others what was happening. I lied and said I had no idea. They wanted to know what time. I told them ten-thirty. Felicia had a reading at eleven but would reschedule. They would be there.

"We've been wanting to see the place anyway. Something we feel we have to do," Crystalline said.

"Let me know if you latch on to anything when you're out there," I said. "Any impressions."

"It's a ghost town, Emily." Crystalline sounded like an old lady clucking her tongue. "Of course we'll pick up impressions."

"I was thinking more to do with Marjory. Just feelings. You know, pick up what the emotions are out there."

"Sure. We do that anyway. Can't help ourselves," she said. "What did you say they were looking for? Did you tell me already? I mean, what you're digging for?"

"I said I don't know. It could be anything, Crystalline. Or nothing."

That part wasn't a lie, what I told Crystalline. I didn't know. I might have had a sinking feeling. But I didn't know.

Back to the messages. News can't be avoided forever—good or bad.

The first caller was a woman. I didn't recognize the voice and so I didn't listen to what she said, thinking her another nice lady from the phone company or the electric company or the gas company. Or somebody wanting to sell me a timeshare in Boca Raton.

"...got it yesterday, took it home with me last night, and read for most of the night. I'm very excited about your work, Emily. Let me finish the book—I have a few things hanging—and I'll call you back. I've got some ideas. We'll talk in a few days."

I pushed the button again. It couldn't be what I thought it was. It couldn't be the agent, Madeleine Clark. She must have just gotten my manuscript. I ticked off days on my fingers. Only a day or so ago. And she'd already called.

"Emily Kincaid?" the very pleasant, soft voice said. "This is Madeleine Clark of the Pietroff and Clark Literary Agency. I just wanted you to know about your manuscript. I got it yesterday, took it home with me last night, and read for most of the night. I'm very excited about your work, Emily. Let me finish the book—I have a few things hanging—and I'll call you back. I've got some ideas. We'll talk in a few days."

I played it again. Then again. Sorrow and I did a wild dance around the room until I stopped perfectly still, went back, and played it yet again—to be certain I wasn't dreaming. No. Same voice. Same words. We danced. Who could I call? I wracked my brain. Dolly? Nope. Jackson? Nope. Bill? Nope. He was in Lansing on a story. A couple of old friends back in Ann Arbor—they'd be thrilled for me. But it wasn't a book sale. It wasn't a contract. Just another step along the way. It might still take months, or even years, to sell the book. Rapture was a little premature. Maybe I'd just hug the news to myself and surprise everyone when I could point to the framed book contract hanging on my wall. Or maybe that was a little over the top. Still, after all this time, some form of celebration had to be in order. Sorrow agreed. We sat at the kitchen table and carved one of my pumpkins into a big smiling face. I would set it at the top of the drive to grin at everyone. Let them all guess what made Emily Kincaid so happy.

THIRTY-FOUR

Still 5 days

I was almost finished with the ghost town article when the phone rang. Two hours to go before I had to get to Leetsville to meet the elusive Arnold Otis. I wanted one thing completed.

After the usual argument with myself—to answer or not to answer—I picked up.

"Emily?" It was Lucky. "Sorry to be calling you but I'm swamped here and with Arnold Otis coming to town this afternoon, everybody's been calling, wanting to drop by and say 'Hi' to him."

He gave a long, deep sigh.

"The thing is, I got a phone call from Delia Swanson's mother. You know, Bertha Swanson. Lives out there on Willow Lake Road beyond you."

"I know the Swansons," I assured him.

"Well, Bertha says Delia's been kidnapped."

"Oh no," I moaned.

"Yeah, I know. The woman's got to be seventy-six or seventy-seven years old. Who in hell would be kidnapping her? It's not like she's some heiress …"

"What else did Bertha tell you?"

"Seems she thinks it's your friend, Harry. Says something's been going on between the two of them. Which—well—that's all right, but not kidnapping."

"I think I know what this is about, Lucky."

"Thought you might. Could you do me a favor? Just get over to Harry's and see what's going on?"

I sighed, deeper than Lucky had sighed. I was supposed to be a writer, not a matchmaker, or a referee, or a cop.

"Sure," I told the overworked man. "I'll call you back."

"Thanks. Bertha's having a fit. Would you tell Delia to go on home—if she's there at Harry's—and see to her mother?"

I promised, though I had the idea that if Delia was out of that house and living with Harry, well, more power to her. At seventy-seven (or whatever her real age was), I didn't think she'd get many offers that good.

Harry let me in and waved me back to the kitchen where his usual pot of road-kill stew bubbled on the white enameled stove. Delia Swanson, all bright smiles on her round face, got up from the table to hug me and wave me to a chair.

"Want to get Emily a cup of coffee?" she called to Harry, dressed in his neat white apron over the funeral suit.

"Sure thing, Delia." Harry was all smiles. Delia was in charge. I imagined, for a woman who had tended to her mother all those years, this was a pleasant arrangement.

"And maybe some of those oatmeal cookies you baked last night..."

Harry nodded briskly and put the cookies on a cracked plate. He set them between me and Delia, on the table, then went back to the dish cupboard and pulled down two mugs for coffee.

Delia, a Cheshire Cat smile spreading over her happy face, pushed the cookie plate toward me. I took one. She took two, arranging them in front of her on the table. Perfect order. Two cookies waiting for a cup of coffee to go with them.

Harry set down our coffees and went back to stirring his stew. After a while, he turned to me. "What brings you over, Emily? Tree fall? I could come in the morning. Tonight me and Delia got to get into town. Things getting pretty serious, with the world ending and all. We don't want to miss one of those meetings out to the campground."

I cleared my throat, washing the last of the cookie crumbs down with a gulp of Harry's chicory coffee. "I kind of came to get Delia," I said.

"Oh dear..." Delia fluttered a hand to her lips.

Harry turned squarely around to face me. "Why would you want to do that?"

"Your mother called Lucky," I said to Delia, "at the police station, to say you'd been kidnapped."

"Well, of all... Mother knew where I went. And nobody forced me to come down here."

"She reported it." I shook my head, hating to be in the middle of this obviously happy couple. "Could mean trouble for Harry. I mean, if your mother presses charges."

Delia frowned hard. "That's just Mother. I told her I'm not leaving her alone, just wanted to be with Harry. I left her plenty of food—all cooked and ready to be heated in the microwave. No reason for her to get like this. Just being mean…"

"Maybe, if you went home and talked to her…"

"I was going to anyway."

"Today?"

She looked over at Harry and then back at me. "I suppose so. When Harry's stew's done. We'll go together. I wasn't going to live here. We just wanted… oh, I don't know… one time in our life."

I looked down at my cracked fingernails. This wasn't a role I relished, breaking up a Romeo and Juliet moment in the lives of these two lonely people. I finished the coffee and got up to leave. "I'll call Lucky and tell him you're going home this afternoon. If that's all right."

Harry looked to Delia and then to me. He nodded. "I'll have her there in 'bout an hour."

Delia got up to go stand at the stove. She called my name softly. When I turned she was smiling shyly, first at me and then at Harry. She took one of Harry's well-worn hands in hers and brought it to her wrinkled cheek. "Harry didn't kidnap me, you know. I wanted to come stay with him awhile. It's just… oh… you probably wouldn't understand, Emily. You're from a different time."

I thought I understood well enough. About being alone—and needing to be loved.

"What I'd like to do, right here in front of you, is to thank Harry." She looked up at him, old eyes shining, as he stood rigid and serious in his stiff suit and white apron, grizzled chin pushed down into his Adam's apple. "If the world does end in a couple of days … well … you never know the truth of these things until they happen, or don't happen. You just don't ever take the time to think about your life, you know, until you get afraid you might die. I mean … things you might have missed." She blushed slightly. "If the reverend is right and I'm going to die … well … at least I'm not going out a virgin."

THIRTY-FIVE

I WAS LATE INTO town, but so was he. At six o'clock my Deward fisherman walked in, surrounded by a retinue of men who turned out to be an aide, a publicist—or something like that—and an attorney.

There was no fly fishing hat and no leather vest, but I knew him immediately: the wire-rimmed glasses, that thick body, the slight air of condescension. My jaw dropped as he took my hand, pumped it a few times, and moved on to Officer Winston, then Lucky.

Arnold Otis, large in his expensive three-piece suit and navy tie with matching silk handkerchief in his jacket pocket, settled into a chair in front of Lucky's desk, stretched his shoulders, undid the button straining over his stomach, and looked directly at me.

"Sorry I didn't identify myself when we met at Deward." He sounded unhappy. Even a little put out. "I thought you were some ghoul out there to see where Marjory died."

I nodded, offering no explanation and no apology. If he'd been in town earlier, why hadn't he let Lucky know?

Lucky caught on right away. "This the guy you were talking about? The one you saw at Deward?"

I nodded.

He gave the politician a dubious look. "Why in hell didn't you tell us you were around? We've got a lot of questions. You could've been helpin'…"

Arnold Otis shook his head and drew in a deep, sad breath. When he spoke he looked at the ceiling, as if needing a backup. "I required time alone. She was my sister, you know."

Lucky looked uncomfortable, maybe a little embarrassed.

"I wanted a chance to go to where she died and see the place for myself. Without everyone"—he indicated me, Officer Winston, and Lucky—"in the way of my grief."

Lucky said nothing for a minute, thinking over, as I was, the man's need for solitude at a time when we were trying to find who killed his sister.

"Still," Lucky started, sitting up and resting his finger-locked hands on the desktop. I knew where he was going and cheered him silently. This Arnold Otis was used to slippery situations or he wouldn't be a politician. And he was used to talking himself out of anything. It wasn't that I didn't like him. It was the type—the kind I'd come up against often in interviews and covered at trial. You could watch in awe as they squirmed and explained away even the plainest fact, but you also knew you would never turn your back on them, or take one whole sentence at face value without breaking it down—word by word. I was going to watch this man. Lucky, as cautious as he was, seemed to have reached the same conclusion.

"I'd think you'd be interested in catching the killer," Lucky said.

"I am! I certainly am." Here Arnold leaned forward and motioned toward the lawyer. "You step in here if you think I'm over my head." The young attorney moved closer, to stand beside him.

To Lucky, Otis said, "I'm coming up to an election next month. Anything at all could be used against me—I mean my background, that my sister was into all that New Age business. Now her untimely death. I want her killer caught, but I've given up enough for my family. Jim, here, will stop the questioning at any time he thinks you're going beyond your ..." He indicated the lawyer.

Officer Winston sat forward. "Mr. Otis," he said. "If I may. You are here to help us in the investigation into your sister's death. Now, you can do that of your own free will ... ask your attorney here if you need to ... or we can work around you and make sure the press gets all of it."

I looked at Officer Winston with new respect.

Arnold scoffed, and indicated me. "You've already let in the press..."

"Emily Kincaid works with us, very closely. We're a tight-knit community. Nobody's putting anything in the paper unless we give the go-ahead."

I started to object—just a little—then figured whatever we had going was working for us, so I kept quiet.

Arnold looked at his attorney again. Jim nodded. He nodded back, and we were into the questions that had been stopping us short at every turn.

Lucky brought out the note Crystalline had found in the Tarot cards. It was encased in plastic now. He read it to Arnold, then asked if he was the brother, and who had written the note for him. The man sat in deep thought, tenting his fingers in front of his face. His eyes moved left then right, mind working hard.

Finally he lowered his hands and nodded.

"It was a friend of mine. Well, my aide here." He indicated a tall young man. The man kept his head down but nodded. "I had George write to Marjory because I'd gotten a threatening letter, telling me that my brother, Paul, was found, that he was in Leetsville, and he was going to the newspapers about what our mother had done—when she ran away with the tractor salesman."

"That might have made you look sympathetic." Lucky leaned back, watching Arnold Otis.

"Not at this level—running for state senator. And that wasn't the worst of it. The letter also said Paul had found our mother and she wanted to see me. Do you have any idea what kind of thing that would have been? My brother turned against me, and then my mother—God only knows where she's been all these years and what she's like now. Bad enough when we were small…

"And bad enough to derail me, here at the last minute. Wouldn't my opponent be happy to blow the information up, into something much bigger than it is? I couldn't take the chance."

"The note said you were afraid…" I began.

"Of course I was. They could have ruined me."

"That's it? That's why you had this man write to your sister?"

He nodded, then thought awhile. "Paul said she needed money. My mother. He said she would disappear if I gave her fifty thousand dollars."

Lucky gave a low whistle.

"You were going to meet Marjory here?"

252

He nodded. "That was the plan but she never showed up. I went to her motel and she wasn't there. I called. Nothing. By that time, I was afraid of being recognized, so I fled. The next thing I knew I got the call that she had been murdered out at Deward. And," he held up a plump hand, "might I add, Marjory hated Deward. That was where our mother always went when one of her spells, or moods, or what have you, came on her. When she would leave for days on end, that's where we found her. In a tent. Living like an animal. Even Marjory agreed that living with our aunt and uncle was at least a step up from living like our mom."

He looked over at me. "None of this is for your newspaper."

"Your bother, Paul? After so many years? Where'd he come from?" I asked.

He shrugged. "Not a clue. I heard he was in a bad accident but that was the end of him. Never heard another word until that letter, saying he was here. I don't think Marjory knew what happened either. He dropped out of sight."

"Do you have this letter from the person who tried to get money out of you?"

He shook his head. "I didn't keep it. Just having it around was unnerving; as I'm sure you can understand. I tore it into pieces and flushed it down the toilet." He spread his hands. "Sorry. I thought I had handled everything. I hope I didn't bring on her murder. I'll … I'd … never forgive myself."

I looked from Arnold Otis' aide, George, to Otis, then back. "Did your aide also steal something from my car? I mean, he seems ready to do anything…"

Arnold Otis' face turned an odd shade of white. "I beg your pardon. Are you insinuating, young woman, that I would have one

253

of my people act unethically? I find your remark close to slander. Your editor had better watch ..."

Officer Winston sat forward fast, deflecting the growing high dudgeon to come. "How are we going to tackle this one?" he asked Lucky. Lucky shrugged. "I don't think it's ours to tackle."

Winston nodded, then turned to the still-simmering Arnold Otis. "You're going to have to contact the police down where you live—is that around Jackson?"

"Flat Rock."

"Contact them and tell them someone's trying to extort money from you. It may take the FBI to find your mother, if she's still alive ..."

Arnold stood. The others stood with him, buttoning their suit jackets, taking a swipe at knife-creases in their city suits. "That's all I have to offer. I will certainly contact the authorities, when I get back. But maybe not until after the election ..."

"Aren't you afraid your mother will come forward before then? That's what the threat was ..."

He put up a hand, stopping me. "I'll have to take that chance. Just a few weeks to go. Then I'll ..."

"Years ago you told a group of young Republicans that your mother was dead."

He gave what I took to be a sneer. "You've done your research, I see. If you had political aspirations, young lady, and at the same time had the background I have, wouldn't you have tried to cover it up? That's what I did."

"Now your sister was murdered. You could be next. Whatever is going on ..."

He stopped me again. "I'll see to it. You can be assured of that. Once I am a senator I'll have the means at my disposal to look into all of this. I know—" he smiled over at Winston and then at Lucky—"you'll be relieved to be rid of this investigation. Probably have other far more pressing matters to look into. You can leave everything in my hands…"

Lucky's face was a brand-new shade of red. Winston's wasn't much better. If I could have placed a bet right then, it was that Arnold Otis had made no friends in Leetsville tonight.

We all got up and followed Otis out to the parking lot. As I opened my car door he stepped in close and rested an arm over my door.

"Emily, could I buy you dinner here in town? I'd like to talk to you—you seem to have the wrong idea about who I am. And, maybe we could call those friends of Marjory's? Have them meet us. I'd like to buy all of you ladies dinner. You've done so much… and I know Marjory's friends loved her…"

The "ladies" part alone was enough to make every hair on my head stand on end and every pore on my body swell with indignation. The oily smile would have sealed it, but I thought fast. What I didn't want to do was close a door on information this man might still have. I'd dealt with enough politicians to know getting under his protective radar wouldn't be easy. Shying away from him was, in a way, cowardly. If there was anything more he knew, he might let his guard down over dinner, maybe with Marjory's friends.

I gave him Crystalline's number and directions to EATS. He got in his big black car, said good-bye to his entourage, and gave me the high sign that he was ready to go.

THIRTY-SIX

THE HALF HOUR I sat with Arnold Otis in EATS waiting for Marjory's friends was awkward. From the moment we walked into the restaurant, the few people there, at this late supper hour of seven o'clock, eyed him. One of the old farmers I'd met at the Feed and Seed leaned back and waggled a finger toward Arnold as we made our way to a back booth. "I sure as hell know you, don't I? Seen you on the TV. Am I right?" he demanded.

Arnold switched into celebrity mode, agreeing that the man probably knew him: "Running for senator. Not in this district, but don't forget to vote next month." He shook the man's hand, then the hand of everyone at their table. He nodded left and right and all around him, then came to where Flora Coy, the town bird lady, sat. She gave him a look that wasn't the friendliest.

"I know you."

"Grew up in Leetsville, Ma'am."

She shook her head.

"You've been around."

He nodded. "That I have."

"You drive an old red Chevy?"

Arnold threw his head back and laughed. "Not that I recall."

He glanced over to see if I was enjoying this as much as he was.

He patted Flora on the shoulder and pushed on, leaving her to straighten her large, pink-framed glasses and turn to complain in a bird-like voice that she knew him from somewhere.

By the time the restaurant had settled down from having a celebrity in their midst, and we'd ordered—Arnold going with the wedge of lettuce, French dressing, and a cup of coffee—Crystalline, Felicia, and Sonia walked in.

Arnold, ever the gracious gentleman, stood and nodded the three women to seats, then grabbed an unused chair from another table, set it at the end of the booth, and sat down. He said how happy he was to meet them and offered menus, telling them to order anything. "Anything at all. I'm paying. The least I can do for Marjory's friends."

Nobody seemed hungry. Crystalline and Felicia ordered coffee. Sonia ordered a diet Coke. Arnold clucked at this, telling them that lovely women such as they were didn't need to watch their weight—surely. He threw back his large head—one hand up to hold his glasses in place—then urged them again to order. "A steak. Chicken. Whatever you want." He accepted their rejection with bad grace, saying how he wanted to do something for his sister's good friends.

This time Sonia muttered that it was too bad he hadn't done more for Marjory while she was alive. Arnold chose to ignore her and turned to Crystalline.

"I was hoping to discuss Marjory's funeral with you." He spread his hands. "There's nobody else to go to."

"We were talking about that," Crystalline said, glancing over at the other two.

"Have you come to any decision?"

Crystalline frowned and pushed her flaming red hair back from her colorful face. "We kind of thought it was up to you. As her only ... well, one of her relatives."

He nodded. "What I'd like to suggest then is that I leave it in your hands. I'll pay for everything. But, seeing that I'm the only relative, I'd like it done quickly. I thought cremation. Maybe internment in a mausoleum, down there in Toledo ..."

Felicia, who'd been looking at Arnold long and hard, snorted. "No ceremony? No memorial service? Marjory deserves better than that ..." She stopped to stare at him harder. "Anybody ever tell you you've got a bad aura?"

He frowned at her and turned to say something to Crystalline.

"You see it?" Felicia turned to Sonia. Sonia nodded.

"Too red," Felicia said.

Sonia nodded again.

"Could be about Marjory."

Felicia made a face. "I don't know. Red aura with flashes of white. You ever seen anything like it?"

Sonia slowly shook her head. Arnold, who hadn't been fascinated up to that point, lost patience.

"I need this taken care of right away. I don't want it hanging on. There's an election coming up ..."

"And your brother?"

"You mean Paul? I seriously doubt he'd care. I don't know where he is ..."

"He wrote to Marjory. Or someone wrote for him."

"That was me. I had a friend write her. There were problems…"

"Really? I don't think Marjory thought…"

"Someone trying to extort money from me."

Crystalline shook her head slowly.

"Even if Paul is really still alive, I'm afraid the problems he had when I last saw him would have worsened."

"Problems?" I asked, getting involved again.

"Much like my mother's problems. Paul was mentally ill. Even hospitalized for a while. Last I heard he was hurt in an accident. At first I thought he had died. I tried to find him but by the time I got to the hospital where he'd been, he was gone. There's no telling… mental home again. Or dead. If Paul's alive he could easily have killed Marjory. The mental illness, you know? Another thing I wish wouldn't get out to the newspapers." He looked pointedly at me.

"I'm not into muckraking," I said, bristling. It seemed this man was in the habit of directing reporters as to what they could or could not print about him. If he hadn't yet heard of freedom of the press, I hoped to get a moment or two to instruct him.

"The world's ending in a few days, you know," Crystalline said. "Maybe that should come first."

"What are you talking about?" He frowned as if exasperation with all of us was finally doing him in.

"One of the reasons Marjory said she was coming here—to settle something about this End of the World cult.

"I saw them in town," he said. "Why would such a thing interest Marjory? I really doubt…"

"She told me there was something she had to take care of with them."

"What?" he demanded.

Crystalline shrugged. "No clue. That's all she said. But I figure we've got to find out what it was. And your mother—there's a question there, too. Emily, here, has more questions."

"Could you please tell me why you can't go back where you came from and see to Marjory's funeral? I've offered..." Arnold let his disgust show. He was finished with us.

Crystalline reared back, nose going into the air. "We're not going to be a party to hurrying what Emily and that chief of police are doing. Doesn't seem you care as much as they do about who murdered Marjory."

He shook his head. "They're not involved anymore. It's all taken care of. I'm bringing in other authorities. The FBI might need to be called..."

"You know she was strangled," I asked, it just hitting me that he'd asked no questions about how Marjory died.

"I heard. A rope, wasn't it? A piece of white, cotton rope? Has anyone gotten a piece of the rope those cult people use for belts?"

I nodded. "Common rope. Could've been bought anywhere. Lucky didn't think..."

"Yes, that's a problem, isn't it? That Lucky doesn't think? I'll feel a great deal better when I have my own people working on poor Marjory's death. She deserves the best minds." He sniffed and looked over my head.

"That was one of the first things I noticed," he went on. "Those people and their end of the world business—they're kooks. Could have been any one of them. Perhaps because of that shamanism of hers. Religious people don't take kindly to things like that."

Crystalline looked as if she'd swallowed something sour. The other two mumbled and examined their thumbnails.

"I'm getting the FBI in on this right away…"

Crystalline looked over at me. "Tomorrow might settle everything, right, Emily? I mean, if you find something out there…"

"Out where?" Arnold demanded, looking from Crystalline to me.

"Deward," she answered. "The digging."

"Digging? Oh, my God! No." He moaned his surprise. "What's this about now? I thought it was settled. Lucky Barnard and that Officer Winston are out of the picture. They'd better not be messing with any evidence the FBI might want to see. What do you mean, 'digging'? Where? What I think is happening here is you and the chief of police have gone off the deep end." He stopped, staring hard at each of us, and stood.

He put his hands flat on the table and pushed the salad Gloria had just delivered aside. He looked menacingly toward each one of us. "I can see you people are determined to hurt my reputation. From what I'm hearing, I'd say maybe you're nothing but a bunch of Democrats. Or somebody's gotten to you; paying you to make my life a living hell. I'm going to say this one time. You get it? One time only. Leave me and my family alone. Take my offer to pay for Marjory's cremation, interment—whatever you want. I want it over. Behind me. If you keep getting in the way I promise you—every one of you." He looked hard at me. "You're going to regret it."

He walked off, cell phone already to his ear, angrily brushing away a proffered hand held out to shake his.

Crystalline, watching him go, called after him, "Marjory's getting a big funeral. She's got a lot of friends in Toledo. You'll see it in all the papers…"

261

She smirked over at me.

"And keep your money, you son of a bitch!" Sonia called toward his retreating back.

A buzz ran through the restaurant. Eugenia, behind her glass counter, fly swatter in her hand, glowered after the wannabe senator as if she wanted to take a swat at him.

I paid for all of us, since the good politician had forgotten his promise.

THIRTY-SEVEN

It was good to get home, kick off my shoes, grab a cup of tea, and congratulate Sorrow, with a sad sigh, for being a good boy. He hadn't pooped or peed in the house. Maybe he wasn't man enough to lift his leg yet, but he was getting the idea of not defacing the place where you ate and slept.

I sipped the hot tea and let my body sink into itself. I didn't want to think or speculate. There was something about Marjory's friends, and especially about Arnold Otis, that had drained me. I didn't eat at the restaurant. I hadn't been hungry. Still wasn't. There were times when being with too many people filled me in ways that I didn't want to feel. Maybe another reason for coming to the woods, so I could pick my times and places to be social. But that was not a choice at the moment, not with so much going on in my life.

I lay down on the brown couch, Sorrow on the carpet beside me, and put one arm up over my eyes. What I needed right then was the forest on a warm, rainy, summer day, when the trees talked to me and clouds lay overhead like the all-encompassing ceiling of a cave. I wanted to be cradled, to breathe and live without complication, but that wasn't possible. Maybe ahead—when the snow came and I had enough money to live without scrounging work, without being involved with death.

How quickly people tired me. Except a few.

The phone rang. It was Bill, back from Lansing.

"Got your October story," he said, all business as usual. "Good job. Come in next week and we'll talk about holiday pieces. I've got some ideas. Maybe you'll come up with something...?"

There was a pause. The kind of pause that happens when the subject is about to change—maybe go to a place you don't want to go, or are afraid to go. I held my breath, then broke whatever was coming in two.

"The brother, Arnold Otis, came to town," I said.

He cleared his throat. Maybe swallowing words. I couldn't think about that right then. Whatever had been about to happen made me nervous. My heart was beating faster and I had a lot of spit in my mouth. "I heard," he said. "We covered the meeting here in TC."

His voice dropped. I sensed sadness there—as if he knew a moment had passed between us that might never come again.

"He came to Leetsville after that," I finally said. "It turned out I'd already met him."

"Where?"

"I was at Deward. Checking something I found in my photographs."

"What?" He was back to being a newsman, not a friend.

"There was an oblong, or more a rectangle—dug over—on the ground. It looked ... I don't know ... odd. And very close to the jack pine where I found Marjory."

"So?"

"Well, I was kind of crawling around the space...you know, like a gravesite...when I found six very dead roses someone had laid there."

"Oh, my God!"

"Yeah. That's what I thought."

"So? Where does this Otis guy come in?"

"He came up behind me when I was on my knees. Never gave me his name. He said he was fishing the Manistee. But no fishing pole."

"You think he was there to see where his sister died?"

"Yup. But later...and I don't know if this is connected or not...I was at Bellaire, seeing Marjory's aunt, and when I came out the roses were gone, the photographs I'd printed were gone, and so was my camera."

"Hmm. Think he did it?"

"I don't think it was him. But he could have called someone. He was the only one who knew what I had." I hesitated a minute. "Anyway, we're going out tomorrow and Lucky and Officer Winston are having that rectangle dug up. See what might be there."

"What do you think it is?"

"No idea. I've got a suspicion. Otis said he thought it could be his brother, Paul, who had murdered Marjory. The guy hasn't been seen in years. In and out of mental hospitals, like their mother. There was a letter to Marjory. Crystalline, her friend, found it. The letter was from someone who claimed to be writing for Marjory's brother, but they didn't say which brother. Arnold said he'd had a friend write it for him. Something about being blackmailed by somebody he thought might be their mother or his brother."

Bill listened and said nothing.

"Or…" I went on. "It could be somebody from the End of the World group. He thinks the rope they wear at the waist is suspiciously like the rope they found around Marjory's neck."

He still said nothing.

"Lucky's coming to rely on me," I added after a while. "I'm not a cop. I don't have the first idea what I'm looking for…"

"I don't believe that. So Dolly's still with that cult thing?" He gave a low laugh. "She's such an odd cuss. That's worrying you, I'll bet."

"Well… yeah, I guess…"

"So, you'll get me the story tomorrow? Whatever they find. Do a recap of the investigation so far. Don't forget to bring in Arnold Otis. It was his sister who was murdered."

"He's going to be furious. You know the story will go out on the wire, once we print it."

"Can't be helped, Emily. You know that. We don't do favors. Not even for people close to us. That's not what news is."

I sighed heavily.

"That bad?"

"Oh, just… I don't know."

"Yes, you do."

We hung up. I first rested my hands on the phone and then disconnected it from the wall. Enough of people. Too much anger boiling around me. What I needed most was Dolly and her easy certainty, her way of stumbling along in a straight line without looking side to side. I needed her firm belief in what was there before her eyes, while I questioned everything. Too much thinking can be bad for you, I'd found, just as my mother used to say too much reading was bad for the eyes. Too much thinking kept you from jumping on moments that could change your life, and left you wallowing in self-pity. Better not to think at all.

I lay down on the couch, had my face licked a few times—which made me happy—then went to sleep.

THIRTY-EIGHT

Friday, October 23
4 days left to make amends

I PARKED ON THE track leading into Deward, beside a couple of state police cars, Lucky's patrol car, Crystalline's car, and a few others—one long and black, with darkened windows. For just a minute I sat still before getting out and going on to the ghost town to get caught in the middle of another problem, or another disappointment. Whatever was going to happen would happen whether I took a couple of minutes to figure out who I was right then or not.

I set my hands on the steering wheel and stared off into the woods. Thick, changing trees, and then the pines and firs. Deep places between them, each with only enough space to exist. The October day was temperamental, clouds then sun then clouds again; dark, moving shadows then a clear, bright blue sky. I closed my eyes but could still see the moving clouds. There was no power that could stop the moody, changeable day. No power that would allow me to understand what was happening to people around me.

I was a little sick of me at that moment—my neediness, my baseless depressions. Learning things about myself wasn't always a pleasant event, but being honest meant looking at the darkest part of who I was, as well as giving myself a pat on the back for the good stuff.

I took a deep breath and got out of the car. Voices came from farther up the trail, toward Deward. The people were already out there: Lucky, Officer Winston, someone from the DNR, diggers, Crystalline and her group, Arnold Otis and his retinue. Maybe they'd finished digging, found nothing, and were on their way out. Was I going to be relieved that nothing was found? As I walked toward the voices, I had no idea what I counted on.

Crystalline came over to greet me, throw her arms wide, and hug me close.

"This isn't going to be a happy day, Emily," she whispered as she pulled me aside. "The thing that frightened Marjory is out here. We all feel it…" She indicated Felicia, standing down the road, flat eyes wide, her expression serious. Beside her, Sonia stood with her head thrown back, eyes closed, arms and hands spread. She looked as if she might be in a trance.

Crystalline stayed close, near the two men digging beside the jack pine. Officer Winston, Lucky Barnard, and another man with a DNR patch on his jacket sleeve, watched. Off to one side, standing as if they had no part in what was going on, Arnold Otis stood with an aide and his attorney. They seemed to be sharing secrets—their heads close together, hands at their mouths.

Lucky nodded in my direction but said nothing. Officer Winston, solid and in charge, said, "Morning, Emily." He introduced me to Dave, the man with the DNR, who shook my hand.

I glanced at Arnold Otis, but he pretended not to see me. I turned my back on him and stood looking down into the hole where the men dug, shovelful by slow shovelful, swinging the dirt to the side, dumping it in a careful stream, then taking another shovelful, first one man and then the other.

"Nothing yet?" I finally asked Lucky, knowing full well if there'd been anything, he'd have said.

He shook his head. "Maybe should've brought a backhoe. Only thing is I worried about what was down there. Doing damage."

"You started earlier than you said you would," I complained.

"Had to," Lucky said. "You know Leetsville. Words been going around that we're hunting for something. I expect they'll start showing up with their shovels any minute now."

"What do they think we're looking for?"

He sighed. "One thing going around is that there's a stone buried that can stop the world from ending. Another one is that there's buried treasure. Something to do with David Ward, the guy who owned all this property."

"Oh geez," I groaned. "Isn't there enough going on for them? We don't need any more high drama..."

Lucky shook his head. "Got a murder. Got the world going to end in a couple of days. Got Dolly shaving her head. Got you trying to do her job..."

"Hit something!" one of the diggers interrupted, beckoning to Officer Winston. The other man stopped digging at the far end of the rectangle and leaned on his shovel, looking down.

Beside me, Crystalline began to moan. Her head was thrown back; her eyes closed. "It's her," she whispered. I think I was the only one who heard. "It's her. The woman. Marjory knew..."

Sonia and Felicia hurried over. They stood beside Crystalline, each holding one of her arms in support.

We moved closer. Winston bent to see where the man pointed, at something in the hole.

"Looks like cloth. Maybe a blanket," the man said. "I'm trying to uncover it. Seems to go from one end of the hole to the other."

The hole was down more than four feet. The thing they'd uncovered formed a mound, the blackened cloth wrapped around whatever was there, stretched from one end to the other. In places, the cloth was torn, or maybe rotted. It wasn't possible, from where I stood, behind the men, to make out what it was.

Beside me, Crystalline bent her head and waited. Felicia and Sonia held still, their eyes fixed on the open rectangle in the dirt.

"You see this, Lucky?" Officer Winston looked down, then over to Lucky. He pointed.

Lucky nodded. "What do you think it is?"

"No idea. Something buried, that's for sure."

"Let's let them dig the earth away. Maybe we'll know better."

I turned to Arnold Otis and his friends. They'd moved closer with the first call from the digging man and stood bent over, staring into the deep hole. Arnold's face was dark red. His eyes were riveted on the blackened cloth.

"What is it?" he demanded of Lucky, who only shrugged.

Arnold quickly turned to his retinue and whispered again.

The tall attorney came forward, talking to Lucky's back. "This is obviously something to do with Mr. Otis' family, or at least with Marjory, and he wants it stopped. We can get a court order, if you insist. You're interfering with his right to privacy..."

"Tell Mr. Otis to can it," Lucky called over his shoulder and stepped closer to the hole, peering down hard. The attorney went into a huddle with Arnold and the aide.

"Can you peel back any of that material?" Lucky called to one of the men standing up to his chest in the opening.

The man bent, leaning over the long package. He pulled at a place where the cloth seemed to be rotted almost through to whatever was beneath it.

"Don't fool with it too much," Officer Winston said. "If we have to, we'll dig it up and lift the whole thing out of there—just the way it is."

The man pulled a little more. The cloth gave easily at the far end. First one layer, then another. As he pulled away what seemed to be the last layer of cloth, I sensed movement in the woods, on the other side of the opening. When I looked up, three cult members, in their cinched robes, cowls pulled far up over their heads, faces shadowed, stood there, among the trees.

I heard a small gasp behind me and turned just at the moment when Arnold Otis and his men noticed the three figures in the woods. Arnold's face went from deep red to near black. His eyes were wide.

"Get those people out of here," he screeched and lunged forward, constrained by his aide's hand on his arm.

Lucky took a step back then stopped. He walked in the direction of the cult members, stopped again, both arms out at his sides like a traffic cop, and waited to see what would happen next.

I didn't need to see their faces to know who the cultists standing there were: Brother Righteous, Sister Sally, and Dolly Wakowski.

Arnold Otis recovered enough to yell at me and Lucky, "See, I told you they're involved. I told you!"

Lucky looked from Arnold to Dolly and her friends. I hurried to where Dolly stood, up a small, tree-covered hill.

"What are you doing here?" I demanded.

Dolly said nothing. Her hand was on Brother Righteous' arm. The arm was shaking. Sister Sally held his other arm. They weren't holding him up as much as holding him together as he moaned.

"You'd better leave," I hissed at all three. "This is police business."

"Will you let us know what they find?" Dolly whispered toward me, her thin voice wavering.

"Why? You've given up the right to know anything about this investigation," I said, enjoying that her lips withered and trembled.

"Because we need to know," was all she said.

Sister Sally put a hand out to me. "Please, Emily. Dolly is only … she is one of us and we care about those who have suffered."

"You mean the saved who will be going to the great Rapture in a few days? Or you mean the rest of us?" I hissed, too angry to be anything but cruel.

Sally hesitated, turning her round eyes on me. "Everyone. We see to everyone."

"Then go home. I'll find you. If I think it is any of your business, I'll let you know …"

They turned and moved back into the woods the way they'd come, all three walking close together, holding on to each other.

"Emily!"

Officer Winston motioned me over. Arnold Otis ran up behind us. Crystalline and her friends huddled together near the edge of the hole. I knelt, looking where Winston pointed. The digger in the hole pulled back the last of the rotted cloth. A fairly large piece came away at once, slowly uncovering something yellow beneath. Not really yellow, but yellowed, and still bright enough to shine, down in that dark place.

"It's teeth," the man said. "A skull."

"A body," Lucky said.

"That's what Marjory knew," Crystalline whispered. The two beside her were still.

"No, no ..." Arnold moaned behind me and backed away from the grave. "I told you. It was them ..." He kept backing away as he spoke, one hand covering his face, the other flailing beside him. His aide followed, speaking in low tones, soothing, I imagined. "I know who did this. I know ..."

THIRTY-NINE

Friday
4 days until the end of all time

I DIDN'T NEED TO be told it was Winnie. Something had been nudging me in that direction from the first glimpse of the shadow on the photo. I might not have the power of a Crystalline or any of her friends, but I'd had a sinking feeling that hadn't left me. It had to do with symbolism—Marjory under that particular tree.

After the body—or what was left of a body—was removed from the grave and taken to the lab at Grayling, a very tarnished gold ring was found on one of the fingers. Later that morning, Officer Winston called to tell me there was an inscription on the ring.

"'Winnie—Love of my Life—Charlie,'" Winston said, his voice reading off the words with military precision. "Not much doubt as to who she was."

I agreed there was no doubt at all. Winnie Otis had been dead all along. If only we could follow the trail backward, to when she went missing, find out who passed the word she ran off with a tractor salesman. But it was too late for that. If Aunt Cecily didn't know, there was no one else. Maybe Marjory—too late. Maybe the brothers.

"You'd better get back to Arnold Otis before he leaves town," I said. "Ask him who started the rumor about his mother running off. Did you ask him what he was talking about when he said he 'knew'? And who's the 'they' he thought were involved?"

His voice got stiff. "I've done all of that, Emily ... Ms. Kincaid ..."

"Call me Emily, please." I think I rolled my eyes, a bad habit I'd had since childhood when dealing with blockheads.

"I've already spoken to him. Well, that aide who protects him. He said Mr. Otis was too broken up at learning his mother was dead. He wouldn't come to the phone. Through the aide, I asked our questions and he said he had no idea who first said she'd run away, nor who had claimed it was with a tractor salesman. He thought it came from the police—when she was reported missing. Lucky says they have a missing person's report—filed a month or more after she was gone. There's only a notation that the case was closed. Nothing else. A dead end."

"So, what he said there at Deward, did he mean Brother Righteous? Was that what he was talking about? About him being involved? Or maybe Reverend Fritch?"

"The aide said he was insisting the Reverend Fritch's group had something to do with Marjory's death. He's got to take care of something first, before he'll say anything more—but after he's done what he has to do—he'll be happy to talk to us."

"Does he know that Brother Righteous is a mute? I mean, the man can hardly take care of himself, let alone ..."

There was a pause from the other end of the phone. "I ... eh ... didn't know that myself. I was going to go out to where that group is camped … eh … you think maybe we could go together? I mean, you seem to have some knowledge …"

We agreed to meet that evening, six-thirty at the campground. It was the earliest Winston said he could get over from Gaylord.

And that was that. Now I knew why Marjory was afraid to go to Deward. She had to have known her mother was buried there. Maybe Winnie's body even explained why Marjory was killed—to cover up her mother's murder. But why so many years later? And why, unless she killed her, had she never told anyone? Too many questions. My head hurt, but the questions wouldn't stop.

Why had Dolly and those cult members come out? Why was Brother Righteous, or Sister Sally, interested? There had to be a connection between Marjory, Winnie, and the Reverend Fritch. Did Arnold know what that connection was? If so, why hadn't he told us? Lord, how I wished I could put everyone in a room together, throw out accusations, and have somebody confess. Life could be so much easier if I could write it instead of live it.

―――――

I called Bill with the story of the exhumation of Winnie Otis. "Two murders," I said, and filled him in on Winnie's body being found next to where her daughter had lain.

"A lot going on. Think you can handle it?"

"Think so," I lied, and hung up.

Jackson called. Since I wasn't doing manuscript pages for him, he didn't call as often. I was almost to the point of missing him. At least he didn't bring me dead bodies and old tragedies. Well, some—all those Chaucer people on their pilgrimage.

"I'd like to take you out for a drink on Sunday." He had a slight touch of hesitance in his voice. "To make up for Bill's dinner party…"

"Have you asked Bill?"

"No. I thought maybe we could just talk, the two of us, have a quiet drink together…"

"Talk about what?"

"Just… you know… talk."

"Ok. Where? When?"

"In town. Maybe the Blue Tractor. Eighth and Union."

I almost groaned. Of course it would be me taking the long drive. "Five o'clock?"

I hung up. I had a date.

Later, in town, the vestibule at EATS was packed with people. I thought there must be a line again, maybe the End Timers back for a nearly last supper. But these were townspeople. They crowded the small space, standing with their backs turned to the door.

I gave Gloria, who stood among the rest of the Leetsvillians, a confused look. She made a face and pointed to the wall where one of Eugenia's genealogy papers fluttered.

A picture of Cate, the odd old lady Eugenia had taken under her wing, hung above the cigarette machine. A nice, if grainy, picture, from an era when she was young, but recognizable—well dressed, hair swept up into what looked like a chignon. I blinked a few times, not getting it. I turned back to Gloria. She nudged me with her elbow and said, "Read it, Emily. You'll never believe…"

I read the neat typing beneath the old photograph.

Catherine Thomas, it read.

I knew the name. I'd seen it recently...

Dolly's grandmother.

The news knocked me back into people standing behind me. Gloria put a hand on my arm. "Eugenia knew all along. She found her through genealogical research. Remember, she told Dolly she was going to do it? They've just been waiting for the right time. With Dolly, that never seemed to happen."

"For God's sakes, Gloria," I was disgusted with all of them. "The woman's been here for a couple of weeks."

"They were waiting. And now, with this cult business she's got herself into...well...ask Eugenia. Never was the perfect moment."

"And this is? And the right way? Somebody's going to go running out there and tell Dolly, and then the crap will hit the fan..."

Gloria nodded. "Nobody's got nerve enough to be the one to break the news. She'll probably have to walk in here herself..."

"And?"

"Well, I don't know..."

"Sure you do. She'd tear down this whole place, board by board. That's what she'll do."

Gloria shrugged. People around us added comments, about Dolly, about Cate, and even about Eugenia and her patience and how she'd been taking care of Dolly's grandmother.

"Personally," Flora Coy, beside me, said, looking up through her thick glasses. "I think somebody better tell Dolly soon. Not a lot of time left to any of us, you know. With the world about to end and all."

"Oh, Flora, not you! You don't believe that preacher," I groaned.

"Ernie Henry and some of the others say we gotta be out there Tuesday, just in case."

"Like you would miss it, if you didn't show up?"

She clucked at me. "Now Emily. This isn't the time for blasphemy. You know for certain we've got any more than a few days left to live? You got an answer? If you do, I'll just stay to home and take care of my birds."

I had to shake my head—but very slowly, more exhausted than done in by her argument. No answer. Common sense wasn't enough, not in the face of this enormous uncertainty.

"Well, there, you see?" she said. "I'll be out there Tuesday morning. Same as you, I'll bet."

Others around us turned and nodded.

"Somebody's got to tell Dolly," I groused, hoping for a volunteer.

"Nobody's seen her in days," Gloria said.

"Yeah," Jocko Whitney, owner of the discount food store, said. "Heard she was there when they found Winnie Otis in Deward. And, you know what else? Heard there wasn't a magic stone buried after all."

"And sure as hell no treasure," Jake Anderson, the tall, thin owner of The Skunk Saloon, added, disgust at a lost opportunity thick in his voice.

I worked my way through the marveling crowd into the restaurant. Eugenia, behind her glass counter, handy flyswatter in her hand, looked hard at me. I would save her for later. It was Cate I wanted to see.

The old woman sat in her usual place. Her black, lace-gloved hands were wrapped around a white coffee cup. Her wild hair sported

280

a kind of tiara—a few bright stones winking out from her head of white hair. Cate saw me coming. She gave a weary nod. I didn't know if it was a "yes," telling me what hung in the vestibule was true, or if it was an attempt to hide.

I sat down without asking, ordered the meatloaf from Cindy, the only waitress actually working, and let out a deep sigh.

"Is it true?" I asked.

She nodded. "Eugenia found me. Since Delores was little and they took her away, I didn't know what happened to her. My daughter, well, what I told you was the truth. I don't even know if Audrey's alive or dead. But here's my granddaughter. If I'd known Audrey was going to throw her away, the way she did, I'd have taken her myself. I'd have been glad to have Delores. Couldn't get Audrey to say a word about her. I guessed maybe the baby was with her, there in France. Like maybe they took in her and the child. Still, I should have tried ... something."

I nodded, completely out of pity for anyone. All I could think of was Dolly hearing this news. No preparation. Just that she had a family—at last.

"Eugenia shouldn't have done it this way." I lifted my chin toward the vestibule and the people trickling in. "You should have gone to her."

Cate shook her head. "Whatever's happened to Delores, it's changed who she might have been. Eugenia says any way we tell her there's going to be an uproar."

There was truth in that statement. Uproar was what we were going to get.

I finished my plate of meatloaf, set in front of me in a record four minutes' time, persuaded Cate to come with me, and headed over to Dolly's house.

The little white house had the look of being empty. It had that dark-window, old-newspapers-on-the-stoop look that signaled no one was home.

I could only think of one other place to go. Since I was meeting Officer Winston there anyway, it seemed the place I was meant to be. Cate and I were off to the campground.

FORTY

Still only 4 days before the end

THE CAMPGROUND WAS MORE crowded than it had ever been before. Four days before the end of the world and people were coming from everywhere. A parking place wasn't easy to come by with only tight spots left between vehicles. There were license plates from as far away as California, some from Canada, many more for East Coast states, and then the South. Trailers and tents and RVs were stuck wherever there was an open space. More and more bald people hugged cowled robes around their bodies, even little children, walking along, tripped on the too-long, white ropes tied about their small waists.

I took Cate's hand. Best not to lose her now.

It wasn't time for Officer Winston yet. I wanted to take care of our business with Dolly before he got there. This was separate from the investigation. This was about Dolly's life. I'd known her for a couple of years, but I had no clue what her response to Cate would be. Dolly was full of surprises, like this cult thing. I would

283

never have picked her out as religious, or even mildly superstitious, but here she was, as anonymous as the others, waiting for the world to crumble around her.

With everyone dressed the same, it was impossible to tell one person from another. I bent to look at faces under hoods. Most glared back at me. I held tighter to Cate's hand, going slow so she wouldn't trip. We headed to the open area and the stage. People milled about everywhere. We pushed through. Behind me, Cate looked tired, and more than a little concerned about the crowd.

"We'll find her. I know she's here," I said, urging her on, over the uneven ground in her down-at-the-heels, fancy shoes.

We rounded one end of the raised stage and were stopped by two large figures, robed as all the others. I stepped to one side, and then the other. They blocked my way deliberately.

"I'm looking for Dolly Wakowski," I said, peering up into a face I didn't know, hadn't seen before.

"Not here," one of the men said.

"Yes, she is," I countered and pushed at a bulky body. Broad shoulders closed the space between the men, pinning me there. I stepped back, almost running into Cate, and looked into two set, indistinguishable faces.

"The cops are on their way out here. You let me talk to Dolly or they're going to shut this place down for overcrowding, for allowing people to live in dangerous conditions, for sanitation problems..." Everything I could think of poured out.

The men weren't fazed by my threats. They stood like a brick wall as I searched my brain for something more dire—maybe child abuse complaints, kidnapping. I didn't care. This time things were going to go my way.

"It's ok." Sister Sally stepped from behind the two men. Another figure, hood lowered, arms up into the wide sleeves of her robe, stood just behind Sister Sally.

"What'd you want to see Dolly for?"

I was too damned mad to talk to Sally. She'd done enough to keep me away from my friend. I was there to do battle.

"For Christ's sakes. Is that you, Dolly?" I said to the shy, bowed woman behind Sally.

Cate moved closer. I sensed her fear. The thought flashed through my head that this could have been the way she'd last seen her own daughter—being sheltered by a cult. Those memories couldn't be happy ones.

Dolly put her hand out toward the two men, then motioned them away with a flap of her fingers. I recognized the signal: Dolly taking over, in charge. At least that much was left of who she'd been.

Dolly flipped her hood back with a toss of her head and leaned forward, looking me hard in the face. "This better be good," she growled.

The men disappeared into the crowd around us. Sister Sally stayed at Dolly's side, following us to one of the picnic tables in front of the big RV. Dolly hitched up her robe and threw one leg over the seat, settling herself there. I thought I caught a glimpse of blue uniform pants but I must've been wrong. Cate and I sat across from her. Cate rode the bench side saddle. Sister Sally moved away, but not too far.

"I've told you I've got my reasons for staying out here," Dolly leaned forward and hissed, ignoring Cate sitting beside me. "I don't want you interfering. We got four more days to get through."

Cate leaned forward. I could see she wanted to reach across and grab on to Dolly's hand, but she restrained herself, her bent hands fluttering in her lap. "You didn't sign over your house or anything to this man, this Reverend Fritch, did you?" she asked.

"The man's not like that," Dolly snapped. "Hey, I've seen you in EATS? You're new around here, aren't you? I was going to have a talk with you before … all this other stuff came up. Sure started hanging on to Eugenia. I hope there was no … what do you call it … ulterior motive? Like scamming people …"

"Dolly," I put my hand on hers, stopping her. "Cate is Catherine Thomas."

Dolly winced, then pulled back. She thought hard, raised her chin, looked at Cate, nodded and went back to thinking again.

"Catherine Thomas," I said. "Your grandmother."

This time Dolly frowned and wound her face up into an odd knot, all caught at the middle, around her little nose. "So *this* is the scam?" She gave a snort and looked away from us. "It was on me the whole time? How do you like that?"

"No scam," I said.

Cate leaned in as close as she could get. We both saw this wasn't going well. Dolly was pedaling as fast as she could mentally pedal, backing away, coming up with anything she could to deny that family was finally right there in front of her.

"Your mother was my daughter, Audrey. I'll tell you about her, Delores, if you'd like." Cate laid a small photograph in front of Dolly, against the bare wood of the table.

"That's her," Cate whispered.

Dolly's hand came slowly up to touch the old photograph. Her fingers closed around the picture and held it there, against the table, as Dolly stared down at her mother's face, then over toward the back of the stage, one eye slipping off slightly as the other lost focus.

Dolly looked at Cate then slowly shook her head. "I don't need no damn family now. Been doing fine by myself all these years ..." Her hand closed tighter on the photo.

"Dolly," I said. "Cate didn't know anything about what happened to you ..."

"I would have taken you to live with me if I'd known," Cate said, her voice low and hurried. She drew her black shawl up to her neck, against the chill. Dolly's hand opened slowly. She looked down again, into the face of Audrey, her mother. Her small, rather homely face didn't crumple so much as melt into the kind of longing other human beings shouldn't ever have to see. I wanted to put my arms around Dolly, just hold her and tell her this was good, that she finally knew where she'd come from. Not just foster homes. Not just a pawn of an unworkable system, but from a woman, out of another woman. A person with a name and a history.

Dolly swallowed hard and glanced toward Sister Sally, who watched us. She pulled her leg back over the bench, thumped her fists on the tabletop, and got up. No one said anything as she stood, stretched, then drew her cowl back over her head. The photograph wasn't on top of the picnic table. It was either still in her hand, or slipped into a pocket. Her face was blank and under control.

"Come on, Sally," she said. "We've gotta get inside. They'll be coming out soon." They walked off toward the RV.

With no choice left us, Cate and I went to stand beside my car, me thinking the yellow Jeep would be easy for Officer Winston to spot among all the old pickups. I kept Cate talking about everything but Dolly, going over the weather, the parking problem, the crush of people—anything, until I'd figured out, in my own head, what had happened back there.

Officer Winston, in his blue and gold state police car, arrived exactly at six-thirty. He was nothing if not a man of his word, and a man dedicated to keeping his life in precise order. He nosed his car in behind two pop-up campers, got out, and nodded first to me and then to Cate, who asked to wait in the car. Her face was drawn, dark circles under her eyes. I helped her into the front seat and made sure she was all right.

"Just tired," she said, smiling wanly up at me. The old bravado was gone. I couldn't imagine being her at that moment. Two children—off into cults, to be absorbed, made impersonal, made into robots afraid to love their own mother.

"We have got to speak to that Brother Righteous," Winston said as I hurried along beside him, figuring he had to have been in the military. Though he was a squat little guy, his stride was wide. He out-loped me as we made our way back toward the open space and that RV. "And the other one. That Reverend Fritch."

"I think they're getting ready to start a service…" I said, out of breath.

He nodded. "Won't take long."

"I wouldn't count on seeing either of them. They've got a few thousand people out here. Everybody guards Brother Righteous. The guy seems special. He starts the revivals. Kind of like a wordless cheerleader. I doubt…"

I was right. Winston knocked on the RV door and was told to leave.

"Tell them both I'll be back in the morning. If need be, I'll get a warrant. That Brother Righteous is going to talk to me ..." Winston must have realized what he was saying at that point. He backed off. "Well, somebody's got to know sign language. I mean, they're going to have to bring Brother Righteous in ..."

The door closed in his face. Winston was furious but kept the lid on.

"That's all right," he muttered. "I'll be back tomorrow morning. I'll get a warrant ..."

"Don't wait too long," I warned. "After Tuesday they'll be gone."

Winston gave a kind of horse laugh. "You mean with the world ending? Very funny."

I stopped, and then gave him a hard look. "No, I mean the people will be leaving Tuesday. The Reverend Fritch's going to have his hands full. Can't see them hanging around much after noon, if nothing happens."

We fought our way through the crowd gathered in the clearing, in front of the stage. The stage lights were on, overhead bulbs buzzing. Hymns blared from the loudspeakers as before. Winston pushed his way ahead of me, through the throng.

All I wanted to do was be where I could hear nothing but quiet. My mind was still torn between pathos and being happy over my recent news; between wanting the cult gone and needing to know who killed Marjory, and now her mother. All these people were in my way—between me and a place where I could think. I didn't mind pushing; didn't mind the glares I got in return. I stopped at one point, trapped between two large families. I searched for a pathway through the pilgrims. Off to our right, there seemed to be an open aisle where people jockeyed for standing places then moved quickly when they spotted a better vantage point.

Winston saw the cleared path at the same time I did. We hurried together, staying close so as not to be separated and maybe lost in the crowd.

As I passed one man, not in a robe but in a fishing jacket and slouch hat, I looked up. The glint of a bare lightbulb reflected off the man's glasses. Winston kept me hurrying on but I was sure I knew that hat, and that jacket. I pulled at Winston's arm, stopping him finally, and yelled the name of the man behind us. I pointed, wanting Winston to witness that he was there, but the man was gone. Robes and cowls had filled in the spaces. Winston shrugged and pushed on, getting us back to where we'd parked our cars.

Inside my Jeep, Cate slept with her gray head back against the seat, her worn face troubled. There didn't seem to be peace for Catherine Thomas, any more than there'd ever been peace for Deputy Dolly Wakowski. I got in my car as quietly as I could, shut the door behind me, and headed back to town.

FORTY-ONE

HOME FELT DIFFERENT FROM the moment I unlocked the door. Something in the air, a different kind of energy, as if a good friend had been here and left behind good wishes.

I loved the feeling—as illusory as it was.

Sorrow danced himself silly out the screen door to the first spot on the driveway he found to squat—unfortunately it was beside my car, but, I asked myself, what did that matter? In the whole scheme of things—with the imminent end of everything quickly coming upon us—what was a little pee running toward a tire?

The feeling of someone there with me was so strong I had to check the bathroom, the bedrooms, and Sorrow's screened-in porch before I was convinced there was no one in my house.

My next thought was the answering machine, maybe a good voice on it, telling me I'd won the Publisher's Clearing House million-dollar prize; or the guy in Nigeria really was going to put money into my bank account. I had myself well amused by the time I pushed the button showing only one message.

I knew the voice. My stomach dropped; my heart dropped; my chin quivered—here it came, an in-person rejection.

Madeleine Clark—in that high-pitched, languid voice, speaking as if expecting me to pick up at any moment. "Emily Kincaid? Madeleine Clark here. I've finished your manuscript and would very much like to represent you and *Dead Dancing Women*. I need to talk to you, of course, but I'll be in London for a week. What I'd like to do, in order not to hold up anything, is return the manuscript with edits and suggestions for strengthening the story. It might require some work...well...you should have it by the middle of next week. I'm looking forward to representing you and hope our relationship will be a satisfying and successful one. I'll call when I get back from London. I have ideas, where the book should go. A couple of editors I know would be perfect for your book..." Her voice trailed off, ending with a faint "bye-bye."

I played it again. Then again. Then again. After that I leaped into the air, pumping my fists at the ceiling and screaming. Sorrow leaped and barked with me. This was it—the next step. All I had to do was rewrite parts of the manuscript...

With a thud, a new thought struck me. What if Fritch was right? Wouldn't that be the cruelest cut of all—to taste success and have it stolen by four guys with flaming swords? That part of what was going on had to be put out of my mind. I just wasn't going to go there. This was my chance. What kind of god would dangle that before my nose then stick his/her tongue out as it was snatched away?

What I had to focus on was getting back to work on the same manuscript I'd been working on for over a year and make it better, even though I'd thought it was perfect as it was. That brought me down with another jolt, like Mary Poppins at her uncle's tea party.

More work—but who cared? I had an agent! She liked my novel. She was going to sell my novel.

This wasn't the kind of news you kept to yourself. I picked up the phone. I would call Bill. But I couldn't. I'd failed the friend test, or whatever line we'd almost crossed the evening he got back from Lansing.

Jackson? He would turn it around to be about him. This wasn't something he would celebrate. I'd probably get asked again to recommend him to Madeleine Clark, then get blamed and hear what a terrible agent he'd heard her to be, if she dared turn him down.

Dolly wasn't even in the picture, though I had the feeling she would have been happy for me. First thing she'd do would be to claim she'd known it all along, that it was her who kept encouraging me, and if I'd only listened to her in the first place I could have saved myself a lot of my goofy agonizing.

I sat on the floor, folded my legs under me, took Sorrow's head in my hands, and stared directly in his face. He blinked and rolled his eyes. "Did you hear my news? Isn't it great?"

He lifted his head, trying to get free of my hands. I took that for a "yes."

"Just a little more work, Sorrow. We can do it," I whispered and buried my face in the top of his curly black head. "We can do it. You just watch."

He groaned and hit the floor. He stretched his legs out, and closed his eyes. I sat, patting his head as he went to sleep, figuring that though he was my best friend, he was just a little bored with exuberance, and maybe not quite as ambitious as I.

FORTY-TWO

Saturday, October 24
Ready, set, 3 days to go

THREE DAYS UNTIL THE world was going to end. I spent the day cleaning my house and doing laundry so I'd have more than one holey, purple thong to wear—just in case. I changed the sheets on my bed though it wasn't their week to be changed. I got a ladder from the shed and wiped off the ceiling fan, then took a moldy cheese from the refrigerator, then cleaned out the dryer. It wasn't that I thought my cleaning would matter or that I was sparing myself harsh judgment due to the cleanliness of my lint trap; still, I would be a liar if I said I wasn't a little nervous about losing this new world I was coming to love.

Like everyone else in Leetsville, I was on edge. When I closed my eyes, I pictured flames and fiendish faces. Every dark pit and nightmare from childhood came back to plague me. I wasn't nervous about the state of my soul—it had no true state, and if it did I didn't have a clue what that state might be. I was more afraid of facing pain. Even more than me, I worried about Sorrow, out snapping at dead ferns along the path down to the lake. He was only a pawn in this whole big prophecy, nothing to say about anything, and probably with a soul as big as mine, if not bigger—or no soul and the whole thing would end in a flash for him and he'd never be the wiser.

Winston called midday to say he'd gone back out to the campground. Both men weren't available but he would keep trying. "Something going on I don't understand ..." he said.

"Well sure, the world's going to end."

"No." I could almost see him shaking his head. "Something else. Can't find that Arnold Otis. Even his aide says he hasn't seen him. That's three men I can't seem to locate. It's a real puzzle, Emily. Don't you get the feeling when we have them all together we'll know what's going on?"

I had to admit that I did feel both murders were connected in some way to the Reverend Fritch. I just couldn't say how.

My house was clean with nothing much left to do. I lay down on the sofa under an afghan and read my new P. D. James. Later, I picked out clothes to wear to the Blue Tractor, in town, found an egg expired only a few days, boiled it, salted it, and sat down to dinner with half a bagel and the boiled egg rolling back and forth on my plate.

———

Sunday dawned gray and blustery. The weatherman predicted sunshine later that afternoon, but at nine a.m. the trees whipped back and forth, leaves blew in circles, limbs fell in the woods, and rain pelted my windows.

I stepped out to the deck, bracing myself as wind tore at me. I wore only an old sweater over flannel pajamas. The smell of rain was in the air, and the feel of fine mist on my skin. It was a transitional morning—fall and winter in battle. I hugged my arms to my body and was going to go back in when I heard the cry of a single, lonely loon come from down at Willow Lake.

I'd thought they'd all gone for the season. But there it was, that familiar melodious swinging up and down the scales, the two-toned hurrah. I was the luckiest woman alive—to hear the last call of the loon, to share this moment with him—he on his way south for the winter; me staying put, there to greet him in the spring. The thought brought tears to my eyes, from joy to sorrow and then regret. Damn, I thought. What if all of this did end, the way the Reverend Fritch predicted? Some day it would. Everything ended—that was why everything came into being.

I hurried in. I had a freshly washed quilt to snuggle under and my P. D. James to finish. I had a few hours to spend exactly as I wished to spend them. Wasn't I the most fortunate of women, at this precise moment, in this precise place, being precisely who I chose to be?

FORTY-THREE

Sunday, October 25
2 days

THE PROMISED AFTERNOON SUN never materialized. The wind was still raw; the drive to town rocky. Traverse City was empty as only a resort town can be on late fall afternoons. I'd never been to the Blue Tractor Cook Shop before. My budget didn't lend itself to solo drinking binges.

Jackson—and Regina, his assistant, whom I hadn't expected—were seated at a high table in the wood-walled bar, glasses in front of them. A few early diners filled other tables.

Jackson stood and enveloped me in one of his bear hugs. I nodded to Regina, who sat next to him, then hopped up on the other side of the table. I ordered a glass of wine. To celebrate this new place I was in, I made the wine a chardonnay. Not exactly a major break with habit.

Jackson threw an arm over Regina's shoulders, pulling her clumsily in close to him. "I thought this might be the perfect way to get to know each other better. Regina is the perfect assistant. She knows everything about my work—including my ups and terrible downs."

He hadn't mentioned this goal, this "get to know each other" party.

I smiled at Regina, who frowned at Jackson as she shrugged out from under his arm.

"Not this new book, Jack," she said. "You haven't told me a thing about it."

"But I'm telling you both now. You and Emily. My two best girls—together."

The wine came. I buried myself in the glass to keep my mouth busy.

"Here's what I have so far," he went on, not noticing that I wallowed in wine. "It's the mystery I mentioned. Maybe you could tell me if I'm on the right path, Emily. You know, of course, that this will be a literary mystery. Not one of the lighter things, such as you write. Not that there's anything wrong..."

I bared my teeth at him.

"You see." He cleared his throat and leaned back, looking off as if watching his story unfold. "There is this very fine young man. Probably from Bostonian aristocracy. He will fall in love with an older woman."

He stopped speaking and looked from me to Regina, his eyes growing wide with the pearls he was about to drop before us. "Here comes the twist. The older woman is a widow, the widow of his late uncle. What I'm thinking here is that it will slowly be revealed that she murdered the uncle, and is perhaps preparing to murder my young man. There will be all manner of what you might call 'subplots' along the way and..."

I looked over at Regina. She was young, still, maybe she'd noticed what I'd noticed. She gave me an open-mouthed, confused stare.

"Sound familiar?" I asked, trying to put pieces together.

"Please!" Jackson laid his fingers against his forehead, then shook his head.

"No. Really, Jack. I've heard that plot before."

He made a scoffing sound deep in his throat. "There are only so many plots in all of literature, Emily. Perhaps, in another context, in another..."

"Noooo..." I dragged out the word, my brain fumbling to come up with a title.

Regina frowned over at me as Jackson downed the rest of his wine in one long gulp.

"I thought you'd be happy for me—that I've come up with such an original idea." He held his glass up, getting the waitress's attention. "After all, it's you, Emily, who does things like that—rewrites old stories. I can understand a twinge of jealousy, but please don't project your faults on to me. I'm sure a book like mine has never been attempted before. Maybe I shouldn't have brought this up to you. I know how disappointed you've been in your own work..."

It was at that moment that Regina's face lit with the answer. The same time my brain spit it out.

"*My Cousin Rachel*," we said in unison.

Having been where Jackson was now, I sympathized immediately that he'd settled on an old plot from a well-known mystery. But to tell the truth, I enjoyed myself far too much.

Jackson's mouth hung open. He had his *I know you two are wrong* face on.

"Daphne du Maurier," I said. "Came out in the nineteen fifties, I think. Maybe earlier."

First he gaped at me. Then he shook his head. Then he smiled his belittling smile, eyes half closed, chin up.

"You're both teasing me."

"No, Jack," Regina sat forward. Her dark hair framed her face. "Emily's right. I read it not too long ago, in an English Mystery course I took at Michigan."

He frowned. "You don't have to pull one of those female solidarity things on me, Regina. Perhaps I should have asked a male mystery writer about this; a real writer like my friend, Aaron. He would recognize something very new in the genre …"

"Write it," was all I said as I looked around for a waitress and a second glass of chardonnay.

"I thought you could help …"

I shook my head. "You don't listen."

"Perhaps if I get some of the story written. The first five or six chapters. You could read them. I'm sure you'll see that though the storyline might be similar—my approach will be very different."

I shrugged, dreading a return to critiquing his work—futile job at best. "I won't have the time for a while. I'm beginning a new novel of my own …"

He blew away my words with one brushing hand.

"You're always writing a new novel. Surely you'll have time. I mean, it's not as if the world is clamoring at your door …"

Here was one of those supreme moments in life we all wait for but don't often get. I wasn't about to pass up this perfect time. I smiled, enjoying my long smile as if it were licorice. I shook my head—so sadly. Ah, poor Jackson, he had no idea how I was going to lay waste to his ego.

"But the world has beaten a path," I leaned forward, and waited, smiling wider, letting the possibility of what was to come sink into his head.

"I have an agent. Madeleine Clark called. She's excited about my mystery and wants to represent me."

I wouldn't say he fell apart, more that he froze. His eyes took on the vacant look of someone hurriedly thinking, wheels spinning faster and faster. You could almost smell burning rubber. He sat very still then looked at Regina and back to me.

"Well … my goodness … I must say …"

"Just say congratulations," I prompted.

"Of course. Congratulations. I couldn't be happier for you …" He looked off to where a party of late tourists sat eating quietly, then back to me. "I suppose she wants changes, they always do."

I nodded. "She's going through the manuscript now and sending it back with suggestions."

"Ah ha—yes, suggestions. That's what they all say and then they reject the book after you've worked so hard." He clucked a time or two at me as he shook his head in sympathy.

"I doubt that will happen in this case, Jackson. She's excited about my book."

He nodded. "Yes. Of course she would be. I imagine you are very good."

He pulled himself back, blinked a few times, took a deep breath, then smiled as broadly as I was still smiling. "So, moving on … I have news, too."

I waited, almost afraid to hear what he'd come up with by way of retribution.

He looked around until his eyes fell on Regina, who leaned back away from him.

"Why... the reason I really wanted you here today... well... I'm... I mean, I'm about to propose to Regina. I thought it nice if you..." Even he had to gulp getting the words out.

"Who?" Regina and I asked together.

"Regina," he shook his head sadly at her. "Why, the two of us, of course."

"Huh?" Her eyes were bigger and rounder than ever, and utterly uncomprehending.

"You know I've been preparing to ask."

"Come on! We've never talked about anything..." Her voice had a valley girl's "As if'" buried in it.

He took her hand in his and held on tight, though she tried to pull away. "You see, Emily? Like you, I'm full of surprises."

That wasn't all he was full of, I told myself.

I nodded, then looked at the very shocked, and not happy-looking, Regina, who sat upright, tight, and angry.

"I'll look forward to the wedding," I said, smiling at both of them, bestowing my heartfelt blessing. "I assume there will be one."

"Yes, yes, of course. We'll be planning..."

"Shit!" was all Regina said, and knocked back the last of a strawberry daiquiri.

I excused myself, telling them I had a book to write. I got up, giggled a demented giggle I tried to turn into a burp, and walked away, glancing back only once to see them arguing vigorously, Regina's pretty face a mask of confusion.

FORTY-FOUR

Monday, October 26
1 day to go

ALL I HAD IN my refrigerator was a package of American cheese slices and a cucumber. I wasn't going to go to Eugenia's Clean Out Your Refrigerator party empty handed so I stopped at the IGA and picked up a package of hamburger and two bags of frozen vegetables to chip in.

The party was in full swing when I got there. People from Leetsville and people I'd never seen before. Nobody was in robes with cowls and ropes, so I figured the real End Timers were tending to other business.

The restaurant was packed—inside and outside. The day was chilly with the smell of rain coming from the west. Leetsvillians stood in the parking lot, plates of food in their hands. They leaned on cars or stood with feet planted wide. The women kept calling their children close to them. Nobody laughed. Voices were kept low. This wasn't the kind of party where people expected to have fun. It was just Eugenia's way— and probably most of Leetsville's way—of dealing with nerves, and that nagging fear that the Reverend Fritch might be right. What they were doing was what Leetsvillians always did—share their food with everyone, share their trepidations, and share companionship in times of stress.

I pushed my way in the front door, got through the crammed vestibule, and across the restaurant toward the kitchen. Eugenia met me at the swinging doors with her hand out for my contributions. She frowned at the hamburger—obviously just purchased— and the two bags of frozen corn.

"Didn't quite get the spirit of the party, did you, Emily?"

"I didn't have anything in my refrigerator," I told her. "Unless you wanted a cucumber and cheese slices."

She shrugged. "You scared?"

I gave her a smirk and looked around for Catherine Thomas.

"Over there," Eugenia pointed with the hamburger, reading my mind.

"How's she doing since meeting Dolly?"

"Hopeful. Still hopeful."

I left Eugenia to whip up something she could add the hamburger and vegetables to—expecting it to come out looking like meatloaf anyway, and went through the standing crowd to Cate's corner, where she sat with Crystalline, Sonia, and Felicia. Harry and Delia Swanson called out as I passed. Jake Anderson waved from his table of men from The Skunk. Anna Scovil presided over a table of librarians from surrounding towns. There was battlefield humor going on. Jake called out that he was returning his new Cadillac to Sy Huett before he had to make a payment. Anna Scovil turned and told people behind her that she hadn't really cleared out all

304

the risqué books from the library, and that it was safe to come in again. Jokes jumped from table to table. Crystalline, Felicia, and Sonia laughed as Cate regaled us with the story of trying to pare her wardrobe down to one outfit for her last day on earth and not being able to give up one single item. "I'm just going to wear it all," she said, her face pale under her thick makeup, her red lips finally pulling into a half-smile.

I pushed at Sonia and Felicia and settled into the crowded booth. The women greeted me and then demanded to know what was happening in Marjory's murder case. I didn't have much to tell them.

"Poor Marjory. I've been wondering if she had some inkling that her mother was out there. You know, like a vision or a premonition." Crystalline shook her head and settled down into her body.

"Seems she almost said something…" Felicia frowned and thought hard, her long, plain face wrinkled with worry.

"I was trying to think…" Small Sonia raised that pierced eyebrow, sniffed, and settled back against the booth.

"Yeah, well," Crystalline took over again after thinking hard. "And then… well… I just don't know. I remember once her saying how she hoped someday to see her mother again."

"That could mean in heaven," I said.

She shook her head. "No. It wasn't like that. More like she hoped to find her."

"Then we're right back where we began: why was she afraid of Deward?" I asked.

All three women looked at me oddly. "She was a psychic, Emily. Marjory tuned in to things other people couldn't sense. I'm sure she knew there was something to fear there. She just didn't know what."

"So, why'd she go to Deward the morning she was killed?" I asked, hoping to finally hear something that made sense.

One by one, the women shrugged. Crystalline shook her head. "There was that letter, that her brother needed her help. She would have gone anywhere for family."

"Did you get the idea it was Arnold, the politician, the one she rarely heard from?"

Slowly, all three women shook their head.

"Un-uh," Sonia said. "I thought it was the other one. That Paul guy. That's what I took it to mean. Like maybe he was in trouble in Leetsville. Now I'm wondering if he killed his mother and needed to get it off his conscience."

"So he murders Marjory? Great way to jump-start your road to heaven." I said. "And we don't even know if the guy's still alive or not."

They all frowned at me, including Cate, and dug into their plates of what looked like stew with peas.

When two robed figures with shaved heads and the aura of death about them stepped into the restaurant, a slow hush fell over the diners.

Table to table, people quieted each other and pointed.

When the room was still, Sister Sally looked first to Deputy Dolly, cleared her throat, then said in a loud and carrying voice, "There will be a miracle tomorrow morning. Before the End, at noon, the miracles will begin. Everyone must come. It is our last offer of salvation. Be at the campground. If you believe or don't believe, come."

"Hey Dolly," someone yelled out. "Good thing, eh? I mean, I don't have to pay that shitload of tickets you gave me if the world ends."

Dolly lifted her bald head, face stormy, and looked hard around the room. "Who said that?" she demanded, voice not at all reverential. "That you, Jake Anderson? You checked out that liquor license of yours in a while? Could be a problem. Maybe I'll come on over to that saloon..."

Jake, back at a table with his buddies, lowered his head, mumbled something, and returned to his meatloaf.

Sally lifted both of her narrow hands into the air. "Brother Righteous will speak tomorrow."

"Ha!" someone catcalled. "Guy's dumb as a post."

Dolly walked among the tables, stopping to look down and glare at anyone who dared open their mouth. Her swagger didn't fit the robe. And that shiny bald head looked like something out of a Japanese movie—some kind of Ninja Turtle strutting neighbor to neighbor, man to man.

"Brother Righteous will speak," Sister Sally called again.

Dolly got to where the five of us sat. She looked hard at me then leaned down to stick her finger in my face. "Be there," she growled. "I need you."

I didn't have time to ask why. Something was coming. I wasn't sure I knew what would happen, but this was more like the old Dolly. I hoped it was real, and not just that she wanted me there to help her climb on one of those fleet-footed stallions as the Four Horsemen rode through town.

"Will our children really be killed?" a worried woman yelled out.

"I wanna go out stoned..."

"I'm well shriven. Will I get to heaven?"

Raw nerves showed. People put their hands up for attention; others challenged Sister Sally; others wanted reassurance.

The terror that had been tamped down by the sense of occasion Eugenia'd provided, surfaced at the speed of light. People's faces, strained and concerned, turned to the robed women.

Dolly leaned over toward Cate, looking her straight in the eye. Cate raised a hand and touched Dolly's face. At first Dolly reared back, away from her grandmother. It only took a second for her to come close again, to lean down, and kiss Cate's cheek.

"I'll see you tomorrow," Dolly whispered toward the woman.

"Will there be a day after tomorrow, Delores?" Cate asked, her old face a mix of happy and sad.

Dolly nodded. "It will all be over by noon."

"You mean the world?" Cate asked.

"Somebody's world," Dolly said, and turned, making her way back to Sister Sally, then out the door.

FORTY-FIVE

Tuesday, October 27
End of all time

TUESDAY DAWNED BLOODY RED. Red streaks ran in ribbons across the sky. The lake reflected a crimson universe. *Red sky in morning, sailors take warning*—and all the rest of us, too, I thought, and hugged myself.

I figured it was as good a sky as any to end with—if it was all truly over. I got ready early—but not too early—and actually dressed up, a little. I wore an old blue cashmere sweater and a pair of pressed black pants. After all, what did you wear to burn in hell for eternity? And why was I expecting to burn? I'd never been a bad person. I'd done some good. I found myself hoping all of that would be taken into account when . . . well, I didn't know what to expect. This was going to be a very different day.

Sorrow begged to come along but all I could do was pat his black head, look into those distressed, dark button eyes, and tell him I hoped I'd be back. No matter how it worked out, it would be sad. I think he'd picked up on my melancholy.

———————

When I got to the campground it was already after ten. The crowd was huge, reaching back out of the open space to between the trailers, and beyond. I took a place at the edge of the crowd and looked around for Dolly, or Officer Winston, or Lucky Barnard. It seemed no matter what went on out there that morning, it would have to do with the murders.

Everybody from Leetsville had lined around the periphery of the crowd; even Eugenia was there with Gloria, Simon, and Cate. Eugenia had puffed her hair to an impossible height, ready for eternal damnation. I saw a man ask her to change places with him so he could see.

Crystalline, Sonia, and Felicia arrived fifteen minutes after I had. I called out, beckoning them to join me.

"The guy knows how to draw a crowd," Crystalline said as she elbowed her way to my side, nodding her head of red curls caught with tortoiseshell combs.

"What do you think, Emily? We gonna be here at twelve-o- one?" she asked.

I shrugged. "No clue. Something's going to happen. I just don't know what."

"This have to do with Marjory's death?" Crystalline asked, bending close to my ear.

I shrugged.

Slow, mordant music began at eleven o'clock. These weren't the rousing hymns they'd played on revival nights. I recognized Bach. I recognized Beethoven. I recognized a few hymns I'd heard once.

310

I'd gone to a little independent church with a friend of mine when I was twelve years old. I never forgot that clapboard church in the country, nor the slow, chilling music.

The stage we all looked toward was empty.

The men who had milled around up there before weren't in sight. There were the hanging lightbulbs and a long, white tarp draped overhead. Nothing else. We waited. The music drowned out talk. Our nervousness was palpable. It wrapped around, became a thing you could feel coming from the skin of the person next to you.

Overhead, the sky had changed from sunny to an odd shade of yellow—as if wind might be in the offing. The red streaks of that morning were gone, replaced by a deck of heavy black clouds coming out of the north. I heard thunder over the loud music—and felt thunder move through the ground.

At eleven-thirty, the Reverend Fritch climbed onto the stage with two people helping him. He was wrapped in a wide and very white robe that whipped around his ankles. The man was huge, taking up a great deal of space. He seemed weak—holding on with pale-fingered hands to the robed figures beside him, then looking over his shoulder to a third person, as if to make certain he was there.

One of those figures was Dolly. Another was Sister Sally. The third, walking behind, was Brother Righteous, his cowl back, sleeves rolled up, tortured face contorting as he looked over the gathered crowd.

Reverend Fritch shook off the helping hands when he stood at the front of the stage. The women didn't move far as Reverend Fritch raised his arms for quiet. Silence fell. The music died. At that moment, there came a roll of thunder from the north. The ground shook. The air shook. I didn't know about the others, but I began to shake like the last leaf on a bare tree.

"The moment nears," the preacher called out, head back, arms wide, voice gathering strength. "Soon. By noon it will begin. Do you hear the thunder? Only the start, my friends. The wind will grow. The thunder will beat at us. The lightning will strike. And then ..."

He paused, arms raised above his head. "And then ... and then ... and then ... my Lord! The sky will split open and the hand of God will reach out from among the clouds to smite the wicked. The Four Horsemen will be among us, striking left and right with their mighty swords ..."

A woman off to my right fainted dead away. Her friends left her where she'd fallen. Children, throughout the crowd, were crying. A few people moaned.

"This is the moment the Righteous among you have been waiting for." His voice reached the level of a screech, causing the microphones to squeal, the grating noise hurting my ears. "The earthly toil is over. Today ... I said TODAY we will join our loved ones in heaven, to sit among the angels ..."

Moans grew as thunder rocked the campground. In a few minutes I knew I was going to get wet. Maybe I wouldn't be carried away on a bloody sword, but I sure was going to be soaked with rain.

"And we will have miracles ..." the Reverend Fritch shouted out, voice booming around us along with thunder. Lightning split the sky—sideways overhead. The thunder was immediate, roaring, shaking even the trees, echoing off as no earthly sound can echo. A generator behind the stage sparked high arcs of fire. Light bulbs hanging above the stage on wildly dancing wires blew in bright showers of glass as a backup generator whirred to life.

On cue, Sister Sally and Dolly took Brother Righteous by the arms and escorted him to the front of the stage. The reverend stepped aside, with a flourish of his robe, to make room. He turned a benign, fatherly smile on the trembling Brother Righteous, put a hand on his back, and patted encouragement.

The emaciated man opened his mouth. We waited, expecting words that would save us. Sally leaned in close, urging him to speak. He tried again, and then again.

There was no heckling from the audience. Everyone held their breath, including me. The wind picked up and pushed hard at our bodies. Every ounce of will in each of us was directed toward the stage and the trembling man trying so desperately to speak.

Black clouds moved faster, roiling overhead. The stage and the clearing grew dark. People became shadows. Urgency gripped us. We stood as still as statues, waiting as the driving rain struck.

Brother Righteous stepped back, then clasped his hands together near his mouth. He looked up into sideways rain beating at his face, then looked hard down into the crowd. His face changed. His look of fear turned into astonishment. He recoiled, seemed to take a breath, then straightened, his back tall and firm. I tried to find what he was seeing down in the crowd but there were only rows of indistinguishable robed figures lined in front of the stage. He looked down again, squinting hard. He licked rain from his lips.

Reverend Fritch, his robe soaked, took a step toward the Brother, coming to his side, grabbing his elbow to support him then pushing him slowly closer to the microphone.

The two men became as one; their robes blowing out on hard gusts of wind and rain. They became entangled, commingled—two men in a single wildly blowing robe. They bent close, heads together as one person, fighting to stand.

"Five minutes left," the reverend grabbed the mic and shouted, turning to point at the clouds rolling faster and faster over us. "Brother Righteous must speak..."

One of the brother's hands came out from the folds of his robe. His shaking hand formed into an accusing finger. He pointed at something or someone in that first row.

Over the whining microphone came the sound of a throat trying to be cleared, a voice trying to be heard. Brother Righteous' lips moved. An unintelligible sound, coming through the sputtering amp, flew over the heads of the crowd.

"Four minutes!" the reverend intoned around his friend as he fought to keep his footing on the stage floor.

My clothes hung heavy against my skin. The cold grew intense as the wind whipped around us.

"I..." Brother Righteous cried out, followed by a shriek of the mic. "...am not... my brother's keeper."

Quiet was absolute as the words moved off, falling on the heads of the faithful, and disappearing as if they rode on thunder.

Behind me someone whispered, "A miracle!"

The reverend looked down at the place where Brother Righteous pointed. He put a pudgy hand to his lips and whispered something. Brother Righteous nodded and pulled the mic close, leaning in.

"I...buried...my...own...mother," the poor, struggling man blurted. "My brother...I didn't...know. It was...an accident...he told me. But...I...helped bury her...and never told."

We looked quizzically at each other, not understanding.

Brother Righteous, obviously under great strain, leaned forward, speaking to all of us but also to someone in the crowd. "I didn't know...my brother...was a murderer."

Everything that happened after that was a blur. The rain hit harder. The trees bent in half. The wind tore off the overhanging tarp and wrapped the men and women in a shroud they fought hard against. There were screams and shouts and curses. The Reverend Fritch went into amazing motion for a man his size. He launched his body into the air—as if about to fly. There was a terrible, loud crack. I couldn't tell if it was a tree limb falling, or if this was the sound of the heavens opening. Then another crack, and an echoing retort: around and around the clearing, into the trees. Panic set in. People grabbed each other, some screamed; there were frightened cries and pleas for mercy. I fought off clutching hands, dealing with my own terror. I ran toward the stage. Something was going on there. A mass of flying robes, and people, and shouts.

The Reverend Fritch lay on the stage floor, his white robe transformed by the blood, his body like something pierced, stopped in mid-flight. His large hands grasped at his middle. He stared down in wonder as blood streamed through his wide fingers. I heard terrible gasps for air when I got up there. Brother Righteous knelt in the reverend's blood. His hands were clasped together, his head thrown back, mouth filled with a terrible keening.

Dolly was the first to look up from where she knelt near the dying man. She screamed at me and pointed toward a robed figure pushing back through the stunned crowd. There were other shouts and screams. Another shot rang out and everything stopped.

The rain passed on by. The clouds rolled off as clouds always do. There was no more thunder; no lightning. Within moments the sun shone down again and, as with all storms, fear drifted away.

FORTY-SIX

Salvation

Arnold Otis lay in a pool of his own blood where he had fallen after Officer Winston shot him. People in robes and people in blue jeans made a wide circle around the dead man. They stared in disbelief, gaped over shoulders, and pushed their way through to get a look. Horror spread over their faces. Children clutched at their mothers' skirts. Most of the crowd was silent, stunned that they were still alive. Little by little, with eerie quiet, they began to slink away, stopping only to give a police officer their name and address—potential witnesses. They would be needed—some of them—for the inquest; people called to back up Winston's story about the use of his weapon and deadly force. Dolly and I would be there, but more than just the two of us would be needed.

When enough information had been gathered, people scurried off as fast as they could, some to their trailers, some to their tents, where they grabbed stakes from the ground and hurriedly stuffed canvas haphazardly into the backs of their pickups. Little by little the grounds were cleared; the wet and trampled dead grasses left a sea of mud. Before the ambulance arrived to take away the two dead men, a few of us stood looking down at the murderer, Arnold Otis, who had killed his mother and his sister, and had tried to kill his brother, only to bring the end of the world to the Reverend Fritch, just as the reverend had predicted. An honest, if confused, man, the reverend had foretold his own mortality and projected it out onto the world.

After the ambulances left, no sirens blaring because they carried only the dead, Brother Righteous, or Paul Otis, in his bloody robe, had to be helped up from his knees. His long, pale face was streaked with tears. His eyes were terrible—the eyes of a man who had seen his world end more than once.

Dolly helped Sally get him off the stage. They sat him down at a picnic bench and let him rest his head on his arms, all life draining from his thin body.

Dolly was out of her wet robe in a flash, uniform on beneath; her gun strapped at her side. Not the outfit a sane woman would wear to heaven.

"Will he be all right?" I asked Sally, who hovered near the grieving man.

She nodded. "He'll have to live with another death. But he will go on. There is the reverend's work to continue."

I was confused. "The world didn't end…"

Sally shrugged. "The reverend's world ended. Arnold Otis' world ended. Who knows what the messages really meant? Brother Righteous will keep the movement going. Perhaps another message. Perhaps another ending. Who knows but that he was the one, himself, who put this wild day into motion? There are those who must be

317

punished and those who are the catalyst for that punishment. And there are those who are martyred—like our good, dear Reverend Fritch.

"He will be rewarded today. He wouldn't have wanted to live on. People will say he failed. Better to give his life for someone he loved the way he loved Brother Righteous—like a son." She closed her eyes and smiled. "He is in heaven now, with our Father. What better reward..."

"But. . ." I still wasn't understanding. "I'm missing things here. Were you the one who wrote to Marjory?"

She nodded. "The Reverend Fritch asked me to. Something was going on with Brother Righteous. After the terrible accident he had—so many years ago—he came to the reverend's church, hurt, unable to speak, devoid of memory.

"Little by little his memory returned. But something terrible was buried there. We all saw it, how his eyes would widen—as if he'd seen the fires of hell—and he would cower, face in his hands. One day he came out with a name—he wrote it down for Reverend Fritch. That's when he asked me to find the woman—Marjory Otis. It was her name Brother Righteous had written. I found her in Ohio."

She looked over at Paul Otis, his face buried in his hands. She lowered her voice. "More and more came back to Brother Righteous until one day he wrote that he had to confess to a terrible sin before the end. He needed his sister—and it was this Marjory Otis. He had to confess to her first, he wrote. Reverend Fritch thought maybe it was an excess of religious zeal—people get like that when the spirit moves among us; when the predictions are dire."

"He knew about his mother being buried out there?" I asked.

Brother Righteous looked up at me. "I helped ... Arnold. My ... sin too."

"You put the roses on her grave?"

He nodded. "I needed to ... honor her. After what ... I helped Arnold do."

"Why did he kill his own mother?"

Brother Righteous hung his head. "He wanted ... to live with our ... aunt and uncle. He ... said ... we had ... no chance with ... our mother. He made ... me help ... bury her. He said I would ... go to jail if anybody found ... out what we ... did. I believed him."

"Too bad Marjory didn't come to us first." Sister Sally, shivering now, moved close to Brother Righteous and rested her hand on his bent shoulder. She bowed her head to his and whispered in his ear.

She straightened. "Marjory came to Leetsville, as we'd asked her to do. But not to us. She must have called Arnold, telling him of my letter and her mission. She didn't know what she was doing. Arnold knew. All I can imagine is he arranged to take her to Deward. He told her what he'd done and, while she was in shock, maybe crying, he killed her. So terribly, terribly sad. All so he could escape his past."

"I'm surprised he didn't bury her too." Dolly shook her head.

"He ... didn't have me ... to help him." Paul's voice was sorrowful. "I should have ... warned Marjory about ... Arnold."

His eyes were burdened with new guilt.

Sally drew a deep breath. Paul lifted his head and listened as Sister Sally put the last pieces of his family tragedy together.

"I was the one who saw in the local newspaper that a Marjory Otis had been found dead. I had to tell the Reverend Fritch and he told Brother Righteous.

"We seemed to almost lose him there for a while." Tears filled Sally's eyes. Brother Righteous nodded. "When he came back to us he wrote that he would speak—on the morning of the End Time. He would tell all. But too late for his brother to seek redemption. He wanted his brother to go to his death unshriven, in a state of sin so awful that he would burn in hell forever."

"You've gotten your wish…" Sally leaned in toward Brother Righteous. "He would have killed Marjory anyway. He wanted so badly to be a senator. Once Marjory was dead we all knew Brother Righteous—Paul—had to be next. But there was no way to prove anything. Our word against the word of a powerful man. That's why I was so afraid and needed Dolly's help."

Paul Otis heaved a deep sigh and looked skyward as if searching for something there.

Dolly moved close to Sally's side. "It isn't Brother Righteous' fault, you know, Sally. He wouldn't have wanted the reverend to die like he did."

"I know that." Sister Sally pulled back. "It's the way of all things, Dolly. Out of our hands.

"And thank you," she said, smiling into Dolly's solemn face. "I don't know what we would have done without…"

I looked at Dolly, too, still angry but catching on that more had been behind her instant conversion that I'd given her credit for.

"You knew…" I said.

Dolly made a face. "Later."

Around us, the men of their church quickly dismantled the damp stage. Everything was down and being packed into vehicles. The huge RV was pulled up close, waiting for Sister Sally and Brother Righteous.

"We're not leaving," Sally said as she helped Brother Righteous to his feet. He looked down at his blood-stained robe and hands. He folded those hands up into the thick sleeves of his robe.

"We'll claim his body first, then we'll continue his ministry," Sally said. "That's what he would have wanted."

Brother Righteous looked from her to Dolly, then me. He nodded.

"Death has passed ... on by," he said in his halting, flat voice.

Sally patted his arm. "Yes. It was as it was supposed to be. Now we walk into the future."

He looked back at Dolly, pleading written across his face.

"Thank ... you."

"I'm sorry ... about your friend," Dolly said, her small face, under that bald head, almost melting with regret.

"I'm staying until ... We will ..." He gulped hard, as if reaching down inside himself for words. "... bury my sister ... and my mother. And my ... friend."

Later, at EATS, over warming cups of tea, Dolly had to tell her story again and again. How Sister Sally had gotten her off in a corner on that first night at the campground and begged her to help. She knew Brother Righteous was in trouble; that Leetsville was more than a place to wait for the End Time. And then his sister was found murdered. No one knew what to do. They only knew Paul was in trouble and had to be protected.

"Sister Sally told me that they were afraid Brother Righteous would be next. They feared he would die without cleansing his soul of the awful sin bothering him. He'd never been in a mental home, the way Arnold Otis hinted. But he wouldn't share what was so troubling to him, with the flock, until the last day. That was his wish—the last day. He would speak—he'd been working on one word at a time. He would tell everything, be absolved, but curse his brother. A real Cain and Abel kind of thing going on, I guess."

Dolly took a deep breath and looked around at the people gathered, listening.

"Sally told me they couldn't get it out of him. Whatever the terrible thing was he carried inside him. Brother Righteous promised to tell everything in his last confession, on the day of the End Time. But that tied everybody's hands. Who were they supposed to protect him from? Eventually we knew, but had no way of proving anything."

Dolly shook her head and leaned back, stretching her arms wide. "I figured all along we'd find out this last morning."

She put up a hand, stopping the questions bubbling around her. I jumped in anyway.

"You couldn't trust me?" I was madder than ever now that I knew she might have spared me so much misery.

She gave me her usual sour face. "Lucky said I'd better get into character and stay that way. If anybody suspected what I was up to, the whole thing would have been blown. Just like out there at Deward, when Arnold found you there at his mother's grave. He must have had that aide follow you and steal your camera and the roses. Maybe he'd already told his people that blackmail story. Who knows what makes one man break the law for another?" She turned my way. "I'll get your camera back. Don't worry."

I moved right on from that bit of good news, on to the other thing she'd said. "Lucky knew? He pretended he didn't."

"I had to tell him, Emily. What could we do? I guess you really gave it to him about your allegiance to the newspaper. Something like that. Anyway, poor guy, he's been trying his best to include you." She stopped to take a deep breath. "And poor Winston, never shot anybody before. Your newspaper'll be making a big deal of the whole thing—Arnold Otis being a candidate for state senate and all."

"That's my job," I said.

"Yeah, well, keepin' it a secret was ours." She shook her head.

"I feel bad for Omar. I kinda like the guy," Dolly said. People around us nodded. All firmly in his corner.

"Omar?" I asked.

"Yeah. Officer Winston. That's his name. I think he's top notch."

"You would," I groused. "Peas in a pod and all of that. Next time you try to get me into one of these things you keep stumbling into, drive on past my house, ok? You left me holding the bag. Why, I …"

Crystalline, Felicia, and Sonia moved up behind me. Crystalline touched my shoulders, quieting me and holding me in place. Felicia set her fingers gently on top of my head. Sonia reached down to take my hands. Between them they had me pinned where I sat, soothing the anger I hugged close.

"You've got wonderful things ahead of you, Emily," Crystalline said, in what must have passed for a mystical voice. I could feel the warmth of her fingers on my back, coming through the cashmere of my sweater. I tried to shake the calming hands away, but couldn't. "Why, you will do something spectacular with your writing."

Dolly cocked her head my way, lifting her chin at me. "You hear from an agent or somebody like that?"

I wasn't about to share great news with somebody who could shut me out of her life so easily. I said nothing, holding my secret to myself.

"An agent? You sell the book?" she prodded, leaning closer. "Well, what do you know? I'm gonna be famous." She settled back in her chair, a fatuous smile spreading over her face.

"The hell you will." I tried to get my rage back. "I changed your name. You won't even be in there …"

"Yeah, like you got any stories without me."

"I don't need you or …" I complained, but the real venom was gone. I was at ease, the hands on me working magic, the warmth of touch moving along my skin. I gave up fighting.

I finally grinned at her. "Sure I do, Dolly. I need you and you need me."

She gave a thumbs-up that took us right back to where we used to be.

"And, you know what?" I said. "I'm going to throw you a birthday party. You've got it coming." I reached down inside for something mean to follow with, but Dolly nodded. The delighted look on her face gave away her pleasure at the thought of a birthday, and a party to go with it. She folded her hands in her lap and set her chin down on her chest, no doubt contemplating the big wish she'd been saving for just such an occasion.

Sonia tightened her grip on my hands, kneading and patting. I was pure putty. "Maybe love coming your way," she whispered close to my ear.

Felicia, hands still on the top of my head, moved the pads of her fingers back and forth. She leaned down to look hard into my face. "I don't know ... maybe you don't want to hear this one. Ooh, ooh ... it's your poor dog, Emily. He wants you home. He's peeved and put out with you. It looks like ... oh, my heavens. He's lifting his leg on your sofa."

No doubt the women couldn't comprehend my smile. At last, on this, the first day of the rest of my life, my little boy had become a man.

EPILOGUE

IT WAS AN ORDINARY northern Michigan morning; late into the fall. No drama in the heavy sky above our heads. A few ragged clouds floated by, some outlined in bright white, most the color of pewter—the kind of sky that would stay until spring, soon dropping snow, day after day after day.

We stood on the high banks of the Manistee River: Dolly, her grandmother Cate, Crystalline, Sonia, Felicia, Officer Omar Winston, Lucky Barnard, Sister Sally, Brother Righteous, Bill Corcoran, and I.

We'd slowly filed by Winnie Otis' longtime grave, which was filled in but still rough from the recent digging. We'd passed Marjory's last resting place. At each spot we'd stopped, bowed our heads, said silent prayers, then moved on, farther into Deward, the place where it all began.

High on the Manistee switchback, we stood side by side, looking down at the near-motionless water as three crows fluttered by with weak, muted "caws." Crystalline held an urn with the ashes of

Marjory Otis. Felicia held the urn with Marjory's mother's ashes. Brother Righteous held the ashes of the Reverend Fritch.

I took Bill's thick arm and held on. A slight breeze sprang up, forcing us to huddle down into our warm coats as we stood in silence, above the river. The wind rose and pushed the water along faster. It blew dead leaves around our feet, then sighed softly away through the pines. Crystalline stepped forward, pulled the top from the urn she carried, and held it up first to the east, then to the south, to the west, and finally to the north—land of the dead. She turned and, leaning over the embankment, sent what was left of her friend, Marjory Otis, into the air above the water. As the ashes fell, a veil of brown sinking toward the river, the breeze grew stronger, lifting the ashes, then twisting them into a spiral hanging in space.

Felicia opened the urn she carried and sent Winnie's ashes over the edge, into the spiral.

Brother Righteous launched the ashes of the Reverend Fritch at the same time—into what had become a small cyclonic squall. The ashes mingled, turned, then rose together in a graceful dance. They became one veil of ash. They skimmed along the Manistee's surface, flew until they were a momentary shadow above the river, settled down to the water, and then they were gone.

Karen Youker

ABOUT THE AUTHOR

Elizabeth Kane Buzzelli is a creative writing instructor at Northwestern Michigan College. She is the author of novels, short stories, articles, and essays. Her work has appeared in numerous publications and anthologies.